Maybe I was jumpy from the murders. Or maybe it was the smell that made me look up—the smell of fresh earth, a new grave.

Framed in the window was the face of a chimp, with fresh earth clinging to the hair on its head. The face was a dead ringer for Susie.

The face disappeared. I went outside and found—nothing. It could have been Susie the chimp all right. The only trouble was—Susie had been buried yesterday.

If I had been afraid inside, I was terrified out here in the dark.

•

•

•

the DEAD RINGER

By Fredric Brown

BANTAM BOOKS  NEW YORK

THE DEAD RINGER

A BANTAM BOOK published by arrangement with
E. P. Dutton & Company, Inc.

PRINTING HISTORY

Dutton Edition Published March, 1948
1st Printing ....January, 1948
Bantam Edition Published March, 1949
1st Printing ....February, 1949
2nd Printing ....April, 1954

Copyright, 1948, by Fredric Brown

No part of this book may be reproduced in any form without permission in writing from E. P. Dutton & Company, Inc., except by a reviewer who wishes to quote brief passages in connection with a review written for inclusion in magazine or newspaper or radio broadcast.

The Dead Ringer was published and copyrighted, 1948, by Mystery Club, Inc.

Bantam Books are published by Bantam Books, Inc. Its trade mark, consisting of the words "BANTAM BOOKS" and the portrayal of a bantam, is registered in the U.S. Patent Office and in other countries. *Marca Registrada*

PRINTED IN THE UNITED STATES OF AMERICA
BANTAM BOOKS, 25 West 45th Street, New York 36, N. Y.

THE DEAD RINGER

CHAPTER I

IT DIDN'T SEEM in the least like a prelude to murder. It had been a dull gray afternoon, but warm, and there'd been a good crowd at the lot and we'd done all right. It was the fifteenth of August, a Thursday, our fourth day in Evansville, Indiana.

Then, at about half-past six, just as we were beginning to get set up for the evening's business, it started to rain. That's usually tragedy to a carnival, but this time nobody minded much. The weather had been giving us a break for weeks, all through southern Ohio and Kentucky. We'd been working every day, and everybody was in the bucks. An evening off, for a change, looked good.

My Uncle Am had just run up the canvas front of the ball game concession that he and I operated, when the first big drops came down out of the dusk.

He tilted his hat back and looked up at the sky; a couple of drops hit his face and glistened there. Then he let the canvas down again and grinned at me. He said, "Well, Ed, we got an evening off."

"Could be just a shower," I said.

"Nope, it's good for all night. Could be some wind coming, too. Let's grapevine some rope."

We put away the baseballs and the wooden milk bottles and two racks of prizes, and got our raincoats, and I got a hat. Uncle Am always wears one except when he sleeps, so he already had his on. It's a soft black slouch hat like the one The Shadow wears, but otherwise my uncle doesn't look much like The Shadow; he's short and fat and has a cheerful round face and a not-too-neat brown moustache.

We got rope and grapevined the side walls of our booth. It was beginning to rain hard by now. All around the midway carneys were letting down banners and running rope. We grapevined our sleeping tent back of the booth, too.

By then the rain had slowed down to a drizzle, but Uncle Am said it was just fooling. "We won't open tonight. I think I'll go over to the G-top. Why don't you go into town and see a movie?"

I said, "I'll stick around. I want to practice trombone, and I got a detective magazine."

He nodded and wandered off and I went back to our tent and turned on the light. I got out the swell trombone my uncle had given me when I'd joined up with the carnival the year before, after my dad died.

I was still nuts about that trombone. I just sat and held it awhile, getting the feel of it. It had a featherweight slide that moved so easily you couldn't feel the friction or the weight. It was gold-plated and I kept it polished like jewelry. It felt good just to hold it and look at it.

After awhile I started to practice scales, and then played a few tunes from memory, and that went all right. But when I started working on the high notes, one split on me, and I guess it must have sounded pretty godawful.

I heard a laugh and looked around. Hoagy had stuck his head in through the tent flap. He grinned and came on in, dripping rain from a bright yellow slicker. He was so big he seemed to fill one end of the tent, and he had to stand with his neck a little bent to keep his hat from scraping the canvas.

He said, "I thought somebody was getting killed in here, Ed. Looked in to be sure."

I grinned back at him. "Just get back, Hoagy?"

"Few minutes ago. Everything's okay for next week in South Bend. Good lot there, too." Hoagy was spending a few days a week as advance man since our regular one had quit. His regular job as sex lecturer in the side show had been sloughed in so many towns they'd decided to skip it the rest of the season.

I asked him, "How's the chimp, Hoagy?"

His face got serious. "Still pretty sick. I dropped in the trailer first thing to check on her. Where's Am, gambling?"

I said yeah, and he went out. It was raining harder again, a steady drumming on the canvas over my head. And the thunder was starting now. It was a low, far-off rumbling, and it was scary. You knew it was just clouds bumping together, but it didn't seem like that; it was more like an animal growling, some big animal you couldn't identify by its voice, but that sounded as big as the night, and far away but deadly.

I put on my raincoat and went out to the midway. The rain beat down on my hat like it was a drum, and the lot was beginning to get muddy. Luckily, though, the lot sloped off and there wouldn't be any lakes of standing water, and shavings would take care of the mud.

I crossed the midway and headed for the green trailer back of the freak show top. There was a light on and when I rapped on the door Lee Carey's voice called out for me to come in.

He grinned at me and said, "Yeah, you can play the phono. I'm going out awhile though."

"Any new records?"

"A Jimmy Dorsey album. Some pretty good stuff."

He put on a slicker and went out, and I plugged in the portable and played the Dorsey album. It was good stuff. But the thunder kept getting louder, and I couldn't concentrate on the music. I decided the hell with it and went out again.

It was raining a lot harder, almost a cloudburst. I hurried back to our booth and Uncle Am was there, standing in the lee of the popcorn wagon with an eye on our canvas. The wind was up, but not really dangerous.

I stood with him until the rain slowed down, and the wind with it, and Uncle Am went back to the G-top. The G-top, if you don't know, is the gambling tent that some of the big carnivals pitch for card games among the carneys themselves. Marks, outsiders, aren't allowed in; it's purely a family affair.

I went with Uncle Am and watched him play rummy awhile, but I didn't sit in.

After a few hands I went back to our sleeping tent. I was wet in spots under the raincoat, so I stripped and rubbed myself dry with a towel.

It was while I was doing that that the lights went out. Not only the bulb inside our tent, but all over carney. I stuck my head out through the flap and there was only utter pitch darkness, everywhere.

I swore a little and groped around until I found matches

and lit the carbide lantern we kept for emergencies. I was getting into a dry pair of shorts when Uncle Am stuck his head into the tent.

He said, "You okay, kid?"

"Sure," I said. "What happened?"

"Lightning hit some wires and fritzed the generator in the Diesel car. They won't get it fixed tonight; burned out all the windings. Storm's over, but it took a parting shot at us."

When he left, I got my detective magazine and tried to read. But I kept getting sleepier and sleepier. The rain started up again, softly, and then died down. Over the soft drumming of the rain I could hear a clock strike, and a far train whistle.

There was the faint sputter of the carbide lamp, the soft drone of the rain, and the dull story that couldn't keep me awake . . . and didn't.

I don't believe I heard the shot. If I did, it was mixed up in whatever dreams I might have been having, and I don't remember it clearly.

What woke me was Uncle Am's voice, from the tent entrance. He called out, "You okay, Ed?"

I sat up on the cot. I said, "Sure. What—?"

"There was a shot just now. I thought maybe—" He didn't finish it; he'd meant he thought I'd been messing around with the thirty-two he kept in his trunk, maybe, and had fired it accidentally.

He'd stepped into the tent, and a big bulk loomed behind him—Hoagy, bending his neck so his head wouldn't scrape canvas. His voice rumbled, "Somebody says it came from the side show top. Going over, Am?"

Apparently Uncle Am was, because suddenly I was alone in the tent, still dopey from sleep. I swung my feet off the cot and pulled on my boots. Outside, now, I could hear a lot of voices, and sloshing footsteps. There was no longer sound of rain.

I grabbed my raincoat and got into it. It felt cold and clammy against my bare skin. I hurried out, buttoning the coat as I went along the side of our ball game booth, out to the midway. There was still a fine drizzle of rain.

There were others running or walking in the same direction. Most of them had flashlights; I'd been too sleepy to think of bringing one, forgetting the midway would be as dark as pitch. But by following the others, I managed to get across to the side show without falling over anything.

I found the fence in front of the side show easily enough by running into it. I climbed over, groped my way to the canvas without tangling with any stakes, and went under the side wall.

Inside, there was light—dancing irregular light from maybe twenty different flashlights, adding up to enough illumination to light the whole place dimly—and one spot very brightly.

The bright spot was near the middle; a knot of people was gathered around it; I couldn't see what they were looking down at. I ran to the edge of the group there and managed to stretch enough to see over shoulders and between heads.

Then somebody ahead of me backed out of the circle and I had a clear view of what lay on the grass. I wished I hadn't been so eager to see.

It was a kid lying there, face down on the grass, without any clothes on. A boy, it seemed, about six or eight years old, with a very white skin and with short-cropped dark hair.

There was the hilt of a knife sticking out of his back. It was a heavily weighted hilt; it looked like the hilt of one of the throwing knives Australia used in his act.

I didn't know the kid; at least I didn't recognize him from his back.

Other people were pushing in behind me, some of them talking excitedly. Pop Janney, across the circle from me, was on his knees putting a hand on the boy's shoulder. He said, "Dead as a mackerel. Stone cold." He took his hand away quick. Somebody else said "Jesus Christ" and it didn't sound like swearing. Somebody else said, "Don't move him; don't touch him." Somebody said something about coppers, and somebody else swore.

I pushed my way backward into the open. I saw Uncle Am and Hoagy in another, smaller group, around someone who was sitting slumped down on the edge of the geek's platform. Whoever it was, was sobbing, and the sound seemed to run precariously along the edge of hysteria. It was a girl, I could tell by the sound. A very scared girl.

I didn't feel any too good myself. Not scared, not like the girl was feeling, but a little sick at my stomach.

I went out the entrance and leaned against the high bally platform at the front. I wondered who in hell would knife a little kid like that, and why. I tried to place who the kid might be, and I couldn't; that was funny, because there weren't many kids with the carney, and I thought I knew them all by sight if not by name.

One kid about that size and age was a favorite of mine, a kid by the name of Jigaboo who was a tap dancer with the jig show. Jigaboo, at seven or thereabouts, had more rhythm in his feet than Krupa has in his hands. But this kid wasn't Jigaboo, not with a dead white skin like that; Jigaboo was as black as the inside of a cave.

But the kid lying there, I thought, *must* be a carney, not a town kid. A town kid might possibly be around the side-show top this late at night, but not without his clothes on. For a carney kid, that wasn't too strange; I mean, a lot of carneys sleep raw in hot weather. Surely a kid would, but—

After a minute my stomach began to quiet down. There was a bad taste in my mouth, literally and figuratively, but I wasn't going to shoot my lunch.

I heard Uncle Am's voice call my name and I yelled back, "Yeah," and started for inside the top again, when Uncle Am and Hoagy and a girl came out of the entrance toward me. The girl was walking between them, and each had an arm across her shoulders. She wore a long green slicker and a green beret and very muddy high-heeled slippers. There was a lot of mud on the slicker and on her bare legs below it. She was leaning forward slightly, with hands over her face. She was still sobbing a little.

Uncle Am was talking to her, very quietly. He said, "Rita, honey, you know my nephew, Ed? Ed Hunter, same name as mine. Look, he's a good kid. Let him take you for a drive, just around a few blocks, till you're feeling better. Let him get you away from here for a while."

The girl's sobbing stopped. She took her hands away from her face. I recognized her now—one of the new girls with the posing show. She'd been with the carney only a week; she'd joined up in Louisville. I'd seen her around a few times. I remembered she was a good looker, although she didn't look that way now, with her face puffy from crying and with mud on her cheeks.

She said, "H-hi, Ed," and tried to smile.

I forgot the feeling that had been in my stomach and throat, and smiled at her. I wondered if the kid that had been killed was a brother of hers, or something. He couldn't have been her son; she wasn't that much older than I, if any. She couldn't possibly have had a kid that old; she didn't look over eighteen.

Uncle Am left her with Hoagy and came closer to me. He took my arm and leaned forward so he could talk quietly enough that the others couldn't hear.

He said, "She found the kid, Ed; fell over him in the dark, cutting across the inside of the side-show top—on her way to the doniker, probably. She nearly went nuts. Look, you take her—"

"Who is the kid, Uncle Am?" I asked. "Do you know him, or does she?"

"No, but forget that. Look, I want to stick around and so does Hoagy. Hoagy'll give you the keys to his car; it's in front of his trailer but not hitched. Take her for a ride and get her mind off what happened." He grinned, looking for a moment like a cheerful satyr. "Give her something else to think about. Maybe you can think of something."

"Sure," I said. "But look—if she found the body, won't the cops be sore if she isn't around when they come?"

He made an impatient gesture. "We'll take care of that. If the cops start questioning her the way she is now, she'll go to pieces and have hysterics. So let 'em wait. Damn it, I'd say *I* found the body, except that so many people heard the gun go off—"

"Hey!" I said. I'd clean forgotten the shot until he mentioned it. "The kid was stabbed. What was the shot?"

"That was Rita's gun. A little pearl-handled outfit she had in her raincoat pocket. She was carrying it because she was a little scared walking around in the dark with all the carney lights off; she isn't used to the carney yet. She had her hand in her pocket, on the gun, and it went off when she fell over the kid in the dark."

"Didn't hurt her?"

"Not even a powder burn. The bullet went in the ground ahead of her as she fell. Put a hole in her raincoat pocket, but that's all. Now quit asking damn fool questions and get the lead out."

I turned back and Hoagy gave me the car keys.

I said, "Ready, Rita?"

She said, "Okay, E-Eddie, let's go," her voice still trembling a little, but not so much.

The rain was a fine mist that blurred the windshield almost as fast as the busy little arm of the wiper could scrape it off. The rest of the windshield, outside the arc of the wiper, was opaque as frosted glass, as were the side and back windows of the ancient sedan. We were in a little rectangular world of our own, shut off from the outside wetness and darkness, seeing into it only through the windshield wiper's arc.

There was a pretty girl beside me, but that didn't mean anything just then, because I had to keep all my attention focused on the shining strip of road ahead, unwinding into unexpected curves. It took all my attention to follow that unwinding asphalt and keep the car on it.

But after a little while it occurred to me to wonder where I was going that I had to drive so fast. I took my foot off the pedal and let the car idle down to a crawl.

I grinned at the girl beside me, then, and she smiled back. She said, "I was wondering what you were in such a hurry about."

It seemed entirely natural that she moved over closer and that I put my arm around her. But, natural or not, it felt nice.

I let the car edge off the road and stop. Almost right away, as the windshield wiper quit, the arc of windshield misted over and we were cut off from the world outside, completely, in a little rectangular universe of our own, the inside of the car.

I turned and looked at her. She was pretty, even with all her make-up washed off by the rain. Her eyes, I saw, were light blue, sort of misty. They met mine, levelly.

She said, "Let's not, Eddie."

"All right," I said. "I'll be good."

"Because—I *like* you, Eddie."

I laughed. "That's a good reason."

"And I want to keep on liking you. Maybe that sounds silly, but— And quit looking at me, please, Eddie. I know I've got mud all over me and I look like hell."

"I wouldn't say that," I told her. "Not quite."

"Well, stop looking anyway."

"Okay," I said. I leaned forward and switched off the little light on the instrument panel. "Now I can't look. Satisfied?"

"As long as you don't try the Braille sys— I'm sorry, Eddie."

"Sorry for what?"

"For talking cheap, like that. I guess I've been on the defensive ever since I joined the carney last week. All the men with the carney are such—such lice."

"Not all of them. There's my uncle, and Hoagy, and—"

"I didn't mean Hoagy. He's a sort of an uncle of mine. Not a real uncle, but he knew my parents once, and Marge was a friend of my mother's. He got me this job with the carney. And, anyway, he and Marge are so nuts about each other nobody'd have to worry about Hoagy making passes."

"Yeah," I said. "I like Marge, too."

"And your uncle—I didn't meet him till tonight. Who and what is he?"

"Ambrose Hunter," I said. "But just call him Am, or he'll turn you over his knee. He's the best guy in the world, just about."

"I—I'd like to know him."

"You will," I said. "And there are other good guys. Like Lee Carey, the magician with the side show. Like swing music?"

"Sure."

"Carey's got a phono and some swell records. We'll go listen to 'em sometime. And you'll like him, too. And I'll guarantee he won't make passes."

"Why not?"

"Because, well—"

"You mean if he made them at anyone, it would be at you?"

I said, "He wouldn't do that, either. He wouldn't do that because— Oh hell, let's skip it. Your guess was close enough. But he's a nice guy, anyway, and you'll like him."

"Okay, then we'll listen to his phonograph sometime. But the other carneys I've met—"

"I think you've got the wrong slant on them, Rita. The morality of a carnival isn't that of a Presbyterian church in the Bible Belt. But if you were in a jam, they'd give you the shirts off their backs—most of them—and not because they expected anything back for it."

"Ummm—maybe you're right."

"Sure I'm right. You got off on the wrong foot, judging them. You've got to see things the way they see them, to get along. They're—well, they're dishonest in an honest kind of way."

"You mean, never give a sucker an even break?"

"That isn't exactly it, but—more or less."

"*I* believe in that, Eddie. Someday I'm going to find myself a sucker. A rich one. I'm not going to be poor all my life. I grew up that way, and that was plenty."

She meant it; there was something a little fierce in her voice. She said, "You think I'm a gold-digger, don't you? Well, I am."

"That's fine," I said. "So you're a gold-digger. So don't get so excited about it. Put your head on my shoulder and relax."

She laughed a little, and then put her head on my shoulder. She said, "You're funny, Eddie. I like you. I wish you were rich, so I could make a play for you. But you aren't, are you?"

"I've got nineteen dollars and a trombone," I told her. "I think I'm rich. Oh, and I've got one good suit, but I haven't got it on and I wish I had because it's getting cool. All I've got on under this raincoat is a pair of shorts. I was asleep when the excitement started."

"Me, too. I mean, I'd gone to sleep and I woke up and had to go to the—what is it you call it, with a carney?"

"The doniker," I told her. "Look, don't talk about what happened. I'm supposed to get your mind off it."

"I'm all right now, Eddie; don't worry. I just—got a little hysterical back there for a minute. I don't mind talking about it."

"Okay. Then, in that case, maybe it'll even do you good to talk about it. Look—do you always carry a gun when you go to the doniker?"

"Of course not; don't be silly. It was because the lights were all out, and I couldn't find a flashlight. And I'm afraid of the dark, Eddie. I mean, when I'm alone in the dark; I'm not afraid now.

"I don't sleep on the lot, usually. I've got a room downtown in a hotel. But tonight Darlene asked me to stay with her."

"Darlene? That's the redhead, isn't it?"

"Yes. Her man's out of town for a couple of days, and she wasn't feeling well tonight and asked me to stay with her. In their trailer. When I woke up an hour ago or thereabouts, I couldn't find a flashlight and didn't want to wake Darlene. But I happened to know where Walter kept his gun because I'd seen it before when Darlene opened a drawer. So I took that."

She shivered a little; I thought maybe because her mind had gone back to what had happened after she left Walter's trailer. I tightened my arm around her. I said, "Don't think about it, Rita."

"I'm all right, Eddie. I told you that. Except I'm cold. I haven't got much more on under this coat than you have under yours, and I'm freezing."

I said, "And a fine exhibit we'd make if a state police car came by and picked us up for parking. Besides, the police will be at the lot by now, and they may get huffy if you're gone too long. So shall we go back?"

"Yes."

"You're sure you're all right, and set to face the music?"

"Yes, Eddie. Kiss me, just once and nicely. And then let's go back."

I kissed her—just once and nicely. And it was plenty nice. It jolted me a little; I hadn't been expecting anything like it.

I whispered, "Are you *sure* we should go back?"

"Yes, Eddie. Please."

"Okay," I said, "But someday, maybe?"

"Someday, maybe."

So I turned the ignition key and stepped on the starter and the windshield wiper started wiping again, back and forth across the glass irregularly, like a drunken metronome. I felt a bit drunk myself.

And again I had to concentrate on keeping the car on that shiny strip of black road, so we didn't talk on the way back.

CHAPTER II

AT THE CARNEY LOT, there were more lights on. The generator hadn't been fixed yet, but oil and carbon lamps had been dug up and hung at strategic spots. It looked weird, somehow; I mean the spots of light made the places in between seem darker and scarier.

There was a light on inside Hoagy's trailer. Uncle Am came out of the door of it as I eased the car back into position. He opened the door of the car and said, "Hi, kids. How was the moon?"

"Brightly shining," I told him.

"I-I feel fine," Rita said. "Is everything okay, Am?"

"Everything's ducky. The police have arrived and, if I may coin a phrase, have the situation well in hand. They've set up headquarters in the freak show top. They want you to show up there, but just for a few routine questions."

"Shall I go with her, Uncle Am?" I asked.

"You stay out of it, Ed. I told 'em we'd sent Rita for a drive around the block and I didn't mention who with. So you can just disappear quietly into your bunk."

It sounded like a good idea because I was cold through, now. My raincoat felt as wet on the inside as it was on the outside, and clammy.

Rita said, "Thanks a lot, Ed. See you tomorrow." She gave me her hand a minute and I said, "Sure. Tomorrow," and then watched her walk toward the freak show top.

I stood there shivering a minute, and then went to our sleeping top. I toweled myself off again, put a couple of blankets on my cot and climbed in under them.

I was sleepy, but not yet asleep, when Uncle Am came in

and started undressing. I said "Hi" to let him know I was awake.

"Like Rita?" he asked.

"She's all right."

"That doesn't sound enthusiastic. Or does it? Anyway, don't fall too hard. She's the type that's out after dough."

"Uh-huh," I said. "She told me so. Said if I was rich she'd make a play for me."

Uncle Am shook his head slowly. He said, "That's dangerous, kid. When they're honest with you, that's dangerous." I couldn't tell from his voice if he was serious or not.

I said, "Then if they're dishonest, they're not dangerous?"

"Not the same way." He stood up and put out the carbide lamp. Then the cot creaked as he got into it.

I asked, "Who was the kid?"

"What kid?"

"The one that was killed, of course. Was he with the carney?"

"Hell," said Uncle Am, "I forgot you haven't been around. It wasn't a kid, Ed. It was a midget."

I sat up. A midget—that could mean only one thing. There was only one midget with the carnival.

"You mean it was the Major?" I demanded.

"No. Nobody knows him. This midget wasn't with the carney, Ed. Nobody around here had ever seen him before."

For a minute I thought he was kidding me. It didn't make sense. A midget who *wasn't* with the carney found stabbed to death and stark naked in the freak show top. A midget nobody with the carney even knew was around.

It sounded fantastic. But then I realized Uncle Am wouldn't be kidding me about a thing like that.

"Where were his clothes?" I asked. "Did they find his clothes?"

"No."

"But how the hell—?"

Uncle Am said, "It's none of our business, Ed. Let the cops worry about it."

"All right," I said. I lay down again. And after a while I went to sleep.

I got up early the next morning. I don't know why, except that I woke up and got thinking, and couldn't go back to sleep. Uncle Am always says thinking is dangerous; that's one of his pet themes—that thinking is worse than getting drunk but not quite as bad as smoking reefers. Somewhere in between. Of course, he doesn't really mean it.

I got dressed, putting on my best suit; I don't know why. Uncle Am didn't wake up.

Outside, the sky was a dull gray, but the rain was over. It was hot, even that early. There wasn't a breath of air and the canvas of the tops hung as still as though it was chiseled out of gray stone, the same color as the sky.

I stood there on the soggy grass in front of our tent, wondering what in hell I'd got up for. Probably, I decided, to keep from thinking.

I turned up the cuffs of my pants to keep them out of the mud and went on out to the midway. Over past the merry-go-round there were some men shoveling shavings off a truck into the mud. Otherwise there was nobody in sight.

I walked down to the end, where Hoagy's trailer was. Marge, I knew, generally got up early. I was honest enough with myself to admit that I wanted to see her solely to lead the conversation around to Rita.

But there wasn't any light in Hoagy's joint, or any sign of life. Nor was there at Walter-and-Darlene's trailer, around the curve of the oval. Not that I'd expect Rita to be up yet; she must have got to bed a long time after I did.

I started back to the midway, and I felt like sloshing through the puddles, but I didn't. I went around the high-dive tank with its platform high up on a tall pole. I looked up and shivered a little at the thought of being up there and diving from that awful height into four and a half feet of water. Not that *I* ever intended to dive from up there, but I had dreams about it once in a while.

When I was back on the midway again I saw a man in front of the freak show who was a stranger to me. He was sitting on the edge of the bally platform, smoking a cigarette. He was a big guy, with a kind of dumb look on his face. He looked like he might be a cop. When I got close enough that I could see his shoes, I decided he was a cop.

But I thought even a dumb cop might be better than nobody at all to talk to, that is, if he wanted to talk.

I said, "Hi" and he said "Hi" back in the right tone of voice —not too interested or enthusiastic, just ordinarily friendly— so I stopped.

"Cop?" I asked him.

"As you can plainly see," he said. "I try to dress and look the part, to please the suckers."

That was better than I'd expected. I sat down on the bally platform too. "How goes it?" I asked him.

"Lousy," he said. "The way these goddamn carneys cooperate— You a carney?"

"Yeah," I said. "I hear the guy was a midget. Who was he?"

"We don't know," he said. "Tie that. Nobody knows him. Nobody ever heard of him. Nobody ever saw him. Nobody ever smelled him. Hell. We get a *freak,* dead in his birthday suit in a freak show, only nobody ever heard of him. They say."

He threw his cigarette down in the wet grass, pulled out a crumpled package and put a new cigarette in his mouth. He lighted it from a lighter that shot a flame four inches high.

I said, "It sounds silly, sure. But I've been with the carney all season. There's only one midget with it."

He nodded gloomily. "That's what they all say. Where were you while the fun and games were going on? I don't remember seeing you last night. Or did I?"

"I was in bed," I said. "Turned in early. I didn't even hear the shot, but my uncle waked me up coming in the tent to—"

"Wait a minute," he said. "We might as well make this official and save time later." He pulled a notebook and pencil out of his pocket and got set for action. "Name?"

"Ed Hunter," I said. "Nineteen—nearer twenty. Been with the carney a year or so. Staying and working with my uncle, Ambrose Hunter. He runs a ball game concession."

"Yeah, I remember him. Shortish, fattish?"

"And smartish," I said. "That's him."

"Then you both sleep on the lot, in a tent back of your booth?"

"Yeah," I said, and went on to tell him how I'd got waked up and had gone to the side-show top after Uncle Am, in a raincoat over my shorts, and about seeing the body. After that I switched it a little because Uncle Am hadn't told them I'd taken Rita for a ride, so I couldn't either. I said I'd gone back to our sleeping tent and had gone back to sleep before the police came.

He looked at me, a little funny, I thought. "Sleep the rest of the night?"

"Sure."

"How long you been up this morning?"

"Not long," I said. "Fifteen-twenty minutes."

"Who've you talked to since you woke up?"

"Not a soul," I told him. "Not a word."

He put the notebook back in his pocket. He gave me a long look that I didn't particularly like. He looked away and said, "God damn," to nobody in particular, unless to himself.

Then his eyes came back to me again. "You carneys don't like cops, do you?"

It caught me a little off guard. I said, "I guess a lot of them don't like cops."

"Why not?"

"Well, I guess they—we—get to figuring the law is against us because it sloughs some of our best concessions in most of the towns we play, and—"

"Do we stop any honest, legal, decent ones?"

"Well—"

"Look, think it over; what a carney would be like if the law let it run wide open, if nobody gave a damn. Your penny-pitch games that slide along the borderline of gambling would be shell games and three-card montes—and all of 'em either as crooked as hell or with the odds so stacked against the sucker you might as well take his money with a gun. Your cooch shows would be strips, and with little tents pitched in back for the customers who really wanted to lay it on the line after the—"

"Who," I said, "gave you the idea carney girls are whores? They aren't."

"Because the law doesn't let—" He stopped. "Wait, don't

look at me like that. I don't mean the same girls, the ones you got now, would do that. Not all of 'em, anyway. I mean the carney would hire broads who *would* put out.

"And your candy floss booth'd sell reefers instead of air, and your side shows— Oh, hell, skip it."

"If a carney peddles stuff the law doesn't like, it's because the mooches want it, isn't it? Your citizens."

He sighed. "Ed, if the *majority* of my citizens wanted gambling and indecency, the town would have it. Nobody'd have to go to a carney for it."

He looked at me gloomily. "So you don't like cops, and you lie like hell to us."

"What do you mean?"

"You went back to sleep before we got here last night. Right? And you haven't talked to a soul this morning. But you knew without my telling you it was a midget and not a kid. How? Up to the time we got here and turned him over, nobody knew that."

"Hell," I said, disgustedly. I did feel disgusted with myself for being so dumb. "I woke up when Uncle Am came in to bed. He told me."

He said, "Oh," as though he meant it, as though he believed me. He shoved his hat back farther on his head. "You don't know the midget that was killed?"

"No," I said. I saw his expression start to change and I said, "Now hold it; don't get your bowels in an uproar. I didn't see his face, no, but just the same I know that I don't know him. For the simple reason that I don't know *any* midgets except Major Mote, and Uncle Am told me it wasn't the Major."

He nodded. "Okay, Ed. Just for routine, though, I want you to take a look at the picture we took of him last night." He took a photograph out of his pocket and handed it to me.

I took it and looked at it.

It wasn't a picture you'd want for a pin-up. It was a wizened little dead face with the eyes wide open and staring. The face had a look that made you think he'd known that knife was going into his back, all right. The picture had been taken right where he'd been lying, except that he'd been turned over, face up. Back of his head was the trampled grass.

I handed it back. "No," I said. "I don't know him. I never saw him before."

"Just one more question then, Ed. Notice anything at all last night that was out of the ordinary? Anything that wasn't strictly routine and kosher?"

"Nothing," I said, "except the lightning fritzing the generator. That doesn't happen every night."

"Yeah," he said, "we know about that. Okay, Ed, thanks."

It sounded like a dismissal, but I didn't feel like moving on, especially as I had no place to go, in particular. I asked him, "You been here straight through? Don't you sleep?"

"Once in a while. Don't talk about it, or I'll start yawning. And I haven't even got a start at making the world safe for midgets. What time does your chow top open?"

"About ten, usually."

He pulled out a big gold pocket watch and looked at it. "Guess I'll live till then. Maybe after then, if they don't put arsenic in my eggs. Will they?"

"I wouldn't bet on it," I told him. "One of the cooks is a two-time loser. Well, be seeing you."

I strolled on toward the front gate. His talking about breakfast made me realize I wanted some myself, and I didn't want to wait till ten. There was a bus waiting at the end of the line, only a block from the carney lot. I got on it and pretty soon it started in to town.

On the bus I could think of some good answers to a lot of nasty cracks he'd taken at the carney. You can always think of good answers when it's too late.

One other thing I realized; right or wrong in his slant on carneys, he wasn't a dumb cop. And he wasn't a bad guy.

Evansville, when I got off the car downtown, turned out to be bigger than I'd thought. Not anything like Chicago, of course, and not even as large as Louisville, but it was more than a crossroads, at that. I had breakfast in a cafeteria and got a shine to get the mud off my shoes and then strolled along the main drag, looking things over.

It was only eleven o'clock and none of the movies were open yet.

So I strolled around looking in windows; music store windows, haberdashery windows, even lingerie windows.

But it didn't work. Not even the lingerie could take my mind off what I was trying not to think about—the face of that dead midget.

After a while I told myself, okay, think about it, then, and get it over with. It's none of your business; you didn't even know him. But buy a paper and read about it if it'll make you any happier; that's what you've been waiting to do, isn't it?

So I bought a paper. It had the story, all right. The banner head was MIDGET MURDERED AT CARNIVAL.

I went in the lobby of a hotel and sat down to read the story. I read it all and didn't learn anything new, except the names of the policemen working on it. The chief of police was named Harry Stratford and the captain of detectives was Armin Weiss. That might have been interesting to somebody.

There were two pictures, a little one mitered into a big one. The little one was the picture of the dead midget—his head and shoulders, that is—lying on the grass, the same picture the cop at the carney had shown me. The big picture was a flashlight shot of the inside of the freak show top. It had been taken after the body had been moved, but the usual X marked the spot. It was taken from just inside the entrance, and you could see the empty platforms, and the grass and canvas and poles, and nothing else. No people, I mean. Either the police had cleared the top by then, or the carneys had got out of the way when the photographer had set up his camera.

I looked back at the streamer head, MIDGET MURDERED AT CARNIVAL. It sounded so simple. I mean, what more logical place is there for a midget to be murdered? Only it wasn't right; there was a word missing. It should have read MIDGET MURDERED AT *WRONG* CARNIVAL.

One little word that took it out of the plane of the ordinary and made it screwball.

I got to wondering what it would be like to be a midget. You wouldn't seem like a midget to yourself, I thought. Everybody around you would be giants. Every one of them big enough to pick you up and break you in two. Or stick a knife in you—

I remembered the way his dead face looked and I thought again, *he knew that knife was coming.* But he hadn't yelled, or nobody had heard him yell. Maybe some giant, somebody twice his height and four times his weight, had held him and held a hand over his mouth and—

I didn't want to think about it. To get my mind off it, I read the rest of the paper. There'd been a holdup at a filling station, and a burglary. Neither of them sounded very interesting.

A hundred miles away, in Louisville, there'd been a kidnaping. The seven-year-old son of James R. Porley, of the Porley Cosmetics Co., had been stolen from his bed and a note demanding fifty grand ransom had been left pinned to his pillow.

Almost as nasty a crime, I thought, as murder. And—like murdering a midget—a case of somebody not picking on someone his size.

There'd been a riot in Calcutta. And a defeated candidate for the Illinois legislature was charging an election fraud and making quite a stink about it.

I did what I should have done in the first place, leafed over to the comic section. After that I read the movie ads.

I wondered if it was going to rain some more. If so, I might as well see a movie, now that I was in town. If not, I ought to go back to the lot to help Uncle Am.

I walked over to the window of the lobby and looked out. I could see the sky between the two buildings across the street, but it didn't tell me anything. It was the color of old type metal, like it had been all morning. No clouds, just solid gray nothingness. It could be going to rain the rest of the month, or never again all summer.

Damn, I thought. I felt restless; I wanted to do something and I didn't know what. You get in those moods once in a while, when nothing seems to have any meaning and you don't know what you're hanging around for. I wanted to go back to the carney, and I didn't want to.

I turned around and looked at the clock over the desk of the hotel to see if it was noon yet. It was a quarter to.

There was a girl standing at the desk speaking to the clerk, handing him a key. From a back view, anyway, she didn't look like anything you'd expect to see in Evansville. She looked like a million dollars in gold. That's the color her hair was, and it was in a sort of page-boy bob that hung down to her shoulders. She wore a mauve silk dress that fitted her curves like a bathing suit on a Petty girl. She was as far out of this world as a Louis Armstrong trumpet ride.

So I let the view out of the window take care of itself; I wanted to wait until she turned around, to see if the front view matched the back.

Not that I had any ideas, understand; I was just a carney punk with eighteen bucks in my pocket and to my name, and even outside of money I wasn't in her class. You know what I mean.

Let me put it this way: The hotel lobby had been a fairly nice one, with good furniture and decent decorations, until she stood there in it—and then by contrast she made it look like a shabby, down-at-the-heel flophouse. And she did the same thing to me; I mean, until then I'd been a fairly well dressed, fairly good-looking guy, but if I was with her I'd feel like a high-school kid and look like I'd slept in my clothes.

Anyway, that's what I was thinking, and then she turned around and I guess I did a double-take.

From the front, she was exactly what I'd expected and hoped for, except for one thing: I knew her. It was Rita.

I wouldn't know, but probably my mouth fell open. I felt that way.

She started toward the street door and then she saw me and smiled at me. She changed direction a little and came over to me. She said, "Hi, Eddie." Her voice, at least, was the same as last night.

I stammered something.

"How did you know where I was staying, Eddie?" she asked.

"I didn't." I said. "I came in out of the rain, only it didn't rain. Look, could I buy you a drink, or something?"

She hesitated just a second. "Breakfast, maybe. Have you eaten yet?"

"No," I said.

We had coffee and doughnuts in the coffee shop off the hotel lobby. I kept looking at her across the table. I still couldn't believe it. It didn't seem possible that muddy shoes and ankles and a shapeless slicker and hair being tucked up under a beret could have made *that* much difference.

Over the coffee, she asked, "Have they found out anything, Eddie, about the midget?"

I shook my head. "Not according to the newspaper. They don't even know who he is."

"But that ought to be easy to find out. There can't be so awfully many midgets, can there?"

I'd happened to have talked about that with Major Mote once, and I had the answer. I said, "There are a couple of thousand in the United States. Real midgets, that is. There are about fifty thousand dwarfs."

"What's the difference, Eddie? The midgets are smaller than the dwarfs?"

"Well—I guess most of them are, but that isn't the difference. A midget is perfectly proportioned. A dwarf has a head as big, or almost as big, as a full-sized person. And their bodies, their torsos, are long. They have very short legs and arms."

"Oh. Then just the midgets would be in show business, huh?"

"Generally speaking, yes. No side show would exhibit a dwarf as a midget. But some circuses have dwarf clowns. And some of the troupes of midgets, in vaudeville or in the bigger carney shows, have a dwarf as a comedian—and, I guess, for contrast with the real midgets. Some dwarfs make pretty good clowns."

"Can I have another cup of coffee, Eddie?"

"I guess I can afford it. I told you last night I had nineteen dollars. I've still got eighteen of it."

"Eddie! Have you been spending it on other women?"

"Not yet. And if we stick to coffee, that much money will go a long way."

"Umm-hmm. Then we'll stick to coffee. With maybe a doughnut now and then. I can't get over it, Eddie."

"Over what? The doughnut?"

"No, over how different you look dressed up, from the way you looked last night."

I couldn't help it. I leaned back and laughed. I had to explain, of course, and then she laughed too. She was beautiful when she laughed, and even her laughter was beautiful. It was funny, too, that I hadn't even noticed what a nice voice she had.

"You didn't stay the rest of the night with Darlene?" I asked her.

She nodded. "Yes, but here at the hotel instead of the trailer. After the cops questioned me, I found Darlene up and dressed, and neither of us wanted to stay there. We came in to town and slept in my room here. Only Darlene went back to the lot earlier because she expected her man back this morning."

After the second cup of coffee, Rita looked at her wrist watch. "We've got to get out to the lot," she said. "That is, I have to. And I've got an errand first, at a bank. It's next door. Will you wait here for me; that is, if you're going out to the lot too—?"

"I'm going out," I told her. "Sure, I'll wait here."

Coffee was practically running out of my ears by then, what with the two cups I'd had with my first breakfast an hour before. But I had another cup while I waited.

Then we took a bus out to the lot. She told me we had to watch my eighteen dollars, and wouldn't let me take a cab.

CHAPTER III

UNCLE AM WAS UP and dressed when I got back. He'd dug up some shavings somewhere and was spreading them on the ground in front of our booth.

He said. "Hi, kid. Been in town?"

"Yeah. Woke up early and couldn't sleep. What do you think about the weather?"

"Might drizzle a little. But there ought to be some business, with the town coming out to see the spot marked X."

"You saw a paper, then?" I asked him.

"Nope. But I remember my high-school algebra; X always marks the spot. And the police wonder Y."

I winced. "They're still wondering this time," I told him.

"If you were all the way in town, why didn't you stay for a movie?"

"I ran into Rita in town—accidentally. She was coming out to the lot, so I trailed along."

He said, "Oh," and looked at me. "Careful, kid."

"You didn't warn me last night when you told me to take her for a ride." I grinned at him. "Anyway, I'm safe. She wouldn't look at me twice."

"Once might be enough, if she looked at you the right way. And don't underestimate yourself, Ed. You may not be good looking, but you're romantic looking. Any one of these days now, you'll have to start using a baseball bat to chase the women off you."

"Uh-huh," I said. "Anything new, otherwise?"

He knew what I meant. He said, "Not much. Weiss was around a little while ago."

"Weiss?"

"Armin Weiss, captain of detectives or something. I judge he talked to you earlier in the morning."

I nodded.

Uncle Am said, "He's a thorough sort of cuss. Wanted to know if you'd been awake when I turned in last night. I told him you were. What'd you do, cross yourself up by knowing something you shouldn't have known?"

"That's it," I told him. "I knew he was a midget—and I'd told him I'd gone back to sleep before the cops came and hadn't talked to anybody this morning."

"I figured it was something like that. You'd make a hell of a criminal."

"Okay, then, I'll stay honest. Weiss, by the way, thinks all of us carneys are a bunch of crooks."

Uncle Am grunted and went back to spreading the shavings.

"Can I help?" I asked him.

"Not in those clothes."

I went in and changed, but by the time I got back, he'd finished all the work there was to be done and was sitting on the low counter, juggling three of the baseballs in a tight little circle.

I tried it, but spent most of my time picking them up.

"Kid," Uncle Am said, after about the tenth time I'd dropped one, "you just aren't cut out to be a juggler. Better give up."

"What am I cut out to be?"

"I dunno. A trombone, maybe."

"No," I said. "I haven't got what it takes. I can learn to play the spots, if I struggle hard enough. But I can't *think* on a tram, like a real player. When somebody takes a ride, I can go along, but I can't drive the car."

"A lot of musicians can't, and make a living."

"I wouldn't want to be that kind. Oh, I'm going to keep on playing, but I don't want to make my living at it. I want it to be for fun."

He nodded, and after a while I asked it again; what he thought I was cut out to be.

"Maybe you're cut out to be Ed Hunter. Ever think of that?"

I thought it over. I said, "There's no money in it."

He stopped juggling the baseballs and looked at me. "You want some money, Ed? We've been doing all right. I can let you have some. What do you want? Fifty? A hundred?"

I shook my head. "I've got some left. Look, Uncle Am, you sure you won't need me for a while? I might take a walk around."

"Go ahead."

I walked the long way around, past the entrance gate. There were a few people beginning to trickle in, not many. The sky still looked as though it might let go any minute.

I found myself thinking about the copper, Armin Weiss, and his cracks about the carney. Down inside of me, they rankled.

I looked over the concessions as I walked by them. On plenty of them, he was pretty near right. Like the shooting game I was passing. Spud Reynolds charged two bits for three shots—at fairly short range—with a twenty-two rifle at a card with a red diamond printed on it. If you shot all the red diamond out of the card, you got a prize. A big one, your choice of a lot of flashy stuff he had standing around. But nobody had won a prize yet by shooting all the red out of the card. It was theoretically possible maybe, but just not practical. It looked easy—that was the gimmick—but the best marksman in the country would have to have God sitting in his lap to do it.

I had to give Weiss that one. And plenty of the others: the game where you tried to pitch your coin so it stayed in a floating dish, the cork-guns with which you tried to knock a pack of cigarettes off a rack, the disk game. They were all pretty heavily loaded against the sucker.

But our own game wasn't so bad. For one thing, we didn't offer expensive flash that the mark couldn't win. About one out of twenty-five could knock all three milk bottles off the box with the three baseballs and win a kewpie doll that cost us fourteen cents, sure.

But what the hell, he was paying his dime for the fun of trying, the fun of showing off in front of his girl or the other fellows, the physical fun of whaling those three baseballs as hard and straight as he could. The damn kewpie doll didn't mean anything to him, except as a symbol, so it wasn't really a gambling game. And there was skill involved, even if you had to have some luck besides the skill.

I walked past the mitt camp and the unborn show and the loop-a-plane and the terminus of the scenic railway and the jig show.

When I got to the freak show, Harry Stulz, the talker, was starting a spiel. He had a small tip, mostly kids, but every sentence or so he'd interrupt himself to thump hurry-hurry-hurry on the bass drum, and more people were gathering.

I walked around the crowd, intending to go on past. But when I got even with the far end of the bally platform, somebody said, "Hi, Ed," and I looked around.

It was the copper, Armin Weiss, and he was still, or again, sitting on the end of the bally platform. I went over.

I said, "Don't you ever sleep?"

He laughed. "Tonight, maybe. I'm good for the rest of the day, with coffee now and then."

"But what are you doing?"

"Sitting here waiting for the lightning to strike me, I guess. Like it struck the generator last night, if it did."

"Huh? You mean—it didn't?"

"That's on my list. A talk with the electrician who fixed it. As soon as I get back to town. How do you like Evansville?"

"A nice town," I said.

"We try to keep it that way." He pulled out cigarettes and offered me one, and we lighted up. He said, "Ed, my wife is the best cook in forty miles. You like dumplings?"

"I guess so."

"Then you've never eaten any good ones, or you wouldn't guess so. My wife makes them so light you have to weight 'em down to keep 'em on your plate. And she makes gravy that's just what you need to weight 'em down. I'll bet all the dumplings you ever ate were soggy."

I said, "I guess they were."

He shook his head sadly. "The world is going to the dogs. Look, Ed, this is Friday and we have pot roast and dumplings every Friday night for supper. 'Tain't far from here; walking distance. How'd you like to have supper with us?"

I said, "Mr. Weiss, I don't know anything about the midget, or about the murder. What you could pump out of me wouldn't pay for the gravy, let alone the pot roast and dumplings. Honest to God."

He grinned. "I know that, Ed. Or I think so, anyway. But there are other angles. First, you and Am are the only people around here who don't treat me like I got something catching. And then Am tells me you play trombone. I thought you might bring it around and we could make some noise together, kind of. I got a trumpet myself that I played in a band once when I was younger, and my wife doesn't do as good on the piano as on the stove, but she can play some."

I said, "I'm weakening. But there's no ulterior motive?"

"Sure there's an ulterior motive, son, only it ain't ulterior. You know the people around here, most of them, and the setup. You can tell me who's who and the general background, and give me something to get my teeth into. You can help plenty."

"Well—" I said.

"Good. It's thirty-two sixteen Arlington, only six-seven blocks from here, toward town. We eat at six and my wife'll be mad if you're late, and don't forget the trombone."

"Okay," I said.

He eased himself down off the edge of the platform, said, "So long, then," and lumbered off toward the main gate.

I stood there wondering what I'd said yes for. I didn't want to get mixed up in it. It wasn't my business.

Somebody was looking at me; I felt it on the back of my neck. I turned around. Skeets Geary, who runs the freak show, was standing there in the entrance looking at me. He had a grin on his face, but it wasn't a nice grin. It wasn't a nice face, either, for that matter. Skeets looks like a caricature of a race track tout. But as far as I knew, he didn't have anything against me.

I put my hands in my pockets and walked over. I said, "Hi, Skeets," and he straightened his face out. It went sour when it straightened out. He said, "Listen, Ed, for your own good. Sucking up to coppers won't get you anything around here."

"The hell," I said, "I thought it might get me redlighted."

People were walking past us; the barker was grinding now, and he was pulling them in. Practically all the adults that had been in the tip for the bally.

I stepped away from Skeets and walked in with them. There was something new inside the top, I saw right away. It was a wooden railing about five or six feet square. The marks were gathering around it.

I walked over. Inside the railing was a spot of grass where the body had been lying last night. The body wasn't there, but it had been outlined, like the police outline a body in chalk before they move it.

Only the outline was with a piece of heavy string, because you can't mark with chalk on grass. And a knife with dried blood on the blade was lying inside the string, just where the heart of the body had been. It wasn't the real knife, of course —the police would have taken that. But it was another of Australia's throwing knives, just like the one that had been used for the murder. I don't know where Skeets got the blood, but it wouldn't have been his own.

A couple of marks shouldered up beside me along the railing and I stepped back. I was mad. It probably showed in my face when I walked over to Skeets.

When I got there, there wasn't anything I wanted to say. Not a damn thing. Instead, I just put my hand against his chest and pushed, and he went down backward over a guy rope.

I stood there and waited while he got up, hoping to hell he'd want to make something of it. My knuckles were itching for him to.

Instead, he got up slowly and didn't say a word. He looked at me and his eyes were like little marbles. He turned and went back inside.

The minute it was over, I knew I shouldn't have done it. And, because he hadn't fought back, I even felt a little foolish, a little out on a limb.

When I knocked on the door of Hoagy's trailer, his voice called out for me to come in. He and Marge were sitting one on each side of the breakfast nook that was built into the trailer. Hoagy hadn't been in the trailer company's mind when they'd designed that nook; he more than filled his half of it, and looked uncomfortable.

He grinned at me and said, "Hi, Ed. Pull up a chair. Don't talk loud, though."

He nodded toward the back of the trailer and I saw that Rita was taking a nap on the bunk back there. She'd taken off the mauve silk dress so as not to muss it, and wore only a cream-colored slip. The outlines under the slip were so beautiful that I caught my breath a little.

"Some coffee, Ed?" Marge asked me.

I didn't really want any, but I said "Sure" and got myself a cup and a spoon from the cupboard before I pulled a chair up to the end of the breakfast table. Facing that way, I couldn't see the bunk and the cream-colored slip and maybe that was just as well.

Marge poured coffee. Her eyes looked tired, and for the first time I noticed that there was gray starting to show in her black hair. It wasn't combed very well, and she didn't have any make-up on yet.

She must have read my mind. She said, "Don't look at me, Ed. I know I look like hell."

"Not quite," I told her, and she grinned.

She said, "Anyway, don't compare me with Angelface."

"Angelface?"

"Rita. That's what my husband calls her. That's why I don't worry about him."

"Oh," I said.

Hoagy chuckled. "Wonderful to have a trusting wife. You can get away with murder."

He didn't mean it that way, of course, but the word grated, somehow. I saw Marge look up sharply, too. I thought she was going to bawl him out, so I changed the subject. I asked, "Is the posing show going to run this afternoon?"

"Maury said he'd open a little after three if it hadn't started to rain by then. We're supposed to wake Rita at three. Guess the poor kid didn't get too much sleep last night. You've been out, Ed. *Is* it going to rain?"

I shrugged. "I wouldn't know, but Uncle Am doesn't seem so think so, and he's pretty good at guessing. How's Susie?"

Hoagy shook his head. "Not so good. I guess maybe I didn't get a bargain on her after all. She's a pretty sick little chimp."

"For a hundred and fifty bucks," Marge said, "I could have bought a lot of clothes, and with the season about over—"

Hoagy spread his hands. "So maybe we're out one and a half C's, and a little more on fancy foods and medicines. But if I get her well, we're in the bucks. Know what she'd be worth, Ed?"

"How much?"

"Five hundred, easy. That's a nice profit, but that's not what I'm shooting for. I spend the winter training her and if I'm lucky at that, five grand wouldn't get you a slice of her. Next season I take her with the Big Top, and we're in the money."

"You'd sell her, or go with her?"

"I'm not crazy about the carney, Ed. Give me the circus any day. We'd go with her. I got a trained-chimp routine figured out that'd knock their eyes out. A new angle, and easier to teach a chimp than the regular stuff."

I asked, "Have you had Susie to a vet?"

Hoagy chuckled.

Marge said, "Don't you know Clarence is a vet, Ed?"

It took me a minute to figure out who Clarence was; it was almost the first time I'd heard Hoagy called anything else than Hoagy.

"No kidding?" I asked him.

"Any time you get distemper, Ed, just call on me. Sure, I got a degree. Want to see my diploma? It's around somewhere. Only instead of going into practice, I got with the circus; that's where I met Marge. That's where I picked up what I know about chimps. And dogs. I never got on too well with the cat animals."

"You mean you did vetting or training with the circus?" I asked him.

"A little of both. For a while I ran a dog act."

Marge said, "That's where he picked up his stuff he uses in his sex lectures with the side show, Ed. Only instead of talking about women, he's really talking about bitches."

Hoagy said, "I won't say it."

I got up and strolled to the front end of the trailer to take a look through the slats of the makeshift cage Hoagy had built across the front, from wall to wall and about three feet deep.

Susie, the chimp, was curled up asleep in the middle, on a pile of straw. At least I hoped she was asleep; she lay as still as though she were dead. Then, in the dimness inside the cage, I could see there was a slight movement of her chest that showed she was still breathing.

Hoagy said, "Be quiet, Ed. Don't wake her."

As I straightened up, the sound of bedsprings made me turn around. Rita was sitting up on the edge of the bed, yawning, stretching her arms high.

She said sleepily, "Hi, Eddie. Turn around again till I slip my dress on, huh?"

I turned back toward the wooden cage, but this time I wasn't thinking about Susie.

By three o'clock the sun was out. I walked with Rita to the posing show top, and then went back to our booth to see if Uncle Am could use me.

He was getting a fair play, as good as you could expect from an afternoon crowd. He was glad I'd come back, because he was getting hungry and hadn't wanted to run down the front. So I took over while he went to the chow top.

When he came back, I told him about Captain Weiss's inviting me over for dinner and duets. Uncle Am laughed. He said,

"So the Cap doubles in brass! He did get interested when I mentioned you played trombone, but I didn't know why. Sure, Ed, take the whole evening. I'll get Marge to help me for a change. The joint can use a little sex appeal."

"Marge?"

"Sure, why not? She's always glad to pick up a few bucks. I guess Hoagy's a little tight with her on clothes."

"Okay by me," I said. Then I remembered something else and told him about my run-in with Skeets Geary at the side show.

Uncle Am grinned first, and then looked serious. He said, "Kid, you got to watch that Irish temper of yours. Sure, it's a lousy stunt to cash in on murder that way, but you aren't arbiter of Skeets' morals, as long as they don't step on your toes. And even if you don't like something he does, you don't have to push him over a guy rope to prove it."

I said, "It was one of those things that seem like a good idea at the time. I guess I was a sap."

"I guess you were. Only, damn it, I wish I could have seen it. *All right, folks, step right up. Knock over the milk bottles and win a beautiful kewpie doll . . .*"

I stuck around until almost half-past five. Then I got dressed, took my tram, and hunted up the address Weiss had given me.

It was a nice-looking little cottage on a big lot, well back from the street, and with trees around it. It was the kind of place that makes a carney wonder for a minute whether he's a sucker instead of the other guy.

Weiss opened the door. He said, "Hi, kid. Come on in. Ma, this is Ed Hunter."

Ma was one of those bird-like little women. Around forty, I guess; Weiss was a little older than that. She fluttered over me for a minute, and then went out to the kitchen.

Weiss hadn't been kidding about the trumpet. He got it out right away and set up some easy duet stuff on the piano. I put my trombone together and limbered it up, and we played for a while.

It wasn't anything for Carnegie Hall, but it went pretty well at that. The music was strictly off the cob, of course, but it's funny; you don't mind corn when you're playing it yourself. The stuff was all written for two trumpets and that gave me a disadvantage; I had to read treble clef instead of bass and play it an octave down to fit trombone range. But we were both in B flat, so it didn't take any transposing.

Once in a while Ma would come to the door and tell us how good we sounded, as though she really meant it.

Then we got called out into the kitchen to eat. It was a swell big kitchen and I liked the fact that she didn't—like most people would—apologize for eating there. Kitchens *should*, I think, be eaten in. Food tastes better there.

Anyway, that food did. Weiss hadn't exaggerated a bit. It was just plain grub—meat and spuds and dumplings and gravy —but it tasted out of the world. That gravy would have made sawdust taste good, and we didn't put it on sawdust.

I stuffed myself so thoroughly I had to turn down the mince pie for dessert. Weiss called me a sissy and had two pieces himself, even though he'd been a helping ahead of me on the other stuff.

Ma Weiss wouldn't let either of us help with the dishes, not even on wiping them. So the Cap and I sat over coffee and cigarettes and talked about everything except what I'd expected him to talk about. He still hadn't even mentioned the murder.

He asked if I wanted to play some more, but I told him I was too stuffed to blow a horn, and he admitted he felt kind of that way himself.

He got a couple of bottles of beer out of the refrigerator and opened them, and still we talked about everything but.

I broke down first. I asked him if they'd identified the murdered midget.

"Nope," he said. "That's what makes it tough, Ed. We can't even get a start—an intelligent one—till we get an identification on him. We'll get one, though."

"How?"

"Publicity. If a midget turns up dead in Evansville, then there's got to be a midget missing somewhere else. So we get the A.P. and the U.P. to put the story on their wires, and it's a good enough story that it'll make the newspapers all over the country. And pretty soon now somebody will come up with a missing midget to match, and then we got a place to start from. That story's in evening papers all over the country right now, and a phone call from headquarters any minute wouldn't surprise me."

I said, "Wouldn't *Variety* and *Billboard* be the best bets? Damn few carneys and show people read the regular local papers."

"Sure. We're writing *Variety* and *Billboard*. But they don't come out daily like newspapers and it'll take longer if we have to wait for results from them. And the carney'll move on meanwhile. So I'm hoping for results from the dailies. And when we find out who he is, then we can start trying to tie him in with someone in your carney."

I said, "Or someone in Evansville who isn't with the carney."

He shook his head slowly. "That won't wash, Ed. I don't mean we ain't got murderers in Evansville, but none of 'em did this little job.

"For one thing, Ed, look at the knife angle. It belonged to your knife thrower. It was in his trunk under the platform he works on, inside the side show—only a dozen yards from where we found the midget's body. A carney must have got it out of that trunk. A carney would have known where Australia kept his shivs. An outsider wouldn't know."

I said, "Suppose it was a thief hunting around inside the top for something to steal. He finds the trunk and the knives, and—"

Weiss's quiet chuckle stopped me. He said, "And then he took a naked midget out of his pocket and stabbed him. Hell, Ed, it ties in with the carney. You can't get away from it."

I asked, "Have you talked with the electrician who fixed the generator?"

"Who's pumping who, Ed? Yeah, I saw him. It was lightning all right. The murderer took advantage of the darkness, but he didn't manufacture it. You know, Ed, you ought to be a detective. You got a hell of a big bump of curiosity."

"Have I?"

"Haven't you? You know damn well you're as interested in

finding out what happened last night as I am. And I get paid for wondering and you don't. Another bottle of beer?"

He got up and got two bottles without waiting for me to answer so I didn't say no.

He said, "Ed, I did have in mind pumping you a bit when I asked you here. But I thought it over and decided it wouldn't do any good. Until I get some lead to work on, find out who the midget was, I don't know what questions to ask, and you wouldn't know what to tell me.

"I may want to pump you later. But, meanwhile, I'll ask you something else. I'll ask you to keep your eyes and ears open. Just notice anything unusual you see or hear around the carney, anything that might, even remotely, tie in with the murder. And keep me posted. You'll do that?"

"I—I guess so."

"I wish you sounded more enthusiastic about it. You don't like murder, do you?"

"Does anyone?"

He said, "Murderers do. Hell, that ain't exactly right. Let's say they dislike it less than they dislike some alternative they have to face. Like a torpedo who kills a man for five hundred bucks, let's say. Unless he's off the beam mentally, he doesn't get any actual pleasure out of pulling the trigger, but he dislikes worse being without that five hundred bucks. Without it, he might even have to take a job and go to work."

He poured the rest of his second bottle of beer into his glass and drank it.

He said, "A psychopathic murder might be something else again, but this wasn't a psychopathic murder, Ed."

"How do you know?"

"I don't know how I know. But I'm pretty sure it wasn't. It's too screwy to be a psychopathic murder. It—it ain't the pattern."

I nodded. It wasn't very logical reasoning, but I felt that it was right, because I had the same hunch, too.

I said, "You mean you want me to be a spy in the enemy camp. I don't like that."

"You're right," he said, "in putting it that way. *If* you admit that the carnival is the enemy camp. *If* you admit it's the enemy of law and order to the extent that it'll condone cold-blooded murder. *If* you feel you're on the side of the killer, just because he happens to be a carney. Do you feel that way about it, Ed?"

I grinned a little. I said, "Kind of got me out on a limb there."

"Kind of," he said. "Well, think it over and let me know. I won't push you any more. And be careful."

"Careful?"

"I mean, don't go around asking questions. That could be dangerous, and I'm not kidding. People who do murder don't like people who ask questions about it. Say—nobody besides your uncle knows you came here tonight, do they?"

"No," I said. "All right. I'll think it over, Cap. But probably I won't hear or see anything anyway." I drank the last of my beer and stood up. "I think I better go now. I want to get back in time to help Uncle Am a little."

He didn't argue to get me to stay. He shook hands kind of solemn when I left, and Mrs. Weiss came in the room, wiping her hands on her apron. She shook hands, too, and it made me feel kind of foolish; I don't know why. But she said, "Don't let him talk you into anything, Ed."

"I won't," I said.

And, walking back to the lot, I decided I wouldn't. I mean, that I wouldn't do anything active about it or stick my neck out. Just minding my own business wasn't being on the killer's side.

There was a fine mist in the air; it made haloes around all the lights on the lot. It made the ferris wheel seem a mile tall. It muffled sounds and made everything seem unreal. Even more unreal, that is, than a carney usually seems.

I stood there at the curb outside, looking at the big entrance gate, big and bright and gay like the gates of Paradise, that was set back forty feet or so from the street. Through it and around it I could see the tops and the midway; I could hear the screech of the Whip, the thump of a bass drum call to bally, and the thousand voices blending into one big voice, a voice of the crowd and the carney mixed, all one strange sound. It was as though I'd never seen a carney lot before, or heard that sound.

People were brushing past me, there was a real crowd streaming up to the entrance. A bigger crowd than most Saturday or Sunday night crowds, in spite of the mist and the threat of rain. It looked like a good crowd, too, a crowd that didn't have its pockets sewed shut. There's a difference between a good crowd and a big crowd; this one was both.

I started up toward the gate and then changed my mind and went around the outside to our sleeping tent and stashed my trombone; I didn't want to walk down the midway with it and get somebody wondering where I'd been playing it.

Then I ducked under the side wall of our ball game booth. You can get a baseball in the eye doing that, but I didn't.

Uncle Am and Marge Hoagland were running the booth, and getting a good play.

Uncle Am said, "Show must have got out early, huh, Ed?" I knew he was tipping me off what he'd told Marge, so I played along.

I said, "I didn't stay to see all of it. It smelled."

Uncle Am pulled me over to one side of the booth, out of Marge's hearing and said, "Don't hang around, Ed. I promised Marge a cut on what we took in, and if you're here she'll think she ought to leave; that I don't need her. So run along and play somewhere else, huh?"

"Sure, but—"

"No buts. Look, Marge can use the money. Hoagy hasn't been doing too well lately, Ed. And he's been dropping some gambling. He lost fifty bucks the night of the blackjack game early this week, and sixty last night at gin rummy and—"

"And you won it?"

"I won the sixty, yeah. So I'm letting Marge get some of it back for pin money. So run along."

"Okay, okay," I said. "Don't push."

"I'm just shoving. Here's a dime; get yourself a hot dog." He stuck something into the breast pocket of my suit coat. I couldn't see it, but I knew it would be a fin instead of a dime.

I said, "Thanks. I take it you don't mind if I leave, then?"

He grinned and gave me a push and I had to step quick to

get over the low counter in front of the booth without falling over it.

I joined the crowd drifting down the midway. The mob was even thicker than I'd thought. I let myself be carried along with the current and found myself in a thick jam in front of the side show. I got stuck there, nobody around me was moving either way. That seemed funny, because there wasn't any bally going on up on the platform. Just Skeets Geary sitting on one of the two chairs up there, his back to the crowd, and his hat shoved back at a cocky angle.

But the two ticket boxes to the right of the platform were selling tickets like mad, without even a grind going on. An elbow caught me in the side. I turned my head and it was a fat woman, a really big one. She was as tall as I and must have weighed three times as much. She was panting a little.

She said, "Sorry, Mister. Lord, what a crowd."

We were being pushed nearer the ticket boxes. I said, "What goes on? I didn't see the bally. What's the crowd about?"

She looked at me as though I were crazy. "Why, that's where the midget was murdered! Didn't you read about it?"

"Sure, but—"

"Somebody says they doubled the price. Know if that's right? Well, if it is I guess it's worth it. They got the knife he was stabbed with, and blood still on it, my sister says, and the place where the body was found and all that. And you can get a pitcher of the body but that's extra."

"Oh," I said.

I turned around and bucked my way back through the crowd, out to the clear. I went to a lemonade stand and had a glass of it to take the taste out of my mouth. While I was standing there, I took the bill Uncle Am had slipped into my pocket out, to put it into my wallet with the rest of the money I had left.

It wasn't a fin; it was a double sawbuck, a twenty. Business must have been good for Uncle Am, too, I thought and for a black instant I felt disgusted with that, and then I realized that it wasn't his fault if he was making more money tonight because a man had died last night. There'd have been no point in his closing up or turning away customers just because there were more customers than usual. He wasn't deliberately cashing in on what had happened, like Skeets was.

After the lemonade, I walked on around the midway, only cutting across to keep from passing our ball game booth near the front. A ride boy yelled at me as I started across the tracks of the scenic railway; then he recognized me and waved instead.

I watched the bally at the jig show for a while, getting a kick out of the few fast shuffle steps Jigaboo—the seven-year-old kid wonder dancer—gave the crowd for a teaser. He was really good.

After he went inside, I moved on. There were good tips at all the shows. Even the penny arcade was getting a good play. Everybody was making money—even me, if you figured the twenty Uncle Am had slipped me.

With a mob like that the lot would be busy till one or two in the morning, raking in dollars by the thousands. And on a week night, a wet night, an off night.

If the murdered midget had really been a carney, I thought, he hadn't died in vain.

CHAPTER IV

THERE WAS A BIG TIP in front of the posing show. Rita was with the other four girls up on the bally platform. All of them wore bathrobes.

The barker was giving the mike hell. He was Charlie Wheeler, one of the leather-lungers of the old days before P.A. systems, and he'd never got quite used to the idea that he could spiel at less than the top of his voice when he had a mike to amplify it.

Rit had too much make-up on, but then so did all the other models. She was the prettiest one up there, and the youngest. I tried to catch her eye, but couldn't.

Charlie hit his climax, waved the girls inside, started up the music on the P.A., and began to turn the tip. He got a good play, plenty of them went in.

I stood there, wishing to hell I could go inside, and at the same time being kind of glad that I couldn't. Uncle Am had explained that to me when I'd first joined up with the carney. It's funny till you think it out, and then you understand why it's taboo, practically.

What I mean is, if you're a carney you stay out of the posing show. The models don't mind posing in practically nothing at all for the marks, the suckers. They don't count; they're outsiders; you might almost say they aren't human beings. It's strictly impersonal. But it would be indecent for somebody who knows them to go in and watch. It'd be as much Peeping Tom stuff as looking in trailer windows or over hotel-room transoms. It sounds silly, but it makes sense when you think it out.

So I strolled on, wondering if I could date Rita after the show. But damn it, I didn't have a car. I thought, if Hoagy would offer to lend me his again, that would be swell. I didn't want to ask him—but maybe he'd offer it.

There was a light on in his trailer. He'd yell to come in if I knocked, but I hesitated. I don't know why; I just had a hunch I shouldn't.

But I told myself hunches are the bunk, and rapped on the door, and he called out and I went in.

Marge had done some house cleaning in the trailer since I'd been there in the afternoon; it was in spick-and-span order, all but Hoagy. He was sitting just as he'd been earlier in the day, wedged in between the breakfast table and the seat on one side of it. But this time, instead of coffee, there was a three-quarters empty bottle of whisky on the table in front of him, and he was as drunk as I'd ever seen him. Which meant, in Hoagy's case, that he was still under control, but you could tell by the slackness of his face, and by his eyes.

He said, "Sit down, Ed. Get a glass and have a drink." He spoke clearly, but used exaggerated care to do it.

I didn't exactly want one, but I got a glass. "Not much," I told him as he started to pour it. "A short one."

Hoagy's idea of a short one turned out to be to fill the tumbler only half full, a good three or four ounces.

I said, "To Susie," and took a sip of it. Hoagy drank with

me, grunting an acknowledgment of the toast. Then he sat there staring at me, his eyes hooded. Somehow, I think I'd have been afraid of him if I hadn't known him. Or did I? I hadn't known till now that he was a solitary drinker.

I got a little leery of the silence after a while and I took some more of my drink and then asked. "How is she, Hoagy? Susie, I mean."

"Afraid she's going to die, Ed. Well—God damn it, I did the best I could with her."

"That's tough."

"It isn't all the money, either. I don't mind losing a hundred fifty bucks; I knew it was a long odds bet when I got her. I knew that was why I got her so cheap. But, hell, I got to like her."

I started to get up; I was going to look at Susie. But Hoagy said, "Don't bother her, Ed. I gave her a sedative, and it's just starting to take effect."

"Sure," I said, and sat down again. I wondered how I could get the conversation around to the car. I took another drink of the whisky and got rid of all it this time. It burned, and tasted terrible, but I was too proud to run for a chaser.

When my voice came back I asked, "Is Rita coming back here after the show closes tonight?"

"She's got a date."

"Huh?"

Hoagy looked at me and chuckled. He took the bottle up and poured me another drink before I noticed he was doing it.

He said, "Ever hear my sex lectures, Ed? If they don't slough the blow in South Bend next week, come around and find out what's the matter with you. . . . Hell, I'm sorry, Ed. I didn't mean to razz you. I'm drunk. Don't pay any attention to me. But yeah, Rita's got a date with a mooch. An Evansville banker."

"Oh," I said. I remembered Rita's having to stop at a bank while I'd been with her in town. I'd thought it was business.

Hoagy's eyes seemed to get hooded again. He said, "Better not get ideas about Rita, Ed. That's a gal that's going places. She knows a dollar from a piece of paper. But don't get me wrong, Ed; she's a good kid. I knew her when she was in pigtails—and that wasn't so long ago, either. She's—I guess she's eighteen or nineteen. But she smarted up fast after the tough time she had as a kid."

"Yeah?" I said, to keep him talking. I don't know why I wanted him to.

"Her ma died when she was twelve, six-seven years ago. Her old man, Howie Weiman, is a good friend of mine and a nice guy when he's sober, but that ain't often. Rita stuck it out till she was fifteen and then ran away from home—if you could call it a home, living with her old man."

"What's she been doing most of the time?" I asked.

"Knocking around. Worked in a taxi dance joint, stuff like that. Pony in burlecue for a while till they found out she was under age—even at sixteen she could pass for twenty or so. But she got sick and was in a hospital up to a few weeks ago, and while she was there she saw my name in *Billboard* and wrote me, care of the mag. That's how come she landed here."

"Oh," I said.

"But she won't be here long. She's got too much to stay a carney, and too much ambition. One way or another, she's headed for the big time."

"An Evansville banker isn't big time."

"He could be a step uphill. Anyway, Ed—"

"Okay," I said, "you don't need to draw me a diagram. I can take a hint when somebody gives it to me with a baseball bat."

"Have another drink?"

This time I didn't argue, and I forgot to tell him to keep it short, so I got a tumblerful.

He said, "It's none of my damn business, Ed, but you're a good kid and I wanted to save you some—"

"Skip it, Hoagy," I said. "Look, I haven't fallen for Rita, and I'm not going to. She's a swell gal, and I like her. So let's forget it."

I picked up my glass, and we drank. This time I did drink too much and I had to run for a chaser of water.

Hoagy laughed. He said, "I keep forgetting, Ed, that you haven't done too much drinking. Better not have any more after that one, or Am will climb all over me."

By that time I had my chaser down. I took a deep breath and decided the whisky was going to stay in place after all, and that I wouldn't explode.

I grinned back at Hoagy, "Maybe I better not finish that one," I told him. "Thanks just the same, but I do feel it." I took another drink of water and put the glass back. "I better run along, Hoagy," I said. "See you tomorrow."

As I went out, he called after me, "Stay down out of the trees."

I cut through to the midway and managed to nick my ankle stumbling over a stake. But that was probably on account of the darkness and not the whisky.

I really was beginning to feel the drinks, though. I'd had the equivalent of at least six or seven ordinary shots. I found myself walking carefully, concentrating on making a straight line and not wavering.

Physically, I was under control if I kept an eye on myself. Mentally, I wasn't so hot. Learning that Rita had a date with a mooch shouldn't have been a surprise; she'd been frank enough about herself the night I'd met her. But just the same it was a kick in the teeth.

I headed for Lee Carey's trailer back of the freak show top. It was dark, and I stood there a minute wondering whether to go in anyway and play his phonograph. He'd told me to, any time.

Then I heard his voice behind me. "Hi, Ed. God, what a night. Go on in."

He'd just slipped out under the side wall of the freak show top between acts. I went on in, and he followed me.

"Good play?" I asked him.

"What a mob," he said. He wiped his forehead; it had been beaded with sweat. "Skeets is going nuts because he can't get 'em out faster to let more in. We're giving a show every ten minutes; one minute to a platform. I got eight minutes rest left —and I need a drink."

He headed for the kitchenette at the back of the trailer. He said, "Put some music on, will you, Ed? I need a lift."

"Sure. What?"

"Something hot and dirty."

I put "Swamp Fire" on, out of the Dorsey album. He said "attaboy" when the music started and he heard what it was.

He came back with two glasses in his hands. I didn't need another, but I hadn't thought to tell him not to and I couldn't turn it down now; I should have thought before he went back there. And it was a slug the size Hoagy had been pouring.

So I said, "Thanks," and put mine down on the table by the phonograph. I said, "The carney's going to hell, Carey. Everybody's drinking out of glasses instead of bottles. Even Hoagy."

"I can afford a glass; this ought to be a celebration. I'm getting in the bucks tonight, kid. You know how many of those card-trick combinations I've pitched tonight already? Damn near two gross, and at four bits a throw instead of two."

"Swell," I said.

He tossed off his drink and didn't notice that I'd put mine down. He said, "Say, you feeling all right, Ed?"

"Sure."

"Your eyes look kind of funny. Maybe it's me." He looked at his wrist watch and said, "Four minutes yet. I can sit down." He practically fell into a chair.

"Swamp Fire" finished, and I put another record on the phono.

I picked up my glass and took a sip of the whisky. When I put it back down I almost spilled it because I'd put it on top of something tiny that lay on the table in the shadow of the phonograph. I moved the drink and picked up the tiny object.

It was one of a pair of dice, of transparent red plastic, less than a quarter of an inch to a side. I looked again for the mate to it, but it wasn't there.

Carey saw me pick it up. He said, "One of a pair that used to go with a pocket trick I had, a dice box. I lost the other one and the gimmick on the box is busted. Keep it if you want, or throw it away."

I didn't know what I wanted with it, but I said "Thanks" and put it in my vest pocket.

The record finished and Carey stood up and stretched. He said, "Back to the mines. Stick around and play records if you want to. I might drop in once in a while between shows. And get yourself another drink if you want."

"Okay," I said. "Give my love to Skeets."

He went out, and I looked among the dozen albums and picked out a Harry James album, early Harry James. "Memphis Blues" and "Sleepy Time Gal," and stuff like that.

I'd played only a few of them when I discovered that my glass was empty. I had a momentary impulse to fill it up again from the bottle in the kitchen and then I decided I'd better not —if I was going to be able to walk straight.

I played a few more sides and found I was getting definitely woozy. Enough to make me wonder what it would feel like to be really drunk. I'd been on the border line a few times, but never all the way across.

I wondered if I should or shouldn't.

I took the little red cube out of my pocket. I thought, I'll throw it and if it comes low—a one, two or three—I won't. If it comes high—a four, five or six—I will.

I shook it back and forth in my fist, but it was so tiny that I hadn't closed my hand tightly enough and it popped out of the end of my fist; it made an arc in the air and clicked on the linoleum in the middle of the floor. I saw it hit but I didn't see where it bounced.

I swore and shut off the phonograph. I got down on the floor and started looking under things. I finally spotted it way back under the table and had to lie almost flat on the floor to reach it. It wasn't until I'd put it back in my pocket that I realized I hadn't remembered to notice which number was up.

The hell with it, I thought. I took my glass back to the kitchenette and poured myself another drink—but not such a big one this time. And, since there was nobody around, I got myself a glass of water for a chaser.

I played a few more records and took my time about drinking that one. It didn't make me feel any woozier. I felt ever so slightly more sober, I thought. Maybe, I decided, I can drink like a gentleman—but I'd better not crowd it.

I wished Lee Carey would come back, but he didn't. I wanted someone to talk to. I know now it was the liquor, but I felt that I had some pretty profound things to say. About women, for one thing.

But Carey didn't come, so I had one more short drink and then shut up the trailer and went back to the midway.

Things were slackening off a bit, I noticed. The crowds were dwindling, except around the side-show bally platform—where they weren't bothering to bally because they had more marks than they could handle anyway—it began to look like toward closing time of an ordinary night. In another hour, maybe less, it'd be over for the night.

The mist was thicker. It still made things seem haloed and hallowed. It seemed so strange and wonderful I wanted to talk to somebody about it.

The merry-go-round and the miniature railway had already quit running. They're kid stuff, always the first things to close at night.

I leaned against the ticket booth of the merry-go-round and tried to think things out. About Rita, I mean.

I wanted to see her.

And I thought, why shouldn't I? Damn her, she's just a bitch like the rest of them. Just because she happens to be honest about being on the make for money doesn't make it any better, does it? And why—if she's going out with a mooch—shouldn't I see the show if I want to? That ought to make things different.

I went around the midway, the long way around so I wouldn't have to pass Uncle Am's booth. The posing show was starting the last bally of the night.

And Rita was up there, in a bathrobe, with the other girls. Below the bathrobe, her ankles were bare and slim and white.

She didn't notice me at the edge of the tip.

Charlie Wheeler waved the girls in, and started his last-show-of-the-night spiel. It was on the level, too; they weren't going to come out and bally again. I could tell that because he started to disconnect the mike, almost before he was through shouting into it.

I waited until he'd gone inside, so he wouldn't notice, and then I followed the last couple of marks up to the ticket window. I didn't know the ticket taker and I hoped he didn't know me. I put a half dollar on the ledge, got my ticket, and walked in.

It was dim inside. There weren't any seats; the marks—and

I—just stood back of a rope stretched across six feet in front of a stage with a black drop that was supposed to be velvet.

Somebody backstage started a phonograph hooked up to the inside P.A. system. The kind of sensuous, languorous music that goes with posing shows. After a minute of that for buildup, they ran up the curtain of the first tableau. Two of the other girls were in it, not Rita.

It was supposed to represent something; I forget what. Not that anybody in the dim tent cared what it represented, anyway. The girls wore spangled G-strings and the transparent cheeseclothy brassieres the law required. They did have beautiful bodies.

We got maybe fifteen seconds of it and then the black curtain ran down.

The phonograph on the P.A. began to play "My Angel," and the curtain ran up on the second pose. It was Rita, alone.

She was supposed to be an angel, I guess. She stood full-face, her arms outstretched, and some shimmery stuff that was supposed to be wings fell from loops over her white bare arms and came down to points that tied to each side of her G-string waist cord.

Her body was very white, and so beautiful that it made you catch your breath. Anyway, it made me catch mine, and hold it. Instead of a brassière, she wore a piece of white gauze tied loosely back of her neck, hanging not quite to her waist. It was almost perfectly transparent; her breasts were the perfect hemispheres you sometimes see on classical statues in museums and don't expect, or hope, to see elsewhere.

Her head was tilted slightly back, her eyes seeming to stare right into mine. But, I thought, she can't really see me, not in this dimness and across those bright footlights.

Then the curtain went down. I found my hands were clenched so tight my fingers hurt.

I backed through the few men behind me, turned around and went out of there fast.

I stopped out on the midway, because I didn't know which way to turn, or where I was going. I headed back for Carey's trailer.

I thought, I can still walk straight, without staggering.

The trailer was still dark.

I sat down on the step of it and waited awhile, hoping Carey would come. My head wasn't spinning, but my mind was. And I knew now that I wasn't sober at all, because I wanted to cry. Or else I wanted to knock somebody's block off. Or both.

Suddenly I wondered if Hoagy could possibly have lied to me. I didn't know why he would have, but what if he had? What if Rita didn't have a date with a mooch tonight, or at all? Why should I take his word for it?

I'd been sitting there ten minutes or more—Rita must be dressed by now, ready to leave the posing show dressing tent. I got up and hurried back across the midway.

When I got to the rear of the dressing tent, where the entrance was, I could hear girls' voices inside. I recognized Rita's. I stood outside and waited. Darlene came out first, and another girl, one I didn't know. Then, after a minute, Rita came out.

I took a step forward, started to speak to her. I got only as far as "Ri—" when her hand hit me full across the face, hard. It wasn't a slap; it was a hell of a wallop. I was a little off balance and it actually staggered me. It hurt, too; it made my ears ring.

And while I stood there, too surprised to move, she went on around the canvas to the midway.

One of the other girls came out. She said, "Hi, Ed," and I saw it was Estelle, a girl I'd seen around and knew slightly; she'd been with the carney most of the season. She was a small brunette with olive skin and a nice pocketsize figure. She was a nice-looking kid, a little hard, but likable, only a year or two older than I.

I said, "Hi, 'Stelle."

She said, "Eddie, was that a slap I heard?" And at what must have been the expression on my face, she laughed a little. But it was a friendly laugh, not a catty one. There was humor in it, not malice.

She came a step closer. She said, "Don't waste a torch, Eddie. She's got a date with heavy sugar. An honest-to-God banker."

So Hoagy hadn't lied, I thought. I wondered why I'd ever suspected, or hoped, that he had.

Estelle said, "Now me, I play the field. Will you buy me a drink, Eddie?"

Why not, I thought; I've got thirty-five bucks on me. Why shouldn't I take Estelle?

I said, "Why not, honey?" I took her arm and we went out to the midway and toward the main gate. Everybody was streaming that way now, as the carney closed down. Uncle Am's booth was already closed, I saw as we went by it.

I was cold sober now, or thought I was. My ears still rang a little, and in some strange way that ringing seemed to be all fuzzy and muffled, like the other sounds.

We went through the gate and reached the sidewalk. I looked around for a cab, but there wasn't one. I looked down at Estelle and she said, "There's a tavern a block down. Not a bad one. Let's go there for a drink or two and we can phone a cab later, after the rush is over. Huh?"

"Wonderful," I said.

At the tavern we took a booth, side by side, and ordered highballs. Estelle did most of the talking, but she talked enough for both of us. My highball tasted weak, after all the straight whisky I'd drunk—which seemed an awful long time ago, now.

I phoned for a cab and, on my way back from the phone, dropped a nickel in the juke box. I asked Estelle if she wanted another drink while we were waiting. She shook her head.

"Let's have it downtown, Eddie. There's a nice bar in my hotel; we'll have a drink there." She didn't add "— first," but she cuddled a little closer against me in the booth.

She's a nice kid, I thought; it's going to be nice.

I sipped the highball slowly, and kept getting soberer. I was watching the door and when the cab driver came, we gave him the nod and followed him out. Outside, things were still misty and mysterious.

At the cab, I took Estelle's arm before she got in. I said, "Listen, Estelle, I think I better just send you home in the cab. I—I did a lot of drinking with Hoagy and Carey, and that last highball—well, I'm afraid I might be sick. I'm sorry as hell, but—"

She said, "That's all right, Eddie. You don't need to lie to mamma. You're too wound up with that blonde." She laughed a little. "Maybe *I* should get my feelings hurt and slap you. Maybe I should—oh, skip it."

"I'm sorry as hell," I said. "I guess I'm a little nuts."

"Sure," she said. "That's all right. Thanks for the drink, and I'm not even mad enough to pay my own cab-fare. You phoned for it, and you're stuck with it. Pay the man."

I grinned at her and pushed her into the cab. I paid the driver and stood watching until the tail light of the cab lost itself in the mist.

I knew I was being a damn fool.

I thought about going back into the tavern for another drink. But it wouldn't have made me drunk, as I wouldn't have minded being. I was past that stage, and I had the hunch any more would just make me sick. And that would be all I'd need, I thought, for a perfect evening.

Uncle Am wasn't in the sleeping tent when I got there, so I knew he'd be in a card game in the G-top. I was glad; I got into bed quick.

I was still awake when he came in, but I pretended to be asleep. For once—almost the first time—I didn't want to talk to him.

CHAPTER V

IT WAS ALMOST NOON when I woke up the next morning. It was raining again. Uncle Am was gone.

The inside of my mouth tasted pretty bad. I took a drink of water from the thermos jug, and that diluted the taste a little.

Uncle Am came back in while I was getting dressed. He sat on the edge of the cot and watched me. He asked, "How do you feel, kid?"

"Okay," I told him.

"What happened to the other guy?"

"What other guy?" I asked.

"The one that poked you in the puss. It's a little puffed up on the left side. I think bacon is indicated."

"Huh?"

"Applied internally, with eggs, and potatoes. You'll feel better then and I can bawl hell out of you. Ready?"

We went over to the chow top and ate, and I did feel a lot better. I sat back and waited for Uncle Am to start asking questions, but he didn't ask any. So I did.

I asked, "How did you know? Hoagy or Carey?"

"I haven't seen either of them. But when I came in last night, the tent smelled like a distillery. But you look okay, Ed; one side of your puss is a trifle swollen but it's hardly noticeable. Who plied you with liquor?"

"It was my own fault," I said. "Hoagy gave me a few, and then Carey did without knowing I already had a foundation to work on. And then a guy named Ed Hunter gave me the last ones."

I waited to see if he was going to bawl me out, but he didn't, so I asked, "Anything new this morning?"

"About what?"

"About—anything."

"That's a lot of territory," Uncle Am said. "Well—we're moving camp tonight instead of tomorrow night."

"On a Saturday night? We won't get set up in South Bend in time for Sunday business, will we?"

"We won't get any more here, anyway. Weather bureau says this rain's good for three more days at least. So we're jumping a day early with nothing to lose. South Bend's dry. And if the rain's still bad tonight, we'll pack up early and we can be set up in South Bend by noon."

"How about the murder? Will the police let us move early?"

"What's a day's difference? They can't hold the whole carney anyhow. Oh, by the way, I saw your pal Cap Weiss this morning. He was talking to Maury about the jump. He says there's nothing new and he hasn't got an identification yet. But he says you play nice trombone. I gather you made a hit with the Weisses."

"He's a nice guy," I said, "for a copper."

"Yeah. Oh, one other thing. Marge tells me Rita's gone to Indianapolis."

I must have looked blank.

"She got a telegram last night, just before closing," Uncle Am said. "Her father got hit by a truck and hurt pretty bad, might even be dying. He wanted to see her."

"Oh," I said.

Just before closing, I thought; she'd had that on her mind when she was up there on the stage, posing, and had seen me gawking at her like a drunken hayseed.

And she hadn't, then, had a date with a banker; she'd have called it off. I don't know why I was glad about that. I'd sure cooked my own goose with her.

It wasn't logical to feel glad about something that couldn't be good news for me, but I felt that way.

It kept on raining.

Nothing else much happened Saturday.

Early in the evening, when it was raining so hard that nobody was coming out to the lot even to see the spot where the body was found and the knife that the body wasn't killed with, we tore down and packed the vans.

South Bend was a fairly long jump so we decided not to ride the trucks. Uncle Am got us Pullman reservations on a late train. We saw a movie till it closed at midnight, then had a couple of beers to kill the rest of the time, and caught our train.

I had plenty of trouble getting to sleep in my berth. I kept thinking about Rita. I kept being glad she'd missed her date with the mooch. It was silly; I mean, if she was on the make for money, she'd have plenty of other chances and it didn't make any difference that she'd missed that one.

But what if she hadn't missed it? What if she'd told a story about a telegram for a stall? What if she was week-ending with the mooch? Had anybody really seen that telegram?

The noise of the wheels kept me awake.

I tried to tell myself it didn't make any difference to me whether she was with a dying father or sleeping with a God damn banker. Even if I'd ever had a chance with her, she hated me now.

But logic couldn't put me to sleep, if that was logic.

I guess I finally must have slept, though, because the quiet of the train standing still woke me up. I looked at the luminous dial on my wrist watch and saw it was five in the morning, a couple of hours before we were due in South Bend. I wondered where we were and looked out of the window. It was a pretty big station, a city.

Suddenly I realized what station it had to be—Indianapolis. I'd completely forgotten that we'd be going through Indianapolis between Evansville, down on the Ohio, and South Bend, in the northern part of the state.

Indianapolis! I had a wild, screwy idea of grabbing my clothes and getting off the train. I could explain things to Uncle Am later. I had enough money, and I could join him later and he wouldn't mind.

I grabbed my pants out of the clothes hammock and started to pull them on. Then the train jerked and began to move.

I realized what a silly idea it had been.

But the idea had waked me up so thoroughly I didn't even try to go back to sleep. I went ahead and finished dressing, and went through the train to the back platform. I sat there watching the track stream away from the present into the past. We were heading away from Indianapolis now; I'd probably never see Rita again.

It was cloudy in South Bend, but it wasn't raining. We got to the lot ahead of the road caravan and waited for it. The lot was dry, and it was already staked out as to what went where.

The trucks came about ten o'clock and we got our stuff and put it up. While we were pitching the living top, Maury strolled by and stopped to talk.

He said, "We're a day early, but we ought to get some play this afternoon and evening anyway. I bought spot announcements on the local radio and I phoned an ad ahead of us in time for the Sunday morning paper. So people will know we're here. Only, hell, it looks like rain here too."

I asked him if there'd been any word from Rita, realizing afterward it was a silly thing to ask. She wouldn't have written or wired so quick.

He said, "Who? Oh, the dizzy blonde. No, not yet."

I knew I was making a fool out of myself, but I wanted to know, so I asked him, "That telegram she got— Was it delivered, or—or what?"

He looked at me kind of funny, but he answered. "No, it was telephoned in. The office girl wrote it down and I took it over to her."

"Oh," I said.

After Maury had walked away, Uncle Am looked at me and scratched his head, but he didn't ask why I'd wondered that.

That evening it was still cloudy, but we did a fair business. And Monday the same.

Tuesday it rained. It started about three-thirty in the afternoon. We'd been open and doing fairly well up to the time the rain started.

I'd just reached up to let down the front when somebody said, "Hi, Ed. Hi, Am." It was Armin Weiss, the Evansville copper. We said "Hi" back and he said, "I got to see some other guys first. You going to be around?"

"Sure," Uncle Am told him. "We'll be in our living top, in back."

"See you in a few minutes then. We got an identification on the midget."

We finished closing up and went back. Half an hour later Weiss came in. He sat down on one of the cots. I'd had my trombone out, polishing it and working a little fresh oil into the slide; I started to put it away.

"Lon Staffold," Weiss said. "The midget's name was Lon Staffold. Ever hear it before?"

He looked from one to the other of us and we shook our heads to show the name didn't mean anything to us. He went on:

"He lived in Cincinnati. He was thirty-six years old. He lived in a rooming house on Vine Street and had a paper corner downtown selling *Enquirers* in the morning and *Times-Stars* and *Posts* in the afternoon.

"He'd been a carney once, but a long time ago. Six or eight years ago, mostly out on the west coast. He'd been in vaudeville, too. As far as I could find out, he'd never been with a carney in the east or the middle west."

Uncle Am asked, "Who missed him?"

"His landlady. She's an ex-carney, too, and I think she used to be in burlesque. Anyway, she still reads *Billboard;* that's where she read about the murder. If the regular Cincy papers carried it, she didn't notice. That's why we didn't get a response right away; not till *Billboard* came out. She gave a description to the Cincinnati police. It fits."

"She got any idea who might have killed him or why?" Uncle Am asked.

Weiss shrugged. "Not that she told the police there. I'm going to Cincinnati to talk with her. This is a kind of roundabout course from Evansville to Cincy, but I wanted to try around here to see if I could get any reaction to the name Lon Staffold, get a little ammunition to take to Cincy with me. Thus far, it's a blank."

He stood up off the cot. He turned and looked at me. "Well, learned anything, Ed?"

I shook my head.

"Funny thing," he said. "Staffold left Cincinnati about ten days ago. Turns up on your carney lot in Evansville, dead, last Thursday night, five days ago. Where was he the other five days, in between? If we knew that, we'd have something to get our teeth into."

Uncle Am said, "Have a drink, Cap?"

"Well—one won't hurt me. It'll sure wear off before I get to Cincinnati; it's a hell of a long drive from here."

Uncle Am got out of the nested aluminum cups he used to use in a cups-and-balls routine, and a bottle. He poured us three drinks, going light on mine as usual.

After we drank, Weiss said, "He sold his paper corner—got two hundred bucks for it. So he didn't expect to sell papers again when he got back; he could have rented it out instead. But he *did* expect to get back. He kept his room and paid two weeks advance rent. He figured on getting back within that time. He let out a hint that he might come back with more money than he'd ever had before. Kinda mysterious about where it would come from."

Uncle Am said, "The Cincinnati cops did a good job for you."

"They didn't get me all that. I talked to the landlady long distance last night. She's a Mrs. Czerwinski, a widow. Had a right nice voice on the phone."

Uncle Am was grinning; I didn't know why, then. He said, "Another shot, Cap?"

"Nope. I'll run along. Say, Ed, I'm driving—and you can't work in the rain. Want to come along?"

I shook my head. "No thanks, Cap. I—I got something else I got to do."

"Okay, Ed. Well, keep your nose clean. And your ears open."

"All right," I said.

After he left, I wondered why I hadn't wanted to go along.

That evening in the chow top, I saw Charlie Wheeler, the barker at the posing show. I sat down next to him.

I asked very casually, "Anybody heard from Rita?"

He shook his head. "Why should anybody?" He took a bite out of a sandwich and talked around it. "Hell, she won't be back."

"How do you know?"

"I don't know; I'm just guessing. But it's a good guess. Look, Ed—"

"I'm looking."

"For your own good, forget that dizzy blonde. You'd like to get in, but so'd the whole rest of the carney. She's out for dough. Nobody around here's got enough of it for her. I got an idea for you, Ed. The side show's going to take on a tattoed lady on our next jump. Now there'd be something. Leave the light on and if you can't sleep, you can lay awake and look at the pitchers."

"Sure," I said. "Sure, I'll do that, Charlie."

The next day, Wednesday, it was still raining off and on. Uncle Am chased me downtown and I saw three movies.

Thursday afternoon it cleared for a while but we didn't do much business. Thursday evening, it was drizzling again. We didn't bother to open, although some of the concessions were running for peanuts.

I tried to practice trombone, but I couldn't get my mind on it.

Uncle Am said, "For God's sake, Ed."

"Yeah. I know it stinks. I'll put it away."

"I don't mean the trombone. I mean you. What the hell's wrong with you? Or don't you want to talk about her?"

"I—I guess I don't." He knew what was eating me all right; there wasn't any use lying to him and I was too mixed up myself to tell him the truth.

"Kid, I hate to see dumb animals suffer," he said. "Look, the grouch bag is overstuffed. Why don't you put on that suit of yours that makes you look like a goddam matinee idol, let me give you twenty bucks and go out and get plastered and fall in the mud and ruin the suit?"

I said, "I didn't fall in the mud."

"You stopped too soon."

"I don't *want* to get drunk. It wouldn't do any good."

He sighed. "I was afraid of that. I thought I could settle for twenty. All right, here's a hundred. That enough?"

He wasn't kidding. He had his bankroll out, peeling bills off it into a pile on my cot. Tens and fives and a couple of twenties until it made a hundred bucks. "Is that enough?"

"Enough for what?"

He looked and sounded exasperated. He said, "You know for what. Find out what gives and get it over with, one way or the other. But straighten yourself out. There's a late train this evening you can still catch."

I said, "You mean—I should go to Indianapolis?"

He snorted. "Hell, no. I mean Mars. You transfer to the rocket ship in Patagonia."

He got up and went out, leaving the money lying on the cot beside me.

I looked at it awhile, and then I picked it up and put it in my wallet. With what I had left otherwise, it made a hundred and twenty-two bucks. It was more money in actual cash than I'd ever had at one time, in my life. I felt rich.

I started getting dressed, slowly—and then I got in a hell of a rush when I realized I didn't know what time the late train left and I might miss it. I realized, too, that I didn't know how long I'd be gone or what I was running into, so I popped a couple of extra shirts and some socks and stuff into a valise.

Uncle Am had probably gone to the G-top and he wouldn't want me coming there to say so long, so I wrote, "Thanks to hell and back. I'll keep you posted," and pinned it to his pillow.

I got off the lot without having to talk to anybody. I was in such a hurry now that I grabbed a taxi going by out front and took it to the station. When I got there, I found I had almost two hours to wait for the Indianapolis train.

I'd figured it out on the train; there were three angles I could start from: the hospitals, the newspapers, or the police. If there'd really been an accident last Friday in which a man named Weiman had been injured, I could get the dope on it from one of those three sources. And the police would be last choice; I'd have to do too much explaining to them.

It was almost two o'clock in the morning when I got off the train. The newsstand in the depot was open, but they had no back copies of local papers. I got a dollar's worth of nickels and went to a phone booth.

There wasn't any Howard Weiman listed. Not that I'd expected to find one; if Weiman was a widower and a lush, the way Hoagy described him, the chances were against his having a home of his own and a phone in his own name. He'd be more likely to room somewhere or leave his extra shirt in a hotel room.

There was a discouraging number of hospitals. But I was going to do at least something before I turned in, so I started. I called the emergency hospital first, as the best bet.

"No Weiman registered here," the girl said.

"He might have left," I told her. "He would have been brought in last Friday, after an auto accident. Would it be too much trouble—?"

"Just a moment, please."

I held the phone until her voice came back on the line. "Yes," she said. "A Howard Weiman was brought in Friday evening. On Sunday he was moved to a private hospital, Pinelawn."

"Thanks," I said. "That would mean—uh—that somebody arranged private hospitalization for him?"

"Yes, probably. We handle only emergency and indigent cases. As soon as a patient can be moved, we advise it if other hospitalization can be arranged."

I asked, "It was his daughter who arranged the moving?"

Her voice hesitated a moment. I said quickly, "I'm a friend of hers from out of town. The only way I know how to get in touch with her is through her father."

She decided that it was harmless. She said, "According to the file card, a Rita Weiman made the arrangements. The relationship isn't shown, and her address isn't given. Pinelawn Hospital might have it."

"Thanks," I said. "Thanks a lot."

I still had nineteen nickels. I made it eighteen by calling Pinelawn Hospital. Howard Weiman's condition, I was told, was "fair." And that was all the information I could get, except that visiting hours were two to four in the afternoon. If they had Rita's address, they were keeping it a secret.

Well, I'd learned a lot more than I'd dared to hope for from two phone calls at two o'clock in the morning.

I decided I'd wait until daylight to do more. At the latest, I could find Rita tomorrow afternoon by being at the hospital during visiting hours. If she were staying here solely for the purpose, surely she'd visit him every day.

So I checked in at a fleabag across from the station and went to sleep. I left a call for ten in the morning.

After breakfast, I went to the office of the morning paper and got a copy of their Sunday morning edition. I went through it systematically until I found what I wanted, a single paragraph on the local page:

INJURED BY TRUCK

Howard Weiman, 53, of 430 W. Emory St., was seriously injured at about 8 p.m. Friday evening when struck by a moving van at the intersection of Emory and Blaine Sts. He was taken to emergency hospital. The driver of the van was not held.

I took a cab to 430 West Emory Street. It was a three-story brick rooming house in a cheap rooming house district. A sign, "No Vacancies," hung in the window of the downstairs front room.

The outer room was unlocked, and I walked into the hallway and knocked on the door that would lead to the front room where the sign had hung.

A woman who looked something like the house opened the door. I took off my hat and said, "I hear Mr. Weiman's in the hosiptal. I wonder if you could tell me how he is."

"Pretty bunged up, I guess," she said. "Touch and go for a while, but I guess he'll pull through. Tell 'em he'll be back, but nobody can say when."

"Tell who?" I asked.

"The construction company. You're from there, ain't you, where he works?"

"No, I'm just a friend of his."

She wouldn't buy that; her eyes got suspicious. She said, "You don't look it."

I grinned. "More strictly speaking," I told her, "I'm a friend of Rita's. His daughter."

She believed that. She nodded. "She was here. Sunday, I guess it was. Paid his room rent for a while so his room would be held. Nice gal, she is." The barriers were down now and I was a member of the family. She opened the door and stepped back from it. "Come on in."

I went into a frowzy room with an unmade bed, a stove, a sink with unwashed breakfast dishes in it, and an oilcloth-covered table. She waddled across the room and sat down in a chair at the table. I took one near the door, started to toss my hat onto the bed and thought better of it. Not that bed; I kept my hat in my lap.

I said, "I wonder if you could tell me where Rita is staying."

Her eyes got that look again. She said, "I thought you said you was a friend of hers."

"I am. From the carnival. Did she tell you she was with a carnival?"

She nodded.

"She left there in a hurry when she got the message about her father, and she didn't know where she'd be staying. I—I had to come to Indianapolis on other business, so I thought I'd look her up through her father's address."

"Oh," she said. "Well, I'm sorry but she didn't happen to say where she was staying, except she mentioned something about her hotel, so she's staying at one. But I guess you can reach her through Pinelawn Hospital. That's where she had her old man moved to."

"Swell," I said. "Thanks a lot."

There wasn't any more that I could get there, so I got away as quick as I could.

Back in the lobby of my own hotel, I looked over the number of hotels listed in the phone book. There were too many of them to try phoning them all, unless I had to. And it was after noon already, so I might as well wait for the hospital's visiting hours.

I got there at a quarter of two. Pinelawn was a nice-looking hospital, but I wondered where it got the name; there weren't any pines on the lawn, because there wasn't any lawn. It was a three-story building, built flush to the street.

I took up my watchman's job, leaning against a tree on the corner diagonally across from the hospital, where I could watch both entrances. I figured out I'd give Rita until three to get there. If she hadn't come by then, I'd try to get myself in as a visitor to Weiman and if that didn't work I'd have another stab at getting Rita's address from the hospital office, this time with a song and dance in person instead of over the phone.

But I didn't have to try that. At a few minutes after two a taxi pulled up and Rita got out. I got across the street while she was paying the driver, and I was standing there when she turned around. I said, "Hi, Rita."

If she was surprised, she didn't show it. She said, "Hi, Ed," as casually as though we'd met there by appointment.

"How is your dad?" I asked her.

"N-not too good, Eddie. There were internal injuries besides the concussion. They didn't know about them at first. They had to operate, yesterday. They *think* it was successful, but they're not sure. I don't know whether I'll be able to see him today, so soon after the operation, or not."

"Oh," I said. "Rita, I'm sorry about—"

But she wasn't listening. She took my arm and said, "Come on, Eddie. We'll find out."

We went up the steps and inside the lobby. I waited while she crossed to the desk and talked to the nurse sitting behind it. After a minute she came back to me.

"He's a little better. But he's sleeping now and the doctor left word he'd better not have visitors till tomorrow. So come on." She took my arm again.

"Sure," I said. "But what's the rush?"

"The cab's waiting. I told him I might not be able to see my dad, and he said he'd wait a couple of minutes to see if I came out right away."

The cab was still waiting.

As we started downtown, I slipped my arm around her. She leaned close to me. She asked, "Why did you come, Eddie?"

"You know why I came."

"I—guess I do. I wish you hadn't. *Damn* you, Eddie."

I laughed a little. "That's the most encouraging thing you've told me yet. Swear at me some more." I tightened my arm around her. "Love me, Rita? At all?"

"What's love?"

"What I've got."

She leaned back and looked at me. She said, "Maybe it's just hot pants, Eddie, that you've got."

"That, too," I said. "Guess they go together. Oh, I suppose you can have either one without the other, but only a combination can make you as miserable as I've been."

"I—I've been miserable, too, Eddie. But damn you, Eddie, I don't want love. I want money, lots of it. I want a million dollars and you haven't got it and won't ever have it. You're too nice a guy."

I laughed. "Can't a nice guy ever make a million?"

She took that seriously. "Not—not your type of nice guy, Eddie. Honestly, can you picture yourself as a millionaire?"

"No," I admitted honestly. "I guess you're right; I'm not

the type. But would you know what to do with a million dollars if you had it?"

"Wouldn't I?" She laughed a little. "A big house, clothes, jewelry, furs—"

"Could I live in the house?"

"My husband wouldn't like it. But I could set you up in a little apartment somewhere, Eddie, and pay the rent. And two or three times a week—"

"Eight times a week," I said. "Every day and twice on Sundays."

"If my husband will let me. . . . You don't think I'm serious, do you, Eddie?"

"If you are, shut up."

"Shut me up."

I did; I shut her up very thoroughly, and I felt that kiss all the way down to my toes.

It wasn't quite like anything that had ever happened to me before. It left me dizzy when we broke, and the cab was just pulling up in front of Rita's hotel.

Rita led me through the lobby to the bar and grill that opened off it. We took a booth.

She asked, "Hungry, Eddie?"

"Not for grub."

"Behave yourself. Here comes the waitress. I *am* hungry; I haven't eaten since I got up."

She ordered a plate lunch and I settled for pie and coffee.

When the waitress had gone away, Rita frowned at me across the table. Not a mock frown, a faint but unmistakably genuine frown. She asked, "Why did you come in the posing show that night, Eddie?"

"I know I shouldn't have," I told her. "But—I'd been drinking, and I was mad. Hoagy told me you had a date with a mooch, and I—just couldn't take it. So I decided I didn't give a damn what anybody thought, and I didn't until I was inside and saw you, and—hell, it's all mixed up. Anyway, you damn near knocked my block off outside, and I had it coming to me."

"All right, Eddie. Just don't ever do it again. Whether I come back to the show or not." She smiled. "Particularly if that Estelle dame is with it. She's kind of soft on you, Eddie. Has she made a play for you yet?"

"Nope," I said.

"She probably will. Well—"

"You *are* coming back to the carney, aren't you, Rita?"

"I've been wondering, Eddie. I don't like the posing show."

"I don't either," I said. "I mean, I don't like you being with the posing show. Can't you do something else with the carney?"

"A cooch dance, maybe?"

"Damn it, you know what I mean."

"I know what you mean, but you'd better get over it, Eddie. Nature made me for a show girl or a dancer or something like that. A body but no brains."

"How much are two and two?"

"Five. See, Eddie?"

"All right," I said. "I give up."

The waitress came back with our orders.

I sat sipping coffee, watching Rita eat. Even eating, she was beautiful. I was the luckiest guy in the world—maybe. I was just a little scared, at the moment, of crowding my luck by finding out how lucky I was.

I sat there without talking any more until she'd finished eating. Then I asked, "And now?"

"And now—to the railroad station, Eddie. You're going back."

"*Back?* I just got here. I can stay a week or so. I want to stay here until we find out how your father's doing—he ought to be out of danger by that time, and we can go back together."

"No, Eddie. You've got to go back this afternoon. Right away. I—Eddie, I want you to stay, but you mustn't. With Dad maybe dying, it—it wouldn't be right for you to stay."

"We could—behave ourselves."

"But we wouldn't. Not any more than—than gunpowder and fire could be together and behave themselves."

I knew all too well that she was right about that, but I still wanted to argue.

She leaned across the table and put her finger across my lips. She said, "Be a good boy and go back, Eddie. And *if* you do,

I'll promise to come back to the carney. As soon as I can. And then—we'll have fun, Eddie."

I took her finger from my lips and kissed the palm of her hand, warm and moist.

"All right," I said.

We went to the station. There was a train out for South Bend in only a few minutes.

At the iron gate leading back to the tracks, I kissed her. That was the third time I'd kissed her, and the best. Then, with her arms around me, she leaned back a little.

She said, "*Damn* you, Eddie. *Are* you worth a million bucks?"

"I'll try to be."

"You'd better. Good-by, Eddie . . ."

I guess I forgot to wipe the lipstick off. I saw it in the washroom mirror a few hours later when I was getting cleaned up to get off the train at South Bend. There was a silly, fatuous smile on my face, too, along with the lipstick.

I wondered if I'd worn *that* all the way from Indianapolis.

CHAPTER VI

Sunday night after the crowd had gone, we tore down. We were rolling by four o'clock and pulled into Fort Wayne just after dawn. As on all of the short jumps, Uncle Am and I stuck with the trucks.

We weren't opening until evening, but we went ahead and set up our stuff so we'd have all day to sleep. The sun was out bright by the time we hit our cots, dog tired.

Business was good Monday night. That was the night of the second murder, if you can call it that. I mean, it wasn't a human being. It was Hoagy's chimp, Susie.

At two o'clock in the morning, about an hour after we'd closed, some of us were in Lee Carey's trailer. There was Uncle Am and I, Lee Carey, Estelle Beck, and Major Mote, the midget.

We'd been there half an hour. Carey and I had been playing the phonograph, but there was so much talking that we finally gave up and joined in the conversation. Carey had broken out a bottle of whisky and everybody was having a drink or two, but nobody was high. I was going very easy on the stuff myself, nursing my first drink along so I wouldn't have to turn down another.

Uncle Am and Carey started arguing politics. As nearly as I could make out, Carey was for politics and Uncle Am was against them; it was that kind of a silly argument. Carey was practicing the front-and-back palm with a half dollar while he talked, the bright coin flashing, appearing at the end of his fingertips, then vanishing as he turned his hand, palm and then back. I don't think he even knew he was doing it.

I was listening, amused, and Estelle was listening, bewildered and a little bored. The Major sat glumly silent on the edge of the bunk, looking like an oversize doll somebody had stuck there.

That was the way we were when Marge Hoagland pushed open the screen door. She said, "Susie's gone."

Lee Carey said, "The hell! She got out?"

I hadn't taken it that way; I thought at first she'd meant the chimp had died. They'd been expecting her to, any minute, and I'd thought she was too sick to move around at all. The times I'd seen her, she'd barely been able to move. She'd been just an inert ball of monkey fur, barely breathing. I couldn't picture her running away, even if they'd left the cage door open.

But Marge nodded her head, to Carey's question. She said, "She was there at ten o'clock, when Hoagy got back from Milwaukee. We went uptown for some drinks, Hoagy and me. And when we got back a few minutes ago—"

"Where's Hoagy?" Uncle Am asked.

"Hunting for her. He's going through the freak show top now; we saw your lights and—"

"Sure," Carey said. "We'll all help. Drink first, Marge?"

"Had too many already, Lee. Thanks." She turned around and went out and we all followed her—all but Major Mote. I happened to look at him as I was following Uncle Am out the door. He still sat on the edge of the bunk, but he was hunkered up now, as though he was trying to take up even less room than he did otherwise.

He looked up as I stood there, half in and half out of the door, and I saw he was scared of something, scared stiff. I said, "What's the matter, Major? Aren't you coming?"

He looked at me, but he didn't answer. His eyes didn't seem to see me.

I stood there, not knowing whether to go on out or stay and try to find out what was eating the midget. But Uncle Am said, "Coming, Ed?" and I went on out and closed the door behind me.

As I went down the trailer steps, I heard his footsteps patter across the trailer floor. I heard the inner door of the trailer slam and the bolt slide shut. He'd locked himself in.

Uncle Am had turned and was staring back at that closed door. He must have heard the bolt click, too. He asked, "What gives with the little guy?"

"Scared stiff," I told him. Carey had heard, too, and was standing there, looking back. I asked, "How many drinks did he have, Lee?"

"Two," Carey said, wonderingly. "Just two."

I suggested, "He's kind of small. Two drinks might have hit him a bit."

Carey shook his head. "Nope. I've seen him handle seven or eight and still be all right." He shrugged. "The hell with it. One thing at a time; let's find the chimp."

Estelle and Marge were already ducking under the canvas sidewall of the big freak show top. I could see that Hoagy, or someone, had turned on the lights in there; they'd been off when we'd passed half an hour before on our way to Lee's trailer.

We followed them under.

Hoagy was crossing to meet us, inside the top. Behind him, one of the canvasmen, Pop Janney, was pulling on his pants; he'd been asleep on one of the platforms.

Hoagy had a flashlight in his hand. He said, "She ain't here. I looked behind the bally cloths, under all the platforms. It'd be some place like that she'd crawl off to."

Uncle Am asked, "How'd she get out?"

"Broke the catch. Damn, I didn't think she was strong enough."

Marge said, "You should've known. You kept telling me how strong a chimp is. And then you—"

Uncle Am said, "Pipe down, Marge. Give him hell afterward, but let's find the chimp first. Think she'd have gone far, Hoagy?"

"No. My guess is she'd crawl under something. Sick animals do. Let's split up and—"

Marge said, "She might've headed for the woods. There's two-three acres of 'em over the other side of the lot."

Uncle Am seemed to be taking charge. He said, "Let's get some system in this. Sure, she might have gone for the woods, but we'd never find her there in the dark. Once in the woods, she'd go up a tree and— Well, let's let the woods go until it gets light. She's probably still on the lot anyway. Just how sick was she, Hoagy?"

"I've been away two days," Hoagy said. "But when I saw her last she wasn't able to sit up. Let alone walk, God damn it. I damn near decided to put her out of her misery with chloroform before I went away. But Marge—"

Marge cut in, "Wasn't I right? And she did sit up this afternoon and eat a little. Two bananas besides that formula you made."

Uncle Am said, "Okay, then we can figure she didn't go far. Ten to one, she's on the lot. So—" He went on, dividing the lot among the seven of us—it was seven now with Pop Janney, who'd got his clothes on and was with us.

Uncle Am told us, "Get flashlights first. Then cover your territory and meet by my booth in half an hour. Look under stuff, anywhere she might have crawled. And look *up*, too. She might have got a notion to climb."

We started to split up, but Uncle Am called Hoagy back and I stuck around.

He said, "Hoagy, you better call the cops."

"The *cops?*" Hoagy looked as though he thought Uncle Am had lost his mind.

"Sure, the cops. Don't be a dope, Hoagy. You'll be protecting yourself and the carney—and the chimp. You don't want her shot, do you, if she does get off the lot and a cop sees her?"

"Hell, no. If she's well enough to have got out—"

"Yeah. So you report to the cops. Tell 'em she's sick and that she's tame anyway and not dangerous, and that if they get a report on a loose monkey they should call you instead of getting excited and spraying lead. And there's another angle. If she's not as sick as you think and does any damage, well—"

"Hell, Am. She's tame as a kitten."

"All right, she's tame. But she might do some property damage or accidentally scare someone stiff. Or something. And you're going to be in a devil of a lot better spot if you've already reported, as soon as you found her gone."

Hoagy sighed. You could see the idea of calling copper hurt him. But he said, "Maybe you got something, Am. But Maury isn't here and I don't want to burgle the office car to use the phone and I want to stick on the lot in case somebody finds Susie, because I can handle her better. So will you phone?"

"How about me?" I suggested. "I'll do it."

"Would you, Ed?" Hoagy asked. "Look, you might have to hunt for a phone at this time of night, so take my car. Here's the key."

I took it. Uncle Am said, "Then forget the territory I gave you, Ed. I'm going to break up the rummy game in the G-top and get some recruits."

I took Hoagy's car and drove toward town till I found a place that was open, and used the phone. The guy on the desk at the station was pretty dumb. He got all excited at first; I think he got chimps mixed with gorillas and pictured Gargantua or King Kong loose on the unsuspecting community of Fort Wayne.

I finally got him straightened out and calmed down. He promised to notify the beat men out in our end of town, when and as they phoned in from their call boxes. He was going to send a couple of squad cars to the lot, but I talked him out of that.

When I got back to the lot, the search was in full swing. Somebody had turned on some of the lights around the midway, and there were lights in most of the tops. The search party seemed to be growing by the minute as more people got waked up by those already hunting.

I wandered around a few minutes trying to find Uncle Am but I couldn't remember what part of the lot he'd taken for himself, and I didn't see him.

I looked inside the lemonade stand, thinking somebody might have missed searching it, then I sat down on the counter of it to think, to see if I could get any bright ideas that had been missed.

I was beginning to get one when Estelle came toward me down the midway. She waved and said, "Hi, Eddie."

"No luck?"

"There's no chimp in the posing show top or dressing tent. That's what I covered. I'm glad there wasn't. I'd've been scared plenty."

"A big girl like you," I said. "Afraid of a little monkey."

"Wouldn't be if you were along, Eddie. Say, how big is Susie? You ever see her?"

"A couple of times. I was just getting an idea for a place to look. Want to come along?"

I jumped down off the counter and she fell in step beside me down the midway. "Where, Eddie? What's your hunch?"

"The place I bet everybody else forgot to look. Hoagy's trailer."

"Huh?"

"I'll bet when Hoagy found the chimp gone he started out hunting without looking in his own closets and under bunks and around. Maybe she holed in somewhere else right in the trailer."

"My God," Estelle said. "You've got brains too!"

We cut back between tops, off the midway, to Hoagy's joint. It was dark back there. I held Estelle's arm tightly and she hung on to me as we worked our way back slowly so as not to fall over any ropes or stakes. We did that until we were almost there, anyway, and then I remembered she had a flashlight.

I reminded her of it and she turned it on. I thought that she giggled a little, but I wasn't sure.

At the door of the trailer, I reached up and turned the little knob of the screen door. The door opened, but it didn't feel right. I mean, the knob was loose and the door had started to come open before I'd really turned it at all.

I asked Estelle for the flashlight and with it I looked at the knob and the catch. The catch had been broken, all right.

I said, "Nuts. My hunch was wrong, 'Stelle. The monk did get all the way out of the trailer."

The catch, I saw, had been a flimsy one. It wouldn't have taken much strength to have broken it. I wondered if the catch on the door of Hoagy's homemade cage inside the trailer had been as flimsy.

We went on in and turned on the lights. Then I went to the end of the trailer where the monkey had been kept. It was still dim down in that end; Hoagy had shaded his light on one side so the bright bulb wouldn't shine in Susie's eyes. I used the flashlight to examine the catch.

It was on the outside of the door. It was a hinge and hasp affair, with a padlock. It wasn't broken, nor was the padlock; the screws had been pulled out of the wood. There'd been three screws in the end that had pulled loose; two of them were still in the holes in the hasp; the other had fallen out. They were five-eighths-inch-long screws, and the wood they'd been in looked fairly hard. I didn't know what kind of wood it was, but it wasn't pine, anyway.

It would have taken a plenty hard pull, I thought, to yank those screws right out by their roots that way. A man couldn't do it, I was pretty sure. It was a little scary to realize just how strong a chimpanzee really was. And to know that, tame or not, it was loose somewhere.

Estelle was leaning over me, breathing down the back of my neck. She asked, "Finding anything, Eddie?"

I shook my head. I took another look at the cage itself, opening the door and sticking my head in. They'd kept it plenty clean. There was fresh straw on the floor, a couple of inches deep. The only refuse was the skins of two bananas, the ones Marge had mentioned.

The cage— Maybe I'm giving a wrong idea calling it that; it wasn't a cage, really, in the sense of having bars all around. It was just a partition of bars—one-by-three boards—nailed to the trailer floor and the trailer roof, leaving a space three feet deep between the partition and the end of the trailer.

The floor area was about three by seven feet; not an awful lot of room, but then Hoagy had told me that he didn't expect to have to keep Susie locked up much, except at night, once he'd really got a start at training her.

Studying the space back of the door, I realized something that made me feel better. It wouldn't have taken any superhuman strength after all to have sprung those screws in the hasp. The three-foot depth of the space behind the door was what made it easy.

Inside the cage, bracing your shoulders against the wall and shoving against the door with your feet, there'd have been enough leverage for a normally strong person to have done it. Why, even a husky kid the size of Susie might have been able to do it, if the kid had been smart enough to think of using his feet that way. And for a monkey, using feet is as natural as using hands.

Someone opening the screen door made me turn around. It was Hoagy coming in.

He said, "Hi, kids. Bet you had the same idea I did. Have you looked around?"

"I *had* the idea, Hoagy, but she did get out. Of the trailer, I mean. The lock on it's broken."

"Sure, that's why I didn't search in here. But—maybe she came back. She could have got outside, seen something that scared her, or just got scared of the big wide world itself, and come back in. Let's be sure."

We helped him hunt in all the cupboard and closet space; we looked in and under everything. But we didn't find Susie.

Hoagy offered us drinks and Estelle said "Sure," so I did, too. While Hoagy was pouring them I went outside with the flashlight and looked under and around and even on top of the trailer, just to be sure.

Then we had our drinks, and I remembered to give Hoagy back his car keys. And I showed him how I figured Susie had managed to open the cage door. He nodded. He said, "She was smarter than I am. I didn't figure on that. After I put the hasp on, I tried to pull it loose from the outside, and I couldn't."

He shrugged. "Well, I guess a half hour's more than up. Let's go over and meet Am and the others."

When we got there, all the original seven of us were back, and at least a dozen others. Nobody'd found a hair of Susie. We split up and tried again, and still no luck.

By then it was after three. Hoagy said she must have gone to the woods after all, and it'd begin to be light in a couple of hours, so he wasn't going to turn in. Uncle Am and I decided to stay up, too, and so did Lee Carey. Estelle was getting sleepy so Hoagy and Marge drove her downtown to her hotel.

Uncle Am and Carey and I went back to Carey's trailer.

The door was still locked on the inside. Carey hammered on it and called out, but we didn't get any answer even when we hammered as hard as we could. The lights were still on inside, but we couldn't see the midget through the pane of the door.

I walked around the trailer and through the window on the far side I could see him lying on the floor by the edge of the bunk. He was flat on his back with his tiny arms stretched out sidewise. I was scared for a minute, and then I saw him move his head a little, as though he was trying to raise it and couldn't.

I went back and told Carey.

"The damn fool," he said. "Well—guess we got to do it."

It was his door, so we let him break it in.

The inside of the trailer smelled like a distillery. The bottle of whisky was on its side on the floor, most of it spilled out. We walked around the puddle and Uncle Am bent over the Major.

Lee made the rounds of the windows, opening them. They'd all been closed and latched on the inside.

Uncle Am said, "He's just dead drunk." He picked the Major up and put him on the bunk.

"He was sure scared of something," I said.

There was still an inch of whisky in the bottle and we had a drink apiece and Carey got a deck of cards he said weren't readers, and we played rummy at a nickel a hand until Hoagy and Marge would get back.

Carey won a buck apiece from us, anyway, even if the cards were honest. He wouldn't deal, I remember. He said, "Nix. For a nickel a hand I'd cheat like hell, for the fun of it. For real money I might be tempted to be honest."

Uncle Am grinned at him. He said, "Unless there was a mooch in the game."

"That," Carey said, "wouldn't be a game."

It was getting light already when Hoagy and Marge came in. Marge was sobering up and looked better, but Hoagy's eyes were bloodshot. I remembered he'd been in Milwaukee, making arrangements for our next jump, and had driven back. He probably hadn't slept at all yesterday, like the rest of us had. Likely enough he hadn't slept at all in forty-eight hours, since the carney left South Bend.

We waited until it got a little lighter and then the four of us went out and searched the several acres of woods. It wasn't very thick growth and none of the trees was so big we couldn't see up in it. It took us two hours, but we did a good job and we were sure Susie wasn't there.

We were all getting sleepy by then, but we were hungry, too, and the chow top wasn't open yet. So Hoagy drove us all to a restaurant and we had breakfast.

I phoned the police again and learned there hadn't been any reports on a stray monkey.

We went back to the lot and nothing had developed there, either, so there didn't seem to be anything else we could do.

Hoagy said, "She must've got off the lot, and not into the woods. Probably crawled in somebody's garage or somewhere, and like as not died there. But hell, we can't search the town. We'll just have to wait till we hear something. Anyway, thanks to hell and back, all of you."

Uncle Am said, "Now that it's light, maybe we should try the lot once more. We might have missed something."

Hoagy said, "We've done enough. Let's get some sleep."

Carey said, "She *can't* be on the lot." He was wrong, but we didn't find that out until afternoon.

We broke up, and I went to our sleeping tent. Uncle Am came in a few minutes later. We were both too tired to talk.

Uncle Am went to sleep the minute his head hit the pillow. I guess I was too tired to sleep; it took me a while.

I kept wondering what *had* happened to Susie. I remembered the old gag about the half-wit who had found a horse by imagining *he* was a horse and figuring out where *he'd* go.

I tried that, but I didn't get anywhere; I couldn't imagine myself a chimp, no matter how I tried.

I got to wondering what Major Mote had been scared about. I thought, maybe he really knows something that gives him cause to be scared like that. He's a midget and one midget was murdered on the lot ten days ago. Maybe that was why he was scared. And, hell, we'd all walked off and left him alone; we'd been a big help. He'd been unconscious in a wide open trailer all the time we were searching the woods and eating breakfast.

But Carey must have found him okay when he went back to his trailer just now, or we'd have heard.

My thoughts kept going in circles for a while—until I started thinking about Rita and wondering how soon she'd get back from Indianapolis. It might be today!

After a while, I went to sleep.

Despite all the searching we'd done, it was a mark who found Susie on the carney lot. Found her in the middle of a busy afternoon with the carney running around her and Susie floating dead in the water.

In the water of the diving tank where Hilo Peterson, the Death-Defying Dare-Devil Diver (which Uncle Am says is as nice a chunk of apt alliteration's artful aid as he's seen) does his free act once an evening.

The mark spotted Susie from the ferris wheel; at least, from up there he saw something floating in the water of the tank down at the end of the midway. He couldn't see what it was, from that far. But after his ride was over, he went down to the tank and walked up the ramp leading to the edge of it and looked in.

That's how Susie was found.

Word passed around the carney lot and reached Uncle Am and me in our booth down near the entrance, and we ran down the front canvas and went back there.

By that time they'd taken Susie out of the tank and wrapped her in a piece of canvas to take her away. Somebody had told Hoagy and he was there.

The crowd was so thick around the tank that we didn't even try to push through it. Uncle Am said we might as well go back to the ball game and mind our own business, and we did.

But during the supper-hour lull we closed up again and went back to the tank. They were draining it by then. Maury was directing the job, and looking plenty disgusted.

"God damn prima donna," he said. "Says he won't dive into water that's had a dead monkey floating in it all day. So we got to refill it for him."

Uncle Am chuckled. "Would you, Maury?"

"Me? I got sense enough not to high-dive into four feet of water anyway. If I was dumb enough to do that, I don't know what difference a little monkey-flavor would make."

I walked up the ramp and looked down into the tank.

You could figure how it happened, easy. The tank itself was six and a half feet deep, which put the rim just above eye level, even for a tall man. And that was why nobody had discovered Susie until the mark had seen her from the ferris wheel. The tank was advertised to contain four feet of water; actually the water was about six inches deeper than that, so the level of the water was two feet under the rim of the tank.

I could picture how it could have happened. Susie's escape must have been after one o'clock, and this end of the midway was dark. She'd been thirsty, maybe smelled the water, and crawled up the ramp. She leaned over the edge to drink, and, being sick and weak, had fallen in.

When I came back down the ramp, Maury said, "Say, Ed, there's a letter for you at the office."

Uncle Am said, "Go get it, kid. I'll meet you at Hoagy's."

CHAPTER VII

I GOT THE LETTER. It was from Rita, postmarked Indianapolis, and on hotel stationery. It was just a short note:

Dear Ed:
Dad's worse instead of better. I don't know just when I'll get back. But wait for me, Eddie. You know what I mean.

Rita.

I went around to Hoagy's trailer but instead of going in, I called to Uncle Am, and he came out.

I showed him the letter. I said, "I want to call her up, Uncle Am. Maybe—"

He put his hand on my shoulder. He said, "Okay, kid. Want some money, in case you decide to go?"

I shook my head. "I've still got nearly all of what you gave me last time, because I didn't stay then. I've got over eighty bucks. That'd be plenty—if I should decide to go."

He said, "Marge wants us to eat with them, says they've got plenty cooked and it's about ready. Want to call afterward, and eat first?"

"No, you go ahead and eat with them. I—I'd rather call first and get it off my mind. I'll eat somewhere afterward. Say, how's Hoagy feeling?"

"Not too bad. Guess it's better to have it over with. I'll see you later, then. Or will I?"

I told him I wouldn't go to Indianapolis without letting him know, and that I'd have to come back to get some clothes anyway.

I took a bus downtown and phoned Rita's hotel from a booth. She wasn't in, so I ate some dinner and then tried again, and got her.

"Listen, Rita," I said, "can I come? Maybe I can help?" I didn't know how; it sounded silly to me as I said it.

"Please don't, Eddie. I told you why. And you couldn't help. There isn't anything you could do."

"How is he?" I asked. "Any change since you wrote?"

"We don't know, Eddie. It's—not sure either way. It's a sort of crisis coming up, the doctor says. He'll turn the corner in a day or two—or he won't. And—I'll come back to the carney. But don't come here; wait for me."

"Sure. But I wish I could do something."

"You are, Eddie. Just by waiting. I'm coming back. Honest."

"That's swell," I said.

"I hated the carney, Eddie. But I'm coming back because you're there. And—I've got an idea for the two of us, Eddie."

"So have I," I said.

"I don't mean that, you dope. Well—that, too. But I mean something with money in it. And honest, too."

I said, "I suppose there are honest ways of making it. What's the idea?"

"I'll tell you then. Not now. Love me, Eddie?"

"A little bit," I said.

"I love you a little bit, too, then. And damn your hide, you stay away from Estelle, or I'll scratch her eyes out."

"I wouldn't touch her with a ten-foot pole."

"Don't brag, Eddie. 'By now."

"Good-by, Rita."

I felt so swell that I decided to hell with busses and took a taxi back to the lot.

After we'd closed up that night, Uncle Am didn't go to the G-top like he usually did. I went back to our sleeping tent, and so did he. I sat down on my cot and he on his.

I didn't know what I wanted to do; I didn't feel like reading. I felt too good to read. Music wouldn't be bad, except I didn't want to play it myself, and I'd been bothering Lee Carey too much lately.

Uncle Am said, "How's the tram coming, kid? Haven't heard you playing much lately."

"I'll get back to practicing," I said. "Maybe tomorrow."

"What do you want to do tonight?"

"I dunno. Nothing, I guess."

"Sleepy?"

"N-no."

Uncle Am said, "Kid, you're really gone on that blonde? Clear overboard? Hook, line and sinker?"

"I guess so," I said.

"And she's nuts about you?"

"Unless she's after my money."

Uncle Am grinned. Then he asked, "How soon will she be back?"

I told him about the phone call and what we'd said.

He said, "I guess you're gone on each other, all right."

I asked, "Is that bad?"

"Kid," he said, "it's your life. I wouldn't advise you about anything. Anything serious, I mean. I'm not a Dutch uncle."

"No matter what I decide to do?"

"Ed, if you decide to go in for burglary, I'll buy you a crowbar. It's your life. But how about tonight? Feel ambitious?"

"I guess so."

"Dress up, then. Let's hit the town. I haven't seen a floor show for so long I'd like to see if they're still as corny as they used to be. Want to?"

"Sure," I said.

Uncle Am said, "For cripes' sake, kid, what's eating you?"

We were in a roadhouse or night club, I don't know which you'd call it, just outside of Fort Wayne. It wasn't a bad place. The air was a bright haze of smoke, and the band was so loud you couldn't hear yourself think. We'd been yelling at one another, and it was too much trouble.

"Nothing," I yelled across the table. "I'm all right."

"It says here," said Uncle Am. He grinned. "There's a three-buck cover charge at this robbers' roost, and you're showing only three cents' worth of amusement. We're getting gypped."

I glanced at the small, crowded dance floor, and then back at Uncle Am. "Shall we dance?" I asked him.

"We shall not," he said. "But the floor show's coming up in a minute, after this number. Get in the mood for it. Quit sobbing into your beer. It's good beer."

"It's good beer," I told him, "but I don't like beer. Know what beer tastes like?"

He said he didn't want to know, but I told him anyway. He said I should have my mouth washed out with it, so I took another sip, to oblige.

The floor show came on, and it was just about what I'd expected. An emcee, dressed to within an inch of his life, in the fancy exaggerated clothes that only an emcee would wear, telling dirty jokes and getting a big hand for them. God knows why. They weren't funny. And a blues singer, and a magician who wasn't as good as Lee Carey but had a smoother line of patter. And a tap dancer and a stripper.

I pretended to enjoy it, to keep Uncle Am from worrying about me. When they started dancing again after the floor show, Uncle Am called for the check. It was nine and a half bucks; we'd each had a club sandwich, he'd had two bottles of beer and I'd had one.

He saw me looking, and his eyes twinkled. "And you thought the carney was a gyp joint. Kid, we give value. We're the suckers; we ought to take lessons from places like these."

He paid the bill and we went out. There was a taxi in front, and we got in. My uncle asked, "Is there a wheel around?"

"Well—" The driver shoved his cap back and turned around to look at us.

"We're with the carney," my uncle said.

"Oh. Sure, I can take you to the Club Sixty." He started.

Uncle Am said, "Relax, kid. It'll be on the other side of town. Any place a taxi driver leads you to is on the other side of town. If he knows one in the next block, he'd still take us to the Club Sixty."

"Uh-huh," I said. I was thinking about the place we'd just left. I asked. "Where the hell do people get the money to throw away like that?"

Uncle Am shrugged. "They take in each other's washings, I guess. But what's money? Oh, sure, there are times when a dollar bill looks bigger than a nine-by-twelve carpet. But if you've got money, and more coming in, what's it good for?"

"Your old age," I said.

"If you spend it fast enough, your old age takes care of itself. You won't have any. How'd you like the stripper?"

"She was all right," I said. I didn't tell him that every time I looked at her, I'd thought of Rita.

He chuckled. "That's real enthusiasm for you. Say, what do you want to talk about?"

His voice was mocking, but there was real concern in it, too. I felt a little foolish. After all, why was I being a wet blanket? Just because Rita wasn't back yet? Hell, wasn't I a thousand times luckier than I'd dared to hope? She *was* coming back.

"Guess I'm being silly," I admitted. I cast around for something to talk about. I said, "Wonder what's happened to Cap Weiss. Has he given up the investigation?"

"He'll be around. We'll be seeing him. I'll bet we see him tomorrow."

"Why tomorrow?"

"Susie."

"Huh?" I said. "What's a chimp getting drowned got to do with the murder?"

Uncle Am shrugged. "Maybe nothing. But don't think the Fort Wayne cops aren't keeping an eye on the lot, and don't think they aren't in pretty close touch with the Evansville boys, and that means with Cap Weiss. He's probably been busy running down angles on the dead midget—what's his name?"

"Lon Staffold."

"That's it. Kid, I wish I had your memory for details. Well, for pretty damn sure, Weiss hasn't got his teeth into anything that leads back to the carney, or he'd have been back here before this, with a calliope and six machine guns. Say, you been keeping your eyes and ears open?"

"How do you mean?"

"Like Weiss wanted you to. Got anything to tell him?"

"No."

He turned and looked at me, in the cab. "Don't sound so disgusted about it. What's wrong?"

"I just don't like it. I wish he hadn't picked on me. It's too much like stool pigeoning."

Uncle Am was quiet while the cab went a couple of blocks, and light and shadow played alternately across the inside of the taxi.

Then he said, "Kid, you got the wrong slant. Maybe it's my fault. We carneys aren't crazy about cops, but that goes for sloughing concessions, and little stuff. We don't have to like murder. I know I don't."

He was right, sure. But I guess I was feeling cantankerous enough to want to argue about it. I said, "Then why don't you solve it for them?"

He said, patiently, "Because it isn't my business to do Weiss's job for him. But it is my business to tell Weiss anything I might know about it. If I knew who stuck a shiv in the midget, I'd tell him. If I knew any facts that might help him at all, I'd tell him. That's not playing copper—or playing stool pigeon either. Is it?"

"I guess not," I admitted.

The cab was pulling up in front of what looked like an ordinary, but fairly swanky, tavern.

There weren't many people at the bar; it was pretty obviously just a front, put there for decoration. And the bald bartender didn't give Uncle Am too much argument before he nodded and showed us the door at the back that led to the real joint.

Back there, there were plenty of people. All of them were well dressed and nearly half of them were women. They looked like money. I thought, if we could only get marks like these to come to the carney— There were two roulette wheels, three people at one and about a dozen packed around the other. There was a semi-circular blackjack table, a crap table, and a round poker table with seven or eight players.

"What you want to play, Ed?" Uncle Am asked me.

I told him I'd just wander around and watch awhile. He went to the table in the corner where a man with an eyeshade sold chips. He came back with one pocket bulging and a stack of chips in one hand; there were three blues and about twenty whites.

He said, "Here's thirty-five bucks to play with. The blues are fins and the whites are bucks. Play around awhile. When you lose 'em, look me up. I'll be at the poker table if I can get a seat."

I watched the crap game awhile, but it was crowded and I didn't lay any bets. I played a few hands of blackjack at a white chip each. I got twenty the first hand and won, stood sixteen and won the second, then got a pair of nines, doubled down on them and won on both. That made me four chips ahead so I did as all suckers do and played the four bucks. I got a king-ten and felt pretty cocky about it until the dealer gave himself an ace, looked at his under card and flipped over a queen.

That put me back where I was, with my original thirty-five bucks, so I wandered over to the less crowded of the roulette wheels. Uncle Am, I noticed, had a seat at the poker table.

The wheel was an eagle-bird wheel, with a triple zero for the house besides the ordinary zero and double zero. Strictly sucker stuff. I played single chips on the red or black for a while, watching the play of the others at the table.

A fat man in a tux was the heavy player; he didn't have any white chips, just blues and yellows. He was letting the numbers alone, but putting stacks of blues on screwy red-black, odd-even, and high-low combinations. The woman with him, a painted ex-chorine in a backless gown cut so low in front that it must have just barely covered the nipples of her breasts, had the opposite idea. She had white chips, but played the long shots only, scattering whites over at least a half dozen numbers on every turn.

I played along without getting anywhere, one way or the other, on the red-black. After a while I started playing two whites at a time and then three, and sometimes five. I still won just about as often as I lost, and I started getting bored.

I thought, I guess I'm just not a gambler; I ought to be all excited about this. I wanted to quit and go over and watch Uncle Am. Poker is a good game to watch, if you're on somebody's side. There's drama in poker, even just watching it. You can back your judgment instead of blind chance, or a crooked wheel.

Thinking of crooked wheels made me think of the zeros; none of them had come up for quite a while. So next spin, instead of playing black, I put a chip on each of the house numbers, the 0, 00 and 000. It didn't hit, but I tried again.

At least I was getting rid of my chips faster that way, three at a crack. For the next few spins I put two chips on each of the zeros, and that spin and the next cost me six chips each.

So I put three chips on each zero number, and the double zero hit. The croupier put a stack of twenty-one blues—a hundred and five bucks—on top of my three whites on the double zero.

I picked them up and let a spin go by while I took inventory. I had a hundred and thirteen bucks. I put the hundred in one pile and the thirteen in another. I decided I'd cash out either a hundred even, or a hundred and thirty-five even.

I put ten bucks on black and three on odd, and the ball dropped into an even number in the red.

I went over to the corner and cashed in the twenty blues for a hundred bucks and put it in my wallet. Then I strolled over to the poker table to watch Uncle Am.

He must have felt me standing behind him, because he turned his head and looked up. He said, "Bust already, Ed? Want some more?"

I shook my head. "Cashed out a hundred," I told him.

"Attaboy. Watch a while. This is table stakes."

He turned back to the game; the man across from him was dealing. It was five-card stud. Uncle Am had a couple of hundred dollars in front of him, but I didn't know what that meant, because I didn't know how much he'd started with. I'd have guessed a hundred, which would put him that much ahead.

He shielded the corner of his down card with the palm of his left hand, and then lifted it high enough that I could see it. It was the jack of diamonds. He got the king of diamonds up. He stayed for a five-dollar bet from an ace and then a five-dollar raise from a seven that must have been a pair of sevens. He got the nine of diamonds for his third card—still a possible straight or flush or both.

A ten across the table had paired, and bet twenty. Uncle Am stayed, and so did the ace and the seven that had raised the first time, but the seven didn't raise again, not into a pair of tens.

On the fourth card. Uncle Am got the three of diamonds, and raised a fifty-dollar bet another fifty. That knocked out both the other hands, leaving Uncle Am's four-flush and the pair of tens.

The pair of tens drew an indifferent card and Uncle Am drew the jack of spades, busting his flush but pairing his hole card. He had the tens beaten, but was licked if there was anything back of them.

The pair of tens said, "I'll bet 'em. A hundred. Whatever part of it you can cover." He tossed five yellows into the pot.

Uncle Am sighed and counted his chips. "Eighty," he said. "Call. Jacks."

The pair of tens flipped over a trey to match his fifth card.

Uncle Am nodded. "Hold the seat. Got to get reinforcements." I walked with him over to the cashier's table. He bought two hundred dollars worth, and I noticed that it emptied his wallet. He said, "Don't worry, Ed, I've got more stashed back on the lot. We won't be broke."

"I'm not worrying," I told him. "But, say, maybe I'm a jinx. Should I wander off and not watch?"

He shook his head. "No jinxes in poker, Ed. It's just judgment—and the cards."

I watched a couple of more hands in which Uncle Am folded early.

Then he hit aces up, bet the works, and lost to three sixes. He stood up and nodded to a guy who'd been waiting for an open chair.

He grinned at me. "Kid, the rest of the party's on you. Will you buy me a beer?"

I said, "Sure," and took out my wallet. I started to count out the hundred I'd cashed out, to give it to him. He saw what I was doing and stopped me, but after a little argument, I got him to take back the thirty-five he'd started me with.

We stopped for another beer apiece in the bar in front of the gambling rooms.

I was wondering how much he'd dropped; he'd bought two hundred the second time and if he'd bought a hundred the first time, it had been three hundred bucks. He must have guessed what I was thinking. He chuckled.

"Easy came, easy went, Ed. But you worry me. You're no gambler. You quit before you broke the wheel."

"It looked pretty substantial," I told him.

"Maybe so. Well, I guess I'm no gambler either, or else I'd go back and lose this thirty-five bucks—or else get back what I lost."

"Why don't you?"

"Should I?"

I said, "It's your life. I wouldn't advise you."

He laughed and went back into the gambling rooms. He came back in ten minutes, grinning. He said, "Some days you can't lay away a dime."

I ordered us another beer. I said, "Now that that's off your mind, let's get back to murder. I still don't get why you said Susie's dying would bring Cap Weiss back here. How?"

"He'll learn about it from the Fort Wayne police. And he'll come back, just in case."

"In case of what?"

Uncle Am sighed and sloshed his beer around in the glass.

"Ed, I told you I used to work for a detective agency once, for a few years, didn't I?"

"Yeah."

"Well, we didn't work on murder cases much, so I don't know anything about 'em. But if I did know anything, I'd say there were two kinds. First, the kind where the coppers catch the guy with the gun in his hand, or running away, or where a guy calls the police station and says, 'I just killed my wife.' That's one kind. And then there's the other kind."

"Which is?"

"That'll cost you another beer."

I ordered him one.

He said, "The second kind is comparatively rare, but it happens. It's the kind of murder you read about in detective stories. It's the kind of a murder this one is. It's a puzzle for the cops to solve."

"And so?" I prompted him.

"And so the only way they can do it is to dig up facts— a few million seemingly irrelevant facts, maybe, and then try to guess which of them aren't irrelevant so they can fit them into a pattern that spells mother."

"You mean, spells murder."

"Only three letters difference. But my point is, the facts which they try hardest to fit into the pattern are the unusual ones. Just like Weiss had in mind when he asked you to keep your ears and eyes open for anything unusual that might happen. Isn't that how he put it?"

I thought back, and then I nodded.

"Weiss is a smart duck," Uncle Am said. "And isn't it unusual for a chimpanzee to drown in a diving tank? How many chimps have you known to drown in diving tanks?"

"Not very many," I admitted.

"Specifically, one. So it's unusual. Q. E. D."

"But how would it tie in with the murder of the midget?"

He put down his glass of beer and made little wet circles on the bar with the bottom of the glass. Finally he said, "How was the midget brought to the lot? Why was he killed? Who gained what by doing it?"

"I don't know."

"So if you don't know those things, how *could* you figure out how it could tie in with the death of a sick chimp? But you do know that they have two things in common already. One is that they both happened with the carney. The other is that they're both unusual. So why, maybe, wouldn't they have still more things in common?"

I thought it over. "Maybe," I admitted. "But I still don't see how you can fit them together."

"You can't, with what we have. You need other facts. Then it might all make a pattern. But finding those other facts is Weiss's job, not ours. Only, what else have you got to tell Weiss if he wants to know what's been going on?"

I lighted a cigarette, thinking it over. I said, "About Major Mote being scared stiff and locking himself in the trailer."

"Good boy. Now why is that especially good?"

"Because it concerns a midget; so did the murder."

"We'll make a detective out of you yet. How'd you like to be one?"

I thought about it seriously. "I don't know," I said.

"That's the right answer, too. But let's get back to the Major. You do see, don't you, that there's one simple, obvious explanation of it—which might be as wrong as hell?"

I thought again. "It might be he's just afraid of chimps, and knowing one was on the loose gave him the meemies. Come to think of it, a chimp, to a midget, would be as big and dangerous as a gorilla is to a man."

"Attaboy. So, if you really want to help Weiss, you can find out for him, tomorrow, if the Major is still scared now that there aren't any more live chimpanzees around."

"Uh-huh," I said, not too enthusiastically.

"Anybody else been scared?" he asked.

"Ummm—Rita was scared the night of the murder. But that's understandable. She fell over the body. Any woman would be scared."

"That's all?"

"All I know of," I said. "Why? Who else?"

"Marge Hoagland. She's been scared ever since the murder. Hadn't you noticed?"

I shook my head. Then I told him, "Now that I think of it, she has acted a little funny a few times. How about Hoagy?"

"Hoagy wouldn't be scared of the devil himself."

"I guess he wouldn't," I said. "But—maybe Marge is scared of Hoagy. He's been drinking a bit more than usual lately."

"Never enough to get out of control. He can hold it. No, I don't think that's Marge's trouble. Hoagy's not hot-tempered; I don't believe I ever saw him mad, drunk or sober. And, too—"

"What?"

"Marge wouldn't be afraid of him anyway; she's too much in love with him. She'd go through hell for him, if he sent her."

"Say," I said, "about the Major— Did anybody check with Carey to see if he was okay when Carey got back after we searched the woods?"

Uncle Am said, "I did. Carey and I put him in a cab and started him off for his hotel. He was awake by then, but woozy."

"Oh," I said, and felt a little better about it. "Want another beer?"

He did, and I had one with him this time. Then we decided to call it a night and go home. There wasn't anything else either of us wanted to do.

CHAPTER VIII

IN THE MORNING, the first person I saw, outside of Uncle Am, was Armin Weiss. While we were getting dressed, somebody called out, "How the hell do you knock on a tent flap?" and it was Weiss.

He sat down on one of the folding chairs and wanted to know all about the chimp business and we told him. He'd already talked to Hoagy and Marge and had the facts, but he wanted to check them with us and see if we could add anything. He was particularly curious about how the chimp had got out of the cage, and I was glad I'd checked that angle and could tell him how it had worked out.

He told us nobody had seen him come into our tent so it wouldn't matter how long he stayed. He stuck around for quite a while.

He'd run into pretty much of a dead end in Cincinnati. He'd found out a lot about the midget, Lon Staffold, but nothing he'd learned had led to the Hobart Shows. He was pretty discouraged, and admitted that it looked as though he wasn't getting anywhere at all.

"A damned carnival," he said, "is the limit. For any other murder, the *setting* stays put, if nothing else does. But a murder happens in Evansville and a few days later, the whole damned surroundings of it and all the people concerned in it, are in South Bend, and then in Fort Wayne, and then—where do we go next?"

"Milwaukee," Uncle Am told him.

Weiss grunted disgustedly.

"Well," he said, "I get mileage allowance on my car. Say, Ed, outside of the monkey business—and I don't see how that means anything, I admit—have you noticed anything out of the ordinary?"

I told him about Major Mote's being scared the night of the monkey hunt.

"Could mean something," he said. "Then again he could have, like you say, been scared of the chimp being loose. I thought he was a little scared that night, the night of the murder, I mean, when I talked to him. And, if you've wondered, I've checked Major Mote's history back to his great-grandparents since then, account of him being a midget and it being a midget was killed. He never worked at any carney this Lon Staffold midget worked at. I can't find that they ever met or even knew about each other."

He shoved his hat back on his head. He said, "Such a goddam case. It's like hunting a black cat in a dark alley when you don't even know if the cat's there."

He turned down a drink, then changed his mind and took one.

"Sticking around town a while," he said. "I'll be at the Ardmore Hotel till tomorrow noon. Damn if I know why. I don't know of anything to do."

He took a second drink for what Uncle Am called a stirrup cup and finally left.

That was Wednesday, and that night was Wednesday night, the thirteenth night after the murder.

I won't forget Wednesday night; it was the night of the third murder, the one that made us mad, Uncle Am and me. And it was the night I saw and smelled a ghost.

The crowd faded early that night. There was no special reason for it; they just did. By eleven or a little after, the midway was thinning out. The talkers on the shows started to turn their last tips and Maury gave the signal to give the free show—the dive act at eleven-thirty—and get it over with.

We got a few on their way out after the free show, and let down our front before midnight.

As usual, Uncle Am said, "Well, kid?" I think he wanted me to want him to take me the rounds again, but I didn't. I told him I'd mess around on the tram awhile.

I got it out and tried some Dorsey arrangements that were too tough for me to play well, and managed to discourage myself pretty quick. So I did a few scales and arpeggios and let it go at that. The tram just didn't feel right or sound right, and there's no use monkeying around when you feel that way.

Uncle Am had been lying on his cot, reading. He put down his book and watched me polish up the trombone and put it back in the case. He said nothing, but I knew what he was thinking.

"I haven't lost interest in it," I said. "It's just that—well—"

"Yeah," he said. "Ed, we all go through it. Some of us survive. Sometimes we live to a ripe old age."

He shook his head slowly. "Did I ever tell you about the redhead I knew once in Cairo?"

"You weren't ever in Egypt," I told him. "Don't try to kid me."

He looked injured. "The hell I wasn't. This was Cairo, Illinois. But I've been in Egypt, too."

"Yeah?"

"Yeah, damn it. *Little* Egypt. Sometime remind me to tell you about that. Right now we're in Cairo on the Mississippi. It was in—let's see—the year of the big snowstorm. Only this was in summer and the snowstorm was in the winter . . ."

I quit listening until he ran down. Then I said, "Let's go over to Carey's."

Uncle Am said, "Sure," and put his shoes back on.

We went to Carey's trailer. Estelle was there. The radio was going full blast; we'd heard it from clear out on the midway. It was a late dance music program from Chi. Carey and Estelle were dancing.

We pushed in and Uncle Am turned down the volume on the radio. He said, "For God's sake, are you people deaf?"

Carey and Estelle broke, and Carey said, "The mighty Hunters. What do you want to drink? We got whisky."

I said I didn't want anything yet and Uncle Am guessed he'd take whisky. The bottle was on the table and he took a drink out of it.

Lee said, "Am, I got a half-baked idea about a new routine—

tossing broads out of a Svengali deck. I want you to help me work up a patter."

He reached into his pocket with his right hand, but grabbed the air with his left and there was the deck. He sat down at one side of the table and Uncle Am at the other and I heard him start explaining how he was tying in the Mex turnover gimmick of monte with an alternating Svengali. Estelle and I just weren't there.

The music on the radio wasn't bad. It was a small combo with a string bass that stood out. I turned it up a little, not as loud as it had been before, and held out my arms to Estelle. She shook her head. "Let's not dance, Eddie."

That was okay by me; I hadn't really wanted to. I sat down and Estelle sat on my lap.

Here we go again, I thought; well, anyway we're chaperoned, if you could call Lee and Uncle Am chaperons. Thinking about that made me grin.

I said, "Uncle Am, you better protect me."

Estelle laughed. Uncle Am gave me a look over his shoulder and said, "God will protect the working boy," and then turned back to Lee.

Estelle said, "Reach me the bottle, Eddie."

She took a drink and I took one and put the bottle down. It was pretty bad whisky, I thought; it tasted raw and burned my throat on the way down.

Estelle said, "I feel a little dizzy, Eddie."

"You *are* a little dizzy," I told her. "Why shouldn't you feel that way? But you better lay off that white mule, or I'll have to carry you home."

"Will you carry me home, Eddie? Now?"

"No," I said.

"You're *so-o* romantic, Eddie. That's why I like you. That, and you're so handsome."

"Another crack like that, and you'll land on the floor."

"With you, Eddie?"

I said, "You little—" and couldn't think of the right word to finish it. None of the words I knew fitted Estelle. "You've got a one-track mind."

"So have you, only I wish it was on a different track. Say, is that whisky all right?"

"It's pretty bad," I said. "Don't drink too much of it."

"My heart's beating too fast, I think. Feel it." She put my hand over where she thought her heart was.

I took it away again. My mouth felt kind of dry; I had to swallow before I could talk. I said, "Cut it out, 'Stelle. Please. I'm not made of wood, but damn it, I—"

"Answer me one question, Eddie. Honestly."

"Sure."

She sat up a little and turned her head to look at my face. "Are you really in love—I mean, the real stuff—with that— with Rita?"

"I guess so," I said. "I mean— My God, yes."

She gave a little mock sigh and then, surprisingly, she smiled at me. She said, "All right then, Eddie, you win. I'll quit teasing you. We'll be friends?"

"Pals," I told her.

"All right, Eddie. From now on. But first, kiss me. Just once. Nice."

It jolted my memory; they were almost exactly the words Rita had used the first time I'd kissed her, two weeks ago, the night I'd taken her for a ride in Hoagy's car to help her get over her touch of hysteria from falling over the dead midget. She'd signalled no passes, and then just before we started back, she'd asked me to kiss her just once, and nicely.

Estelle leaned toward me and I put my arms around her. I closed my eyes as our lips touched, and I was thinking of that first kiss I'd given Rita. I thought, why not? and let myself imagine it was Rita I was kissing again.

Estelle broke away. She sat up straight again and looked at me. Her eyes were sort of misty and then she smiled and they were all right again.

She said, "Was *that* nice? My God, Eddie. Well, I asked for it, didn't I?"

I smiled at her but she didn't smile back. Her face got serious. She said, "I meant it, Eddie. From now on I won't tease you any more. You're Rita's, and I'll keep hands off. Honest.

We'll be friends. Say, does it bother you if I sit on your lap?"

I lied and said it didn't.

She reached over and got the bottle again and this time she said, "You take one first, Eddie," and I did. I handed her the bottle and it was while she was drinking that I looked up at the open window, over Estelle's shoulder.

Maybe it was the smell that made me look up; I don't remember, exactly, which I became aware of first—that smell, or the sight of what it was looking into the window.

It was a monkey, a chimp. And it was either Susie or a dead ringer for her.

The face was a few inches outside the window, not in the direct light of the bulb in the trailer's ceiling, but I could see it fairly clearly. It was the comic-opera-Irishman face of a chimp, and nothing else. Only it wasn't comic: I was scared stiff.

The smell was the smell of fresh earth, the smell of a new grave. And I could see that there was fresh earth, not yet completely dry, clinging to the hair of the chimpanzee's face and head.

It wasn't my imagination, that smell. Whatever I saw, I didn't imagine the smell. There was a draft that was almost a breeze coming in at that window and for just an instant that earth smell was stronger than the smell of whisky or the smell of Estelle's perfume.

And then the face was gone, and the window was empty. And the smell was gone, too.

Estelle was handing me back the bottle. She was saying, "That *is* lousy stuff, Eddie. But before I put it back, do you want anoth— What's wrong, Eddie? You sick?"

She was up off my lap suddenly, standing there looking down at me, and the sudden change in her voice had made Lee Carey look over toward me, and Uncle Am too turned around and then stood up.

He said, "What the hell, kid? You're white as—"

Somehow I didn't want to say, just then, what I'd seen. And already I was beginning to wonder whether I'd really seen it. Did whisky really— No, I thought, nobody gets D.T.'s suddenly after a couple of drinks. But—

I shook my head as though to clear it. It was easy to see what they thought was wrong with me, and I said, "I'm all right. I—just felt funny all of a sudden. I want some air."

I got up and went to the door of the trailer. Estelle must have started to follow me because I heard Uncle Am stop her and say something about letting me alone; if I was going to be sick I wouldn't want company.

As the door shut behind me I heard Estelle telling Lee to get some coffee going quick.

And if I thought I'd been scared in the trailer, I hadn't known what being scared was. Because, out in the darkness alone, I knew now what I'd come out to do. But I knew if I thought about it I'd make it worse, so instead of thinking, I went around to the other side of the trailer, where the window was.

There wasn't any chimp there, dead or alive. There was enough light so I could see that. But there was a wooden packing box standing almost against the side of the trailer, and almost under the window. A chimp *could* have stood on that box and looked in.

I was less scared now. I don't know what I'd expected to find, but there was a reassuring look about that packing case that took the edge off my fright. I walked up to the packing box and moved it. It was empty and there wasn't anything under it.

I backed off a dozen steps and moved around to where I could get a look under the trailer itself, with the open space silhouetted against the all-night midway lights between two of the tops. I bent down and looked carefully. There wasn't anything under the trailer.

I walked back slowly to the trailer. I thought of striking matches, or going back for a flashlight, to look for footprints, but I could tell by the feel of the ground under my soles that it was too hard. Footprints wouldn't show.

I sat down on the packing box a minute to think it out.

Trying to figure what I'd seen just made me more confused. Susie had been the only chimp on the lot; there wasn't any doubt about that. Also, there wasn't any doubt that I could think of about Susie being dead. Dead enough to bury; one of the wheel men had told me Hoagy'd buried her in the woods west of the lot, the woods we'd hunted through yesterday morning.

Was there *any* chance Susie hadn't really been dead? I didn't see how there could be; I hadn't been there, but plenty of other people had seen her body fished out of the tank of water. Surely Hoagy wouldn't have buried her—

It seemed so impossible, so utterly silly, that I began to wonder if I really *had* seen something that wasn't there. Or, more likely, somebody—maybe from the jig show or one of the colored canvasmen—had looked in the window, and my mind had been tricked into supplying details that weren't there.

I told myself that, but I didn't believe it.

After a while I went back around the trailer and went inside again. Estelle was back by the hot plate, and there was a percolator bubbling on top of it.

Carey said, "Feeling better, Ed?"

"Yeah," I said. "Guess I'm not going to be sick. You can skip the coffee, Estelle."

"You're going to drink some or get it poured down your neck, Eddie. It'll be ready in a minute."

Uncle Am said, "You're still a little pale around the gills, kid. The coffee won't hurt you."

I sat down by the table. I felt silly to realize what the others were thinking—that I hadn't been able to hold two drinks, which was all I'd had, without shooting my cookies.

Carey walked down to the kitchen end to help Estelle find a cup, and Uncle Am walked around the table so he was between me and them, and they couldn't hear him.

"What happened, Ed?" he asked. "It wasn't the whisky, was it?"

I shook my head. Lee was coming back. I said, "I'll tell you later."

Carey picked up the bottle of whisky, still about a third full. He said, "We held an autopsy on this, Ed. The verdict is that it's bad, but it's still whisky. How many did you have?"

"Only a couple," I told him. "It wasn't that. I don't know— something I ate maybe."

He shook his head and put the bottle down. "Maybe it's

acute indigestion, Am. Maybe you should take him to a croaker."

"I'm all right," I said.

Uncle Am said, "He'll be all right, Lee," and winked at me.

Estelle brought the coffee, thick as mud and hot as hell. I had to drink it. I wanted a drink of this whisky now; I felt shaky with reaction setting in. But I couldn't very well take one, as long as Carey and Estelle thought it was the cause of my trouble.

Uncle Am and Carey went back to what they'd been talking about before the interruption, and I sipped at the coffee until I got rid of it. Estelle tried to wish a second cup on me, but I said fresh air would do me more good and I was going to take a walk.

"I'll go with you," she said. And that was all right by me.

We went out on the dim midway, heading for nowhere in particular.

"Want a drink?" I asked her. "At the tavern a block down the drag, where we were the other night?"

"Sure, Eddie, but—you shouldn't drink any more."

"Nuts," I said, "it wasn't the whisky, 'Stelle. I'm all right, no kidding."

"If you're sure—"

We strolled on down to the street and down to the tavern. It was still open. We took a booth and ordered highballs.

Estelle drank her first one fast, but sipped her second.

"Eddie," she said, "what happened between you and Skeets Geary?"

"Not much. Why?"

"I'd watch out for him, Eddie. I don't know what you did to him, but he's got a grudge. And a guy like him—settles one. A guy like that will wait a month or a season, until you've forgotten about it, and then—blooie."

"He's yellow. He's got a wide stripe of—"

"Sure, Eddie. He wouldn't do anything he'd get caught at, or that you could trace back to him for sure. He wouldn't lay a finger on you himself. But—"

"Okay," I told her. "So if a pole falls on my head, or I step in a mudhole, I'll know it's Skeets and I'll look him up and take him apart."

"Don't underrate him, Eddie. He's got dough; the side show's been making plenty this season. He made a killing that one week in Evansville, with that x-marks-the-spot business and the knife. And he doesn't waste his money either, like most of us carneys. He's—rich, I guess, compared with the rest of us. He can hire anything he wants done."

I reached across the table and patted her hand. I said, "Thanks, 'Stelle. I'll watch myself."

She pulled her hand out from under mine. She said, "No passes now, Eddie. We're friends, remember?"

I laughed. "Right. No passes."

"And Dutch treat. *I'll* buy the next round. That is, if you're sure it's all right for you to—"

"I'm okay. Don't worry about me."

I wished now that I hadn't started the gag of the whisky making me sick. But I'd started it and I was stuck with it; I'd have to argue every time I got one.

So I let her order a round. The highballs tasted smooth and harmless after that vicious stuff in Carey's trailer.

"Eddie—"

"Yes?"

"Look, now that we're friends, I was lying to you about Rita."

"So?"

"She isn't a bitch, like I said. She's a swell kid, Eddie. She wasn't with the posing show so long, but long enough for us to know that. And nobody with the whole damn carney got to first base with her, except you."

I hadn't any business asking, but I did. "And the mooch—the banker?"

"I'm not sure about that, Eddie." She was very serious. "There—there was something about her having an appointment with one, but I think it was something about business. Anyway—"

"At closing time? Two in the morning?"

"I know it sounds silly, but—I think it was."

"Uh-huh."

She leaned forward; she was really serious about it. "Now listen, Eddie. Don't be like that. Rita's a good kid. Say it wasn't business. That doesn't mean it was monkey business either, does it? I mean, she met him at the bank, opening an account or cashing a check or something, and he asks her if she'll have a drink with him after the carney closes, that doesn't mean she has any idea of going to bed with him, does it?"

"No-o," I admitted.

"All carney girls aren't easy to make, Ed. Just most of them, *if* they want to be. Rita's no pushover for small-town bankers."

I grinned at her; she was serious. "Just big-town bankers?" I asked.

For a minute I thought she was going to get mad; then she laughed.

"Why not?" she asked, and all of a sudden she was serious again. "You know yourself, Eddie, that gal doesn't belong with a carney. She can hit the big time if she wants. And just by teasing big shots along; she's smart enough not to put out if she didn't want to. Only she wasn't smart enough not to fall for you."

I said, "She ought to have her head examined, for that." I really meant it.

I caught the bartender's eye and signaled for a couple more drinks. I was just beginning to feel the ones I'd had, just a nice edge, feeling just right. The bartender brought our drinks and told us they'd be the last, that the tavern was closing. So we drank them and I bought a half pint of good bourbon to take along in my pocket, and we went back to the lot.

In the tavern, I'd managed to forget what I'd seen through the window; being on the lot brought it back again.

Inside the main gate, I stopped. There was something I *had* to do. I knew now what it was, and I knew I didn't want to wait until daylight to do it.

Estelle asked, "What's the matter, Eddie?"

" 'Stelle, where and when did Hoagy bury Susie?"

"Huh? Why?"

I said, "I just want to know."

"Yesterday afternoon, late. I saw Hoagy and Pop Janney heading for the woods with her. Hoagy was carrying the chimp and Pop had a spade. That was just after they found her. Why, Eddie?"

"Are you sure it was the chimp he was carrying?"

"Eddie, are you *crazy?*"

"A little. Are you sure it was the chimp?"

"It was wrapped in canvas, but— Why wouldn't it have been?"

"Why *would* it? You didn't see it."

"I saw her fished out of the tank, Eddie. We were putting on a bally on the platform then. The posing show's right near the tank. We lost our tip when they found Susie. Everybody went over around the tank, so Charlie gave up and quit spieling."

"Did you go over?"

"No, we could see better from the bally platform. Right over everybody's heads. Anyway, all I had on was a thin rayon dressing gown, and nothing under it but a g-string. I wouldn't tangle in a crowd of rubes, dressed like that. It'd start a clem, with me in the middle. I'm not *that* dumb."

"You're actually sure you saw them take Susie out of the tank?"

"Are you nuts, Eddie? I saw them take a dead monkey out of the tank. If it wasn't Susie, what was it? There *isn't* any other chimp around."

I stood there thinking. Suddenly the whole thing made such monstrous nonsense that it frightened me.

Estelle put her hands on both my arms and shook me. *"Eddie,"* she said, "are you going to tell me what it's all about or—*are* you drunk, really?"

"I'm not drunk," I told her. "Oh, hell, I might as well tell you." I told her what I'd seen through the open window of Hoagy's trailer.

She stood looking at me after I'd finished. Then she said, "Eddie, I'm scared."

"So am I. 'Stelle, you ready to go home? Can I put you in a cab?"

"Why? What are you going to do? You're not going to—"

I nodded. "I'm going to. I've got to know."

"Then I'm going along."

I started to argue with her and then changed my mind. I wasn't too crazy about going out alone into the woods at night to dig up a body—even the body of a dead chimp.

CHAPTER IX

ESTELLE WAITED in front of our ball game booth until I went back and got a flashlight and the little short-handled shovel we used for trenching after a rain. I put on my cravenette coat, too, so I could carry the shovel under it, out of sight.

As we started across the midway, Estelle said, "Eddie, while you were in there I was thinking. What if Hoagy's bought another chimp. He could have."

"He's not that crazy."

"Why not? I mean, if he's crazy enough to buy one chimp, why not another if the first one dies? And if he knew where he could get another right away— Have you talked to him or to Marge since last night?"

"No. But, damn it, it's silly."

"Well, look, we have to go by their place anyway, so if there's a light—Eddie, there is one. They're up."

I said, "It's a million to one shot, but okay. Only let's not both go in; we'll have to stay awhile. I'll wait and you look in a minute. Pretend you're hunting for Lee or someone."

I waited in the shadow of the posing show top. She was back in five minutes. She said, "No, Eddie, I was wrong. I didn't even have to ask. Hoagy'd taken down the bars; there wasn't even a cage any more, so that's proof enough."

"Okay," I said. "Sure you want to come along?"

"Yes, Eddie. But—why don't you talk to Hoagy about it? He isn't there now—but Marge says she thinks he's in the G-top, and you could get him to come outside a minute to talk. And ask him if he's sure it was Susie—"

"No," I said. "I don't want to ask Hoagy. I don't want to ask anybody, to take anybody's word. I want to know."

"All right, Eddie. Let's go."

We gave Hoagy's trailer a wide berth so Marge wouldn't see us. We cut across an open field and we were in the woods.

I'd been through them early yesterday morning, and they weren't very big by daylight. But at night they seemed enormous.

I remembered there was a path through them and I figured they'd have buried her near the path. So, with the flashlight, we hunted along the edge until we found the beginning of the path before we went in.

Estelle was scared. She hung onto my arm so tightly that it hurt. I kept the flashlight moving, watching the path ahead and the open areas on both sides of it, watching for a mound or for freshly turned earth.

We missed it the first time and found it on the way back, a dozen paces off the path. It was a little mound of fresh dirt, about four feet by two, still showing the imprints of the spade that had tamped it down. It was a neat, workmanlike job. It looked like a child's grave.

The same thing must have hit Estelle. Her hand tightened again on my arm. "Eddie," she whispered, "it looks like a grave."

"It is," I said. "But just a monkey's grave. Anyway, I think it is. I'm going to make sure."

"Eddie, *no!* Please don't."

"I'll take you back first," I offered. "I can—"

"No, if you've *got* to do it, I'll stay. I'll hold the light for you."

"Attababy," I said.

I gave her the flash, and she stood a little back and held it while I used our trenching shovel. The earth was still loose enough to dig easily. Two feet down, I came to canvas. I kept on working until I'd cleared the dirt off the top of it.

Then I took the flashlight away from Estelle.

"Better turn around," I told her. "It won't be pretty, I guess."

I held the light for her until she got back to the path. She didn't turn away, but from that distance she couldn't see down into the grave anyway, so it didn't matter.

I didn't like the idea of looking myself, but I was going to be damn sure what was inside that canvas. I wasn't going to settle for a glimpse of fur.

I unfolded the canvas, and made sure. I dropped the canvas back and straightened up.

Estelle said, "Eddie—is it—?"

"It's Susie," I said.

She came back a little nearer and I gave her the flash to hold again while I refilled the little grave and tamped the dirt down again with the flat of the shovel.

Neither of us said anything until we got to the edge of the woods, in sight of the lot, the tops and booths silhouetted against the night-lighted midway, the ferris wheel and the high-dive pole tall against the faintly moonlit sky, the lighted trailer windows, the big silent vans.

Estelle caught my arm. "Wait, Eddie, not just yet. I'll bet I'm white as a sheet—like you were when you saw whatever was at the trailer window. And I'm shaky. I— Eddie, have you got that half pint you bought at the tavern?"

"My God," I said, "I forgot all about it. *I* could have used a drink when I was playing ghoul back there. I can still use one."

For just an instant I turned the flash on Estelle, and she hadn't been kidding. I mean, her face was really pale and she was trembling. She must have been even more scared than I, back in the woods. But she'd stuck it out.

It was different here, out of the woods and past our gruesome job, and in sight of the lights of the carney. I knew how she felt, wanting time to compose herself before going the rest of the way back.

"Sure," I said. "We'll have a drink and rest a minute."

I took off my coat and spread it on the grass for us to sit on, and then I put the flashlight back in my pocket and got out the bottle.

I opened it and passed it to Estelle and she drank and passed it back. It was a good brand; it went down a lot smoother than Carey's whisky had. It put a warm feeling in my throat and a warm spot in my chest.

Estelle said, "Don't be a pig, Eddie. Save me some. I'm cold."

She was shivering a little, and I put my arm around her as I passed back the bottle. She snuggled up a little and said, "You're nice and warm, Eddie. But remember—no passes."

"Right," I said.

It was nice sitting there, in the quiet and the dark, with the carney lights to look at, and nothing to worry about.

Only, I thought, my God I wish it was Rita here with me now. I started to count back how many days I'd been waiting now, but before I finished counting Estelle gave me back the bottle. We killed it, taking our time, because there wasn't any hurry.

Estelle sighed. "I feel better now, Eddie. I feel swell."

"Want to go back?"

"If you do."

"I don't," I said.

"Neither do I."

Her face was a white blur in the dark, very near to mine. And her body was warm against mine.

I thought, to hell with no-passes, and I kissed her. It turned into a long kiss.

Then she whispered, "Why don't you pretend I'm Rita, Eddie?"

That was just what I'd been thinking. But I said, "That wouldn't be fair to you, Estelle."

"Why not, Eddie? It doesn't have to *mean* anything, does it? It could just be—fun."

That, too, was just what I'd been thinking.

When I woke the next morning, Uncle Am was sitting on the edge of his cot, pulling on his socks. There was an alert, listening sort of look on his face, not the usual sleepy look people have when they first wake up.

I sat up quick.

He glanced over at me. "Something's wrong, Ed. Feel it? Listen?"

I opened my mouth to ask what he was talking about, and then I shut it and listened instead. Maybe it was my imagination, because of what he'd said, but there was something a little different. I couldn't decide what it was.

There seemed to be something different in the air, too, a feeling of subdued excitement with a little fear mixed in, sort of like the moment after a flash of lightning when you're waiting for the thunder to come. Or maybe it was like the feeling you have when someone comes up to tell you something and you know by his face that it's bad news—but you don't know what it is yet, and you're waiting for him to speak.

I've wondered since whether I'd have felt that by myself; I mean, if Uncle Am hadn't suggested it by his question and by his manner and the hurried way he went on dressing after he'd said it.

Another murder, was my first coherent thought. And then, *Who?*

But there wasn't any percentage in guessing. I swung my feet off the cot and started racing Uncle Am getting dressed. I didn't beat him; he had too much of a start on me. But I tied him, and we went out of the tent together, and through our passage to the midway.

The place was full of cops.

That was my first impression; on second look it boiled down to about a dozen, and when I counted the dozen, there were only six. They were working in three groups of two each, and they were working down our side of the midway, toward us. Each pair of them was talking to a carney. Some of the cops had open notebooks.

I stepped farther out into the midway and looked around. There seemed to be a center of excitement in front of the jig show. There was a little knot of people, some of them men and mulatto girls from the jig show, a few of them white carneys. It sounded like someone over there, a woman, was crying.

I started over that way and someone said, "Hey, you," and I stopped and looked around. It was one of the cops, walking toward me. He asked, "We got your name yet?"

"No," I said. "What's up?"

Uncle Am came walking over and so did the other cop of that particular pair; the carney they'd been talking to went on down the midway toward the entrance.

The first cop had a notebook and pencil. "Your name?"

"Ed Hunter. What's wrong?"

"You're with the carney?"

I nodded. "What's it all about? What's happened?"

He was writing my name in his notebook; he didn't answer. He looked up and asked, "With what show?"

Uncle Am was standing beside me by then; he nudged me to shut up.

He said, "He works for me, Officer. My nephew. We run a ball game. And we'll answer questions from now till next week, but naturally we're curious as hell as to what's happened. We just woke up. It'll save both you and us time in the long run, and be a hell of a favor to us besides, if you'll take time off between questions to tell us in one short sentence what this is all about. Not the details, mind you, just one sentence. Also we'll be able to answer your questions more intelligently."

The cop grinned. He said, "Okay, Jack, you win. Last night a nigger kid named Booker T. Brent was killed. Now what's *your* name?"

Uncle Am told him and he wrote it down. He said, "Okay, we'll take both of you together. Were either of you off the lot since midnight last night?"

Uncle Am said no, and I started to say no, too, and then changed it and said, "I was a block away—that tavern a block down the drag toward town."

"Feltner's?"

I told him I hadn't noticed the name but that it was a block north of the carney entrance gate and he nodded. "What time?"

I said, "I didn't notice, but it would have been after twelve —not much after. Say between twelve and one. We were there about half an hour, and then came back to the lot."

He wanted to know who was with me, and I told him.

"You know the kid that was killed?"

I shook my head, but Uncle Am said, "Sure you do, Ed. But you didn't know him by his real name. That's Jigaboo."

"Hell," I said.

God damn it, I thought, why did it have to be Jigaboo? He

was so *alive,* so damn good a tap dancer and so nice a kid. It just didn't seem possible that Jigaboo was dead.

The cop was saying, "Yeah, that's how they billed him: Jigaboo. When did you see him last?"

I thought back. "About the middle of the evening. I got hungry and took a few minutes off to go over to the grab joint for a hamburger. The jig show was putting on a bally and he was on the platform, dancing a few steps, when I went by."

"You didn't see him after the carney closed?"

"No."

Uncle Am said about the same thing; that the last time he'd seen the kid had been on the bally platform, only earlier in the evening when he'd gone to the chow top while I'd spelled him at the ball game.

The cop said. "Okay. This your concession here?"

Uncle Am nodded.

"Anybody else work with you or for you?"

"No, just the two of us."

"Always sleep on the lot?"

"Yeah. We got a living top pitched back of the booth."

"Okay," the cop said. "Ambrose Hunter, Ed Hunter. Okay."

He and the other cop went on down the midway. Pop Janney was walking along toward us and they got him between them; the notebook flipped open again.

I started toward the group in front of the jig show platform, and Uncle Am said, "Wait, Ed."

I did, and he said, "That's the kid's father and mother in there. Let 'em alone. They don't want a crowd."

"But we want to find out—"

"Sure, Ed, we want to find out. But not from them. There's nothing we can do for them, so just stay away."

"Where do we find out?"

"Let's get it really straight instead of picking up rumors all over the lot. Cap Weiss is still in town. When he was around yesterday he said he was staying at the Ardmore till noon today. It's a little after that, but this would have come up before he left, so he's sure as hell still in Fort Wayne."

I asked him, "You think this ties in the same bundle as the midget business?"

"How the hell would I know—without knowing how and where the kid was killed? Let's go use a phone. Not the office wagon one—how's about that tavern you and Estelle went to?"

"It's got a phone in a private booth. Sure."

We went to the tavern. Uncle Am ordered a beer and I settled for a coke. While the bartender was getting them, Uncle Am went back to the phone booth.

He came back in a few minutes. He said, "Weiss is at headquarters. He was still checked in at the Ardmore but not in, so I tried headquarters and got him. I told him—"

"What's he doing there? I should think he'd be coming out here to the lot."

"He isn't. He must be working on some angle from there; maybe they got somebody in for questioning. I told him we had some stuff to tell him and that we weren't too crazy about going to headquarters, so he said he'd meet us at his hotel at three."

I looked at the clock over the bar; it was one.

"Why so long?" I asked him.

Uncle Am glanced down the bar at the bartender and saw he wasn't paying any attention to us. He lowered his voice a little.

"Ed, we're not going to hold out on him. I want you to tell him what you told me late last night, about what you saw out of the trailer window."

"Or what I thought I saw," I said. "But what's that got to do with how soon we see him?"

"We want to see Estelle first. Look, it'll tangle both of you up and do nobody any good if you tell one story about what you two kids did last night and she tells another. If they talk to her first and she swears you and she weren't off the lot, she'll be in a jam."

I took a sip of my coke. "Okay," I said, "I can tell them what I saw, but why do I got to tell them we went out in the woods and dug up the monkey? I already told those harness bulls back on the lot that I was away from the carney only to go to the tavern for a half hour. I'm on record."

Uncle Am said, "Yeah, you did. Well, if they get tough about that you'll have to backtrack and say you didn't think of the woods as being away from the lot because they were so close, part of the same property, sort of."

"Sure, but why—"

"Don't be dumb, Ed. You tell 'em you thought you saw Susie or an ape like her, and don't you think they're smart enough to get the same idea you did? They'll go out and dig up Susie, too. And there'll be marks to show she's been dug for already, since she was planted, and they'll find our trenching shovel wherever the hell you left it and—"

"My God, didn't I bring that back?"

"You didn't have it when you came back last night."

I thought back. "I didn't leave it at Susie's grave. I—we stopped a while at the edge of the woods on the way back. I must have left it there."

"Having other things on your mind, I'd guess," Uncle Am said. "Here's the main question right now. You know where Estelle is staying or do we have to hunt for her?"

"She's staying at the Ardmore, same as Weiss. I got a cab for her to send her downtown from the lot last night."

"Then what you waiting for? Go call her up before she gets away from the hotel and make a breakfast date for us. Uh—not at the Ardmore; we don't want to run into Weiss too soon. There's a restaurant in town called Maxie's. Tell her to meet us there at two o'clock."

I went back to the phone booth and got Estelle on the phone.

"Hi, Eddie." Her voice sounded sleepy. "Just woke up."

"You haven't heard what happened, then?"

"What, Eddie?"

I told her the little I knew about what had happened, and that Uncle Am and I wanted to talk to her to get our stories straight before either of us did any more talking to the police. And I told her about meeting us at Maxie's at two.

"Eddie," she asked, "you talking from a private booth?"

"Yes."

"About last night, Eddie. I know it didn't mean anything. We said that, so let's mean it. I—I really didn't mean it to; I honestly meant what I said first, and I don't want to spoil anything between you and Rita."

I felt better. I said, "Thanks, kid. You're swell."

"You didn't tell anybody? I mean your uncle?"

"I didn't tell him, 'Stelle, but I wouldn't put it past him to be pretty sure about it. He's a hard guy to fool; he can read me like a pack of marked cards."

She laughed a little.

"Okay, Eddie. Anyway, it never happened. Right?"

"Right," I said. It was more than that; it was a hell of a load off my mind. " 'By then. I'll see you at Maxie's."

I went back to the bar and told Uncle Am it was all set.

"Come on, then," he said. "We got time to go back to the lot."

"What for?"

"I want you to get that trenching shovel. If you'd left it where you did the digging, that'd be all right because you're going to level about that. But you don't want to have to explain to the cops how come you forgot it at the edge of the woods, do you?"

"I guess I don't," I admitted.

We left the tavern and started back to the lot, and Uncle Am said, "While you're doing that, I want to talk to a few guys with the side show. We never did follow through about the Major and his being so damn scared about the monkey business. Remember? We were going to find out if he had a phobia on chimps or if it might have been something else."

I said, "We told Weiss about it. Maybe he followed through on it."

"He could have tried, but it would be pretty tough for him to get the straight dope—unless the Maj happened to feel like telling him. And I wouldn't bet on that."

On the midway, we were stopped by a pair of cops again and we had to explain we'd been put on record already. We pointed out the cops we'd talked to and they gave us the high sign, so that let us through the blockade.

We split up, then, and agreed to meet at Lee's joint.

I cut off the midway to the south side, nearest the woods, and didn't have any trouble finding the shovel. I went the long way around the outside so as not to have to cut across the midway carrying it, and put it in our living top.

Then, because I had time, I changed clothes and put on my

good suit and another pair of shoes, since we'd be eating downtown. I'd been in such a hurry dressing the first time that I'd put on the clothes I'd taken off the night before, work clothes to begin with and muddy in spots from the digging I'd done.

Uncle Am and Lee Carey were waiting for me. Uncle Am whistled when he saw me coming. "What the well-dressed young man will wear."

Lee said, "A page out of *Esquire*."

"Shall I go back and put on overalls?" I asked Uncle Am.

"Won't be time. Lee's driving in town; we can catch a lift with him. We'll get there in plenty of time for the show." His back was toward Lee and he winked at me, so I didn't say "What show?" I got it that I wasn't to crack to Lee about what we really were going in town for.

CHAPTER X

WE GOT IN Carey's coupé, Uncle Am in the middle and me on the outside. It was the first time I'd been with Lee in his car and I noticed, as we went in to town, that he drove with the same easy dexterity with which he handled cards and coins. He was a fast driver but a good one; he could tool that little coupé through holes in traffic that didn't look big enough to fit a kiddy-car.

As we neared the downtown section, Uncle Am asked, "Say, Lee, happen to know what hotel the Major's staying at?"

Uncle Am turned to me when he shook his head.

He said, "The Maj is scared again. Lee tells me he came out to the lot early today, a little after noon, and then turned around and high-tailed out again, grabbed a cab and beat it."

"When he heard Jigaboo was murdered?"

"Yeah. That is, *if* Jigaboo was murdered. The cops aren't— Okay, Lee, you can drop us here. I got an errand or two before we take in the show."

We got off and headed into a department store and kept going on through to go out the doors on the side street. Uncle Am said, "We're only a block from Maxie's."

I asked, "Why did we give Lee the runaround?"

"General principles, kid. Never advertise your business. If the carneys got the idea we were seeing Weiss, some of them would clam up on us. And if we'd told Lee we were meeting Estelle for breakfast, he might've wanted to come along. If we're going to straighten out your story and hers about last night—well, no reason why he should listen in on that."

"Oh," I said. "Did you find out what happened to Jigaboo? I mean, how he was killed?"

"Lee knew a little about it; I didn't talk to anybody else. Here's Maxie's. Wait, if Estelle's already here, I don't want to have to have to tell it twice, otherwise while we're waiting for her—"

Estelle had taken a table not far back, and was watching the door. She saw us come in, and waved. We went over and sat down at the table. Estelle started to ask something, and Uncle Am said, "Hold it." A waitress was coming.

We ordered, and waited until she was out of earshot, and then Uncle Am said, "Okay, kids, here's the little I found out from Lee that we didn't know. Jigaboo was found about four o'clock this morning, before dawn. Not on the lot—on a road somewhere. Looked like he'd been hit by a car. Took him to the morgue as a routine accident case and didn't identify him till almost noon. His parents missed him then and—"

"He was gone all night?" I interrupted. "And they didn't miss him till noon?"

"Yeah. They sleep all over the lot. He used to sleep in the number four van mostly, with his ma, but she figured he'd bedded down somewhere else and didn't think anything of it for a while. Then she went to Maury and asked about him. Maury figures the kid maybe ran away—he did once early in the season—and he knows the kid being gone will put a crimp in the jig show. So he gets a few canvasmen and ride boys to help look in likely places and to ask around, and when the kid doesn't turn up and nobody's seen him, Maury starts phoning."

I said, "There must be some reason, though, why the police think he was murdered. If it was just that he was hit by a car somewhere, they wouldn't have sent that battery of harness bulls out to the lot."

Uncle Am nodded. "There must be, Ed. But I don't know any more than I just told you. Well, Estelle—"

"Yes, Am?"

He told her that we were seeing Weiss—and had to explain who Weiss was and what he was doing in Fort Wayne—and that I was going to tell Weiss the truth about digging into Susie's grave, and why I'd done it.

He said, "If you want to stay out of it, we can say Ed did the digging alone, after he put you in a cab."

Estelle looked from me to Uncle Am and back again. She said, "I—I guess not. No reason why you shouldn't tell him I was along, and held the flashlight for you. There's nothing they can charge us with, is there?"

Uncle Am shook his head. "No, definitely. There's probably a law about digging into a human grave without official permission. But not an animal's."

"Okay," Estelle said. She looked at me. "But you're not going to tell him—"

I said, "After the digging business, I put you right in a taxi. You were feeling a little shaky, remember?"

"Yeah. I was. Okay, Eddie. Deal me in, then."

The waitress brought our grub, and we didn't talk much while we ate. Then Estelle said she was going on out to the lot, and we put her on a bus and went around to the Ardmore Hotel.

At the desk, the clerk told us Weiss hadn't come in yet, but had phoned and left word we were to go on up and wait in his room. The clerk gave us the key, and we took the elevator up and found his room.

Uncle Am sat on the bed and I went over and stood looking out the window, although there was nothing to see but the other side of a wide airshaft.

We didn't talk.

After a while I heard the door open behind me and turned around as Weiss came in. He looked hot and tired. He said, "Hi," kind of listlessly, took off his hat and suit coat and unbuttoned his vest. Then, before he said anything else to us, he sat down on the straight chair in front of the writing table and picked up the telephone.

He asked for room service and ordered a fifth of Seagram's and a couple of extra glasses.

I wondered why he hadn't brought it along with him, since he'd just come in. He must have been a mind-reader, because he looked over at me as he put the phone down. He said, "Cheaper *this* way. If it's on the hotel bill, which I tell 'em not to itemize too closely, the department pays for it."

He grinned and tilted the chair back against the desk. "Got something, Am?"

Uncle Am said, "Maybe. Maybe not. The kid had a funny experience last night. Get it straight from him."

I told him what had happened, starting with Uncle Am and me going to Lee's joint, and Estelle being there, and then how I'd happened to look at the open window and what I'd seen, or thought I'd seen. I picked my words carefully, trying not to exaggerate it and not to play it down too much, either.

He interrupted me a few times to ask questions, but mostly he let me tell it my own way. When I got to the part about deciding to be sure Susie was still where she was supposed to be, he asked, "Why? Did you think she'd dug her way out again?"

I said, "I don't know exactly what I thought. I'd just seen a chimp, and Susie was the only chimp around. I—I just wanted to be God damn sure it wasn't Susie I'd seen. I just had other people's word she was dead."

He snorted a little. "Several thousand other people. Okay, so you and this Estelle—Beck, you say her last name is?—went out and dug. So?"

"So Susie was there. I filled in the hole again, and that's all."

He ran his hand through his thinning hair. "Way I got it, they wrapped the monk up in canvas to bury her. Did you really follow through, and open up the canvas to be sure what was in it?"

I'd been hoping he'd ask that. I grinned at him. "Why? Do you think she'd dug her way out again, and left something else in the canvas?"

He grunted, and Uncle Am chuckled.

I said, "Yes, I opened up the canvas. It was Su— Wait a

minute; to be strictly accurate, I don't know for sure that it was Susie inside. But it was a chimpanzee, and it was dead."

"A female one?"

"I didn't get that intimate with it."

He grunted again. "How's the level of that trailer window? Could a man look in without standing on anything?"

I said, "A man could. A chimp would have to be standing on something, but there was something it *could* have stood on." I told him about the packing case I'd found outside.

Uncle Am said, "It was still there today; I looked. And I asked Lee about it and he said it had been there before yesterday. So it wasn't put there last night especially to let a chimp look in the window."

"An empty case?"

"Yeah. Came early in the week with stuff from the magic supply house Lee deals with. Twenty gross of the outfits of slum he pitches in the side show, and some other magic stuff, for himself."

"Like maybe a monkey illusion?"

Uncle Am shrugged. "I didn't ask him."

I said, "You're off the beam there, Cap. It wasn't any illusion—I mean, any rigged-up illusion. It was—"

Weiss held up his hand, and I shut up. I hadn't heard the footsteps but there was a knock on the door. Weiss called out, "Come in," and a bellboy brought in the whisky and glasses.

After he'd gone, Weiss poured us drinks. I told him to make mine short. He handed it to me and said, "Okay, Ed. You were saying about illusions—?"

"It wasn't any rigged-up illusion," I told him. "I'll bet on that. It could have been—but I'm pretty sure it wasn't—a trick of eyesight; I mean, sometimes you take a quick look at something and think it's something else till you take a second look."

Weiss nodded. "I've had that happen. Seen a man in the hallway at home, clear as hell. Then you take a second look, and it's the hat rack with a coat on a hanger on it and a hat on top. For just a fraction of a second, your mind, your imagination, supplies the missing details."

I said, "This *could* have been that. I don't think it was. For one reason, it was—well, I'd guess it was a full second I saw it, maybe two or three seconds. It was about a foot back from the window, though, and it was dark outside. The only light on it was indirect, from inside the trailer. I'll give you the possibility that it might have been a man looking in, but I still don't think it was."

Weiss nodded slowly. "A colored man, if anything. You've got lots of them with the carney. A trick of the light—"

Uncle Am said, "Maybe. And maybe not. The kid isn't imaginative, Cap. Well, that's the story. Take it or leave it; we give it to you."

Weiss ran his fingers through his hair again. He said, "Thanks. If I needed anything to help me go nuts, this is it. Well—thanks, anyway. Another drink?"

Uncle Am took one, but I shook my head. Weiss poured a big one himself, but put it down on the desk without drinking it. He sat down in the chair again.

He said, "Now we got another angle. Major Mote—whose real name, if it matters, is Joseph Danton."

Uncle Am said, "I meant to tell you, Cap. He's scared again. He came out to the lot about noon today and—"

Weiss interrupted him. "I know about that. I mean, the other night. He got scared, in Lee Carey's trailer, same as Ed did last night. Did a chimp maybe look in the same window?"

I looked at Uncle Am. His mouth fell open a little.

I said, "Susie would have been drowned by then. They don't know how long she'd been gone and—"

Weiss said, "Susie was drowned by last night, for sure. So why couldn't the Major have seen whatever you saw?"

I thought a minute this time before I answered. Then I said, "No, I don't think it was anything he saw; it was Marge's coming to the door of the trailer and telling us Susie was missing. I was looking at the Maj when she came, and he was all right then. Just sitting looking kind of glum, on the edge of the bunk. Marge came to the door and we were all looking toward her while she was telling us Susie'd got loose and asking us to help hunt. The Major would have been looking that way, too.

"Then when she got up to go out, less than a minute later, was when I looked at the Maj again and saw he was scared. It was what Marge said that scared him."

Weiss said, "Oh. Well, it was a good idea while it lasted." He picked up his whisky from the desk and tossed it off.

Uncle Am said, "Now you tell us, Cap. What we don't know about Jigaboo's death would fill a fair-sized book."

Weiss grinned without any humor back of it. He said, "You bring me that book, Am, and I'll autograph it for you. How much *do* you know?"

Uncle Am told him.

Weiss said, "There isn't much more. He was found on the Dane road, half a mile past the city limits. That's about a mile from the carnival lot. It's not any road that goes by the lot. Early this morning, four-ten to be exact, he was seen by a motorist, lying at the edge of the road. The motorist stopped, found the kid was stone dead, so he didn't try to rush him to a hospital or anything like that. He left his car parked there so nobody else'd run over the body and walked back to where he could use a phone.

"He called the sheriff's office and they sent out a couple of deputies and the wagon. There was only one screwy thing about it." Weiss paused, but we didn't ask any questions so he went on:

"The kid didn't have any clothes on. He was mother-naked."

Uncle Am swore softly.

I said, "Like the midget that was killed on the lot." A kind of funny chill went down my back.

Weiss nodded. "Outside of that it could have been an ordinary enough accident. Cause of death, skull fracture. There were other bruises and contusions. There was blood on the roadway. Everything to indicate the kid had just been walking along the edge of the road and was knocked down by a hit-run driver. Except what would anybody—even a seven-year-old kid —be walking along a road without any clothes on for?

"Well, that worried them, but they took him to the morgue and the best angle they could figure is maybe the kid lived not so far away and might have been walking in his sleep. The carney's not on that road and nobody thought of the carney.

"The county officers made a report to the police that if anybody started asking for a little Negro boy, they had him. If they mentioned the no-clothes angle, it didn't get across or didn't get mentioned to the right people. Because the city police here know about the Lon Staffold murder, and they've been keeping an eye on the carney. The coincidence of another naked corpse would have sent 'em right out there, asking questions. But as it was, nobody tied it in until the call came from the carney lot, from Maury, asking if there'd been a Negro kid turned in to the lost and found. That's the whole story."

Uncle Am said, "That's up till they started investigating. Since then?"

"Nothing. They haven't found anyone on the lot—and they're talking to everybody—who'll admit seeing the kid after midnight. More specifically, after eleven forty-five; that's when his show closed. Nobody on the lot missed him or looked for him till morning so there's no lead as to whether he was on the lot until almost four, or whether he left or was taken away as early as midnight.

"Of course the coroner's physician had a look at him, to make out the certificate. That was after the wagon brought him in, around five. Said he'd been dead an hour or two. That'd put the time of death between three and four o'clock. Not much traffic on that road at that time of the morning. It's unlikely, but he *could* have been lying there since three o'clock, an hour and ten minutes before he was found. More likely he was killed there— or left there—about four o'clock and found ten minutes later."

I asked, "And his clothes?"

"That's the only interesting thing the investigation turned up, Ed. His clothes were in the number four van, where he usually slept, right on the carney lot. All he'd been wearing, which was a pair of overalls. Just as though—"

"How about his costume—for the show, I mean—and his tap shoes?"

"Oh, those. He changed out of them under the jig show top, and put on the pair of overalls. That was the last time he was seen—by several people, incidentally; all performers in the show.

"And then—well, his overalls are in the van. Indications, such as they are, are that he went back and turned in. And then got up and left again, naked, or else somebody or something took him out of his bed,—if you call a roll of blankets a bed."

"What do you mean," I asked, "somebody or *something?*"

"I dunno what I mean, Ed, unless maybe—well, a chimpanzee could carry off a kid, couldn't it? And didn't you see one on the lot that night?"

Uncle Am cleared his throat. He said, "Don't drink any more of that stuff, Cap. You're talking like a double-horror show. You give me the creeps. Let's have another drink, since it's on the taxpayers."

Weiss poured them. I had another short one, myself. I carried it over to the window and stood looking out at nothing, across the airshaft.

Uncle Am got up off the bed, and I could hear him walking back and forth in the space between the bed and the door. He said, "About the Maj. You know what hotel he's at?"

Weiss's voice said, "None. He took it on the lam. If Susie scared him, then what happened to Jigaboo must have given him the screaming meemies. When he grabbed a cab from the lot, we found out, he took it to his hotel and had it wait there till he packed. He checked out, and the clerk says he could hardly talk. He put his stuff in the cab and went to the railroad station.

"Well, a midget's easy to trace. We found he headed for St. Louis, and we've wired ahead for them to hold him there."

I said, "The Maj couldn't have killed Jigaboo. He couldn't have carried him that far, and he doesn't drive."

"Doesn't or can't?"

"He hasn't got a car. And he couldn't drive an ordinary one; I mean, his feet couldn't reach the pedals and he couldn't see over the hood without standing or kneeling on the seat."

"Un-huh. Well, we didn't figure him for that anyway. We want to find out what he's scared of." Weiss stared gloomily at the ceiling. "Not that it's likely to mean anything. Nothing does, in this damn business."

"Yeah, Cap," Uncle Am said. "Too bad the killer doesn't sign his name for you."

Weiss didn't even answer.

I was tired of standing up. I went over and sat down on the bed. Something seemed to be stuck between two of my teeth and I started fumbling through my vest pockets to see if I had a toothpick. I didn't find one, but in the lower right hand pocket my fingers touched something tiny and smooth.

I took it out to see what it was, and it was the tiny red cube Lee had given me, the one of a pair of dice that had lost its mate.

Idly I shook it in my hand and started tossing it on the bed cover with a vague idea of seeing if it was loaded.

Uncle Am asked, "Where'd that come from, kid?"

I told him, and he started pacing back and forth again. He said, "Cap, if you assume Susie's death is a part of the pattern, then there are two things alike in all three killings."

Weiss frowned. He said, "Well, one is that none of 'em had any clothes on. Not that you'd expect a chimp to be wearing any. What's the other?"

Uncle Am jerked a finger at me. "Look what the kid's playing with. That tells you."

Weiss looked. He said, "Huh?" He thought a minute. "What about it? It's a dice."

"Nope," Uncle Am told him. "It's a *die*, Cap. One of a pair of dice is a die. *The little die*. Staffold—Susie—Jigaboo. A midget, a chimp, a kid. But they were all the same size, Cap, within an inch or so."

Weiss said, "I'll be a son of a bitch."

I rolled out the little die again. It wasn't loaded; I was sure by now. I closed my eyes; there was something at the back of my mind that I could almost think of but not quite. I reached for it, but it slipped away.

Uncle Am said, "Come on, Ed. Let's go."

CHAPTER XI

THE JIG SHOW was closed that night. The rest of the carney was running, but not doing much. The carneys all were jittery, too.

I wondered why the marks weren't coming in droves, the way they had in Evansville, after the first murder. That night had been like a madhouse. I asked Uncle Am about it.

He said, "Hell, kid, I don't think the marks know there's been a murder. The kid's death looked like hit-run—at first, anyway. Maybe they gave it to the papers that way, for some reason of their own."

"I'd like to get a paper and see."

"Go ahead. Unless you want to, don't come back. I might close up anyway. The hell with it."

I walked to the nearest drugstore and got a Fort Wayne evening paper. I ordered a malted at the soda counter and while the clerk was making it I looked for the article on Jigaboo's death.

It wasn't on the front page. I found it on the second page, about four column inches. It didn't mention murder, or that the kid had been found naked. It didn't even mention that he was Jigaboo, the boy wonder of the carney show. It identified him only as Booker T. Brent, 7, Negro, from the J. C. Hobart carnival. Just the outside facts, none of the inside ones.

I went back to the lot. I told Uncle Am he'd been right and asked him why the cops had kept it out of the papers.

He shrugged. "Just being cagy, Ed. Cops like to be cagy, even when they don't know why. It makes them feel clever to keep something under their hats as long as they can."

I said, "If you're cleverer than the cops, who killed Jigaboo?"

"I don't know, Ed. Good God, did you think I did know?"

I said, "I think you could find out. You used to be a detective."

"Ed, I was an operative for a private agency; that's all. I traced skips, checked references, did a little tailing, stuff like that. That's different. And that was a long time ago."

"So you're smarter now," I said. "Seriously, why don't you?"

He frowned. "It seems to me, Ed, just night before last you weren't enthusiastic even about keeping an eye open for Weiss."

"I could have been wrong. You told me I was. It could be we've both been wrong from the start, from the time you told me it wasn't our business and I agreed with you. Only it's worse for you because you *could* have done something about it."

"Who the hell do you think I am, kid? Sherlock Holmes or Philo Vance or something?"

He sounded annoyed with me, almost for the first time since

I'd been with him. Uncle Am's got the smoothest disposition of anyone I know; he's pretty tough to ruffle.

I didn't answer. I sat down on the counter of the booth and didn't say anything at all. That must have annoyed him more.

He said, "God damn it, Ed, the police get paid for working on murders. Why should I break my neck doing their job for them? Even if I could."

"*Because* you could," I told him.

I didn't look at him. I said, "When the midget got murdered, it wasn't any of our business. But maybe if we'd made it our business the jig show wouldn't be closed tonight. Maybe it'd be running, and with Jigaboo up on that bally platform."

"God damn it, Ed—"

It was the first time I'd ever heard him sound really mad. At me, anyway.

A mark, a guy with patent leather hair and a flower in his buttonhole, had stopped in front of the booth. He asked, "What do you win if you knock all the—?"

Uncle Am said, "Go to hell. We're closed."

The mark glared at him like he was going to make a beef, but Uncle Am glared back, asking for trouble, and the mark changed his mind and went on.

I said, "He was afraid of you. It's that black slouch hat and the way you wear it. It makes you look sinister."

I didn't look at him; I guess I was a little afraid to, after saying that. I sat there on the low counter of the booth, trying to juggle three baseballs and not having any luck with it.

I dropped one of them and it hit my foot and rolled out of reach back toward one of the platforms the milk bottles were on. I didn't get up to go after it.

I thought, maybe this is the split-up between me and Uncle Am. I felt like hell. My stomach felt hollow.

I said, "You're mad because you know I'm right. You've got brains. More than these hick coppers—even Armin Weiss—have got. And you're on the inside, instead of on the outside like they are. Maybe you couldn't have found out who bumped off the midget and Susie."

Still I didn't look at him. I said, "But God damn it, you

could have tried, instead of playing rummy in the G-top. Me, too. We should have tried, even if it wasn't any of our business. And if we had what it took, then Jigaboo wouldn't have died last night. Don't you see that?"

Then neither of us said anything for a long time—it might have been only a minute or less, but it seemed like a year.

And then another mark stopped in front of the booth. I heard him start to say something, and Uncle Am said, "Sorry, we're closing."

His voice wasn't mad any more. It was just normal; not even with the exaggerated calmness that comes to the top when you shove anger under and hide it. His voice was natural, and that meant it was decided one way or the other. I mean, he might be ready to say, "Okay, kid, if that's the way you feel, we better split up." Or—

Or he might say what he did say when the mark moved on: "All right, Ed. Where do we start?"

It was all right, then. I got up and got the baseball that had rolled to the back. I came back with it.

He was grinning at me when I faced him. He said, "About this hat, kid. Which makes me look the most sinister—like this, or if I turn the brim down all the way around, like this?"

He turned it down all around, and either way—with that grin on his mush—he looked about as sinister as Porky Pig. I tried to keep my face straight, but I couldn't.

When I managed to get things back to a serious plane again, I said, "Listen, Uncle Am, I didn't mean we should close up and go at this full time. I just meant that from now on let's really try to use our eyes and brains.

"As to *where* we should start, I was hoping you might have an idea. Let's skip it till we close tonight, and then talk it over and see if we can get an angle."

He said, "Sure, Ed. But I don't feel like working tonight anyway. Let's close up. We won't lose much."

"Okay," I said.

I reached up to lower the canvas front but somebody said, "Hi, Ed." I looked, and it was Armin Weiss.

"Step on over," Uncle Am told him.

Weiss did, and I lowered the front, with the three of us behind it. Weiss sat down on the counter, his back to the canvas, and asked, "How come closing?"

Uncle Am said, "We just ain't ambitious, Cap. Don't feel like working."

Weiss sighed. "Oh, for the life of a carney."

"What's new?" I asked him.

"Not much. The St. Louis boys picked your Major Mote off the train all right, but he won't come back."

"Won't come back?"

"Not voluntarily. He stood up on his short little hinders and got himself a lawyer. We gotta extradite if we want him back. Be a lot easier for me to go there and talk to him, than to go through all that. Not that it'll do any good, either way."

"Will he talk?"

"Oh, sure; he'll answer all the questions we want. The St. Louis boys held him up to a phone, or held a phone down to him, and he talked. Mostly what he says is that he's coming back to the carney or even to this state over his own dead body. Long distance made a lot of money on the variety of ways he thought of to say that."

"What about why he lammed? Will he talk about that?"

"Oh, sure. He says he was scared stiff he was going to be the next one to get bumped. He's also scared stiff of monkeys."

"What else did he say?" I asked him. "Why was he afraid of getting bumped off?"

"He started getting scared when the midget turned up dead, he says. He didn't exactly reason that somebody was starting a campaign against midgets, but— Well, he was the only midget around and when another turned up with a shiv in his back, it worried him for fear he'd be the next one. He couldn't make his reasons any more definite than that. He still swears he didn't know Lon Staffold, the other midget, and had never seen him or heard of him before.

"Then Susie getting loose gave him a different kind of jitters. He's got a horror of monkeys. Not just because he's little, but like some people have a horror of cats or snakes. Says he's stuck to carneys and never worked for a circus for that reason—because all circuses have apes or monkeys. He says he almost quit the carney when Hoagy bought Susie, but he decided he'd ride out the season."

I said, "But once Susie was found dead, that took care of that, so why'd he run off today? I saw, or thought I saw, another chimp last night. But he couldn't have known that. Nobody knows it now except—let's see, you and Uncle Am and Estelle and I. Or—say, did you ask him if he saw anything last night? Without suggesting a chimp, I mean?"

"Sure I asked him that. No, he swears nothing happened last night. He went right downtown as soon as the side show closed. And I believe him on that—at least I believe that he didn't see anything last night like you did, or he wouldn't have come out to the lot at all today. And we know he did."

I said, "And then scrammed out of town."

"Yeah, when he learned Jigaboo'd been killed. He didn't even ask how or why. He just beat us to the same idea your uncle got this afternoon. Three deaths with the carney in two weeks and all the same size. *His* size. He just didn't want to hang around to find out if that was all or if there were going to be any more."

"He got any ideas about who or why or anything?" I asked.

Weiss said, "Oh, sure. He thinks it's a homicidal maniac with a mania for picking 'em according to size, some nut following the carney, moving from town to town with it."

I said, "The Phantom of the Carnival." But it didn't sound very funny.

Uncle Am said, "It just *could* be that he's got something there. I mean, there's just one thing in favor of it. The first midget not being with the carney. It could be an outsider brought his own midget to the lot. What with the midget himself being an outsider— Hell, that doesn't make sense either."

"Nothing does," Weiss said. "Well, I'll mosey along. I got other guys to talk to. I dunno why, or what about, but I got to earn my pay somehow."

"You going to St. Louis?" I asked him.

"I dunno. I dunno that I could get anything out of that midget face to face I didn't get over the phone. Not unless I get some new questions to ask him, anyway. Only if he's got a lawyer the St. Louie cops can't hold him long either, and if I do want to talk to him, I'll have to chase him to Florida."

"Florida? If he was heading for Florida, wasn't St. Louis kind of out of his way?" Uncle Am asked.

"He didn't care. He just took the first train out of Fort Wayne. He'd have gone to Florida by way of Canada if he had to, to get out of here. Says his grouch bag's in good shape and he isn't going to work any more this year. He doesn't seem to care much, any more, for the J. C. Hobart carney."

I said, "Maybe he's got something there."

"I see his point. Say, the inquest on the Brent kid is tomorrow morning at ten o'clock, downtown. You don't have to come, either of you; you're not witnesses. Hell, there won't be any witnesses, except his parents for identification, and the guy who found him on the road and the coroner's physician that made out the certificate."

"*Want* us to come?" I asked him.

"I dunno what for. How do you get out of here?"

"Lift the side wall," I told him.

"Funeral for the Brent kid's tomorrow afternoon at three. Wiley Mortuary, a Negro outfit on the east side. Closed casket. Well, got to see Maury. So long."

He ducked under the side wall.

Uncle Am said, "Well, Ed—?"

"You name it," I told him.

He thought a minute. "Let's go over to Carey's. He'll be in and out, between shows. We could talk in our living top, or here, but—maybe I'm getting jittery like the Maj. I'd have a feeling someone was listening outside the canvas. I'd rather have a wall, even a trailer wall."

Out on the midway he suddenly stopped walking.

"Flowers," he said. "Ed, we want to get some flowers for Jigaboo. What time is it?"

"A little after eight. Won't tomorrow do?"

"Ummm—better tonight. If we're up late, we might sleep late. There'll be florists open downtown. Will you take a cab and take care of that?"

"Sure," I said. "You'll be at Lee's when I get back?"

"Yeah. Here's twenty. Get something good, put both our names on it. Just first names—Ed and Am."

"What kind of flowers?"

"Anything, just so they're— Wait, get something bright. He liked bright colors. Red roses or something red, like that red costume he danced in. Come on, I'll walk you to the cab."

We headed out the main gate instead of to the trailer. I was glad he'd thought of the flowers; I might not have thought of it, even tomorrow. A cab pulled up just as we got there, bringing some people to the lot.

I took it downtown and had him find me a flower shop still open. I ordered red roses—twenty-five dollars' worth, because I wanted some of it to be mine if both of our names were going on.

Then I went in a hotel lobby, got a handful of change at the desk, and took over one of the phone booths. I called Rita's hotel in Indianapolis and I was lucky; she was in her room and answered.

"Gee it's swell to hear your voice, Rita," I said. "I hadn't heard from you for so long— How's your father?"

There was a second's pause. Then she said, "He died yesterday, Ed. The funeral was late this afternoon." Her voice was very quiet.

"I'm—I'm very sorry, Rita. Why didn't you call me up? I'd have come."

"I thought about it, but I decided not to, Ed. There wasn't anything you could do—and, after all, you didn't know him and hadn't even met him, and—" Her voice trailed off.

"When are you coming back?"

"Tomorrow evening, Eddie. I think the train gets in about seven, if you want to meet me."

"Why not tonight, Rita? Why wait till tomorrow night?"

"There are a few things to do. Some bills to pay—and things like that. I want to get everything finished up before I leave."

"Do you need any money?"

"Oh, no. I didn't know it until he told me when he knew he was dying, but there was some insurance. I knew mother had carried a policy on him, a pretty big one, but I thought he'd cashed it in after she died. I guess he would have, if he could, but she'd paid the premiums and had it fixed so he couldn't cash it in. And before she died, she made it paid-up insurance and had my name put on as beneficiary if she died first."

"That's good," I said. If she'd needed money, I'd have parted with all I had, and even sold my trombone and put the bite on Uncle Am, but I was glad I wouldn't have to.

"Oh, Eddie, I'll be glad to see you again. I—I wish you were here tonight, or me there."

I said, "I can—" and caught myself in time. I was going to say I could go to Indianapolis tonight and come back with her tomorrow night, and I'd just about have given my right arm to do it. But after the way I'd needled Uncle Am into deciding to work on the murders, I couldn't walk out on him tonight. So I caught myself and said, "My God, I wish so too, Rita."

"But—don't come here, Eddie, if that's what you're thinking. It wouldn't be right for us to—to be together too soon, right after my father died. Even when I come back, not right away— You understand, don't you, Eddie?"

"Of course, sure," I said. "I understand."

"Not too long, Eddie. A week maybe. When I come back again."

"Again?"

"I'm just coming back for tomorrow evening, to get my things I left with the show, and to see you, and I have to talk with Maury. Then if everything is all right, I have to make a trip to Chicago."

"Chicago?"

"You sound like an echo, Eddie. Listen, I can't tell you the details over the phone, but it's going to be a swell idea, Eddie, for us. You'll be crazy about it."

I said, "I don't know. But I'm crazy about *you*, anyway."

"You'll be at the train? It gets in around seven; I don't know exactly—"

"I'll find out," I said. "I'll be there."

"Okay, Eddie. Love me a little?"

"A little," I said.

" 'By then."

"Good-by, Rita."

I'm afraid my mind wasn't on murder. I felt too good. I

didn't want to go look up Uncle Am at Lee's joint. I wanted to go to Indianapolis, of course, but next to that I wanted to go to our sleeping tent and play trombone. I was in the mood for it. I felt like I could do things with it, and it could do things to me.

But, of course, I went to Lee's. Uncle Am was there, and Hoagy.

Uncle Am didn't look like he was working very hard at solving murders; he was playing gin rummy with Hoagy. They had a bottle on the table between them, but they seemed pretty sober, both of them, and pretty intent on the game. I looked over at the score pad and saw Hoagy was a little ahead.

I told Uncle Am I'd taken care of the flowers business, and Hoagy said, "Hell, Ed, I wish I'd've known where you were going. You could've sent some for me, too. Oh, well, I guess I'll be in town tomorrow morning, anyway."

"Going to the inquest?" I asked him.

"Huh? What for? You going, Am?"

"Nope." He laid down his hand. "Four points."

"Damn your hide," Hoagy said. He put down his own hand and started counting.

I went over and turned the radio on, and fiddled with it till I got some good music. I turned it soft so it wouldn't bother anyone and leaned back in my chair to listen.

Over the music, I heard Hoagy knock again and go out this time. Uncle Am figured the score and paid off, six dollars and twenty cents. They didn't start another game.

Uncle Am lighted a cigarette, and took his time about it. Then he said, "Hoagy, we've been trying to figure out who's been doing the killing around here. How do you feel about it?"

"How do I— Oh, I get what you mean. Well— The midget I didn't know, so I wouldn't worry who killed him. But if the kid was murdered, and not killed by a car, then a guy who'd do a thing like that ought to fry, sure. I'm not crazy about helping cops, but—"

"He was killed, Hoagy. It wasn't an accident."

Hoagy leaned forward. "I heard the grapevine, but why? I mean, if he was found dead by the roadside—where's the catch on it being an accident?"

"Clothes," Uncle Am told him. "He was naked, like the midget was. That's what ties them together. And—what about Susie, Hoagy?"

Hoagy looked startled. "Susie? What do you mean, what about Susie, Am?"

"It looks like she got out and drowned accidentally. But there's one thing could tie her in, too. Size. Lon Staffold, Susie, and Jigaboo—to put 'em in order—were all the same size. They all died violent deaths within two weeks. So even if Susie's drowning *looked* like an accident, it's a hell of a coincidence, isn't it?"

Hoagy took a drink out of the bottle he'd been holding ever since Uncle Am had handed it to him. It was a pretty long drink. He put the bottle down.

He said, "It sounds crazy, Am. *Why* would anyone want to kill— Hell, it *is* crazy. Is that what you're driving at? That a homicidal maniac did it?"

"I don't think so," Uncle Am said. "Look, Hoagy. When you looked over the cage Susie got out of, and when you helped pull her out of the water tank, you weren't thinking of the possibility of it being anything but an accident. Now think about it, as at least a possibility. Did you notice anything that might—uh—point to it not being an accident?"

Hoagy shook his head slowly. Then he said, "Wait a minute. I remember one thing. I didn't think anything of it at the time, but—"

I reached across the table and shut the radio off.

Hoagy said, "It was something I noticed when I helped fish her out of the tank. I had hold of her by the arms, and the hair on her arm was plastered down flat from the water—flat and sort of parted at one spot and I noticed a couple of little red marks that looked like the puncture a hypo needle makes."

Uncle Am asked, "You hadn't given her any hypos?"

"No. Just oral medicines. I remember wondering for a minute whether anyone had given her a hypo, and then it seemed so silly that I decided she'd jabbed herself on splinters on the bars of the cage, or something. Hell, Am, I still think so. It's silly—why the hell would anyone have wanted to kill Susie?"

I asked, "Why the hell would anyone have wanted to kill Jigaboo, Hoagy? One's no sillier than the other."

Uncle Am nodded. He looked at me and said, "Tell him, Ed."

I told Hoagy about last night, what I'd seen out the window.

He didn't exactly drop his jaw, but his mouth did go open a little. And he turned around and looked at the window behind him as though he expected to see something looking in there.

But nothing was.

CHAPTER XII

AT ABOUT TEN-FIFTEEN Lee Carey came in. He took a quick drink out of the whisky bottle, and sat down. He picked up the deck of cards lying on the table and started riffling them.

"I hear a rumor, Am," he said. "Maury's selling out."

"The hell," Uncle Am said. "Is that straight?"

"I wouldn't know. Likely not; you know how these things get started."

Hoagy said, "It could be, Am. Maury's been talking about retiring."

"Does Maury own the whole carney?" I asked.

Hoagy shook his head. "Old man Hobart still has a slice; kept it when he retired. But Maury has the controlling interest. Why'd you turn the radio off, Ed? That was good music you had."

I turned the radio back on. I watched Lee riffle the cards from one hand to another, until the tubes warmed up. Then I found some good music again. But I kept it soft, for background music, because I didn't want to miss the conversation—if there was going to be any.

It didn't look as if there would. Uncle Am wandered over to the door and stood looking out. Then he opened the screen and flipped his cigarette butt out into the night.

"Getting cooler," he said.

Nobody seemed to get very excited about that and he went over and sat down on the bunk. He leaned back against the wall of the trailer, with his eyes shut. I tried to guess whether he was listening to the music, or thinking, or taking a nap. It could have been any one of them.

This is a hell of a way of wasting an evening, I thought. We had found out one little fact, if it was a fact and not Hoagy's imagination—the hypo marks on Susie's arm. Still, you get together enough little facts and add them up and you get answers, maybe.

But I looked at Uncle Am and I thought, hell, we could have found that out in five minutes—just by asking Hoagy. We didn't have to close up the stand and spend an evening doing it.

Lee and Hoagy had been talking; I'd forgot to listen, thinking about Uncle Am, and I'd missed the conversation until I heard Lee say, "You're crazy," and I looked across at him.

He was shuffling the cards, and between shuffles springing them back and forth between his hands as though they were strung together with thread.

Hoagy laughed. "Go ahead. I'm not kidding. I can beat you."

Lee Carey looked across at me. He said, "Ed, the guy's nuts. He says I can deal him a cold hand and he knows how to win with it."

I turned off the radio and leaned closer.

Hoagy said, "Go ahead; I'm not kidding." He took a wallet out of his pocket and threw it on the table in front of him. He took another drink out of the bottle, then opened the wallet and put a dollar bill in the middle of the table.

He said, "Draw poker, buck ante. Jacks to open; five buck limit going in, and then the lid is off."

Lee put the deck down. He said, "God damn it, Hoagy, how can you win if I deal us cold hands? I don't want to take your money."

Hoagy grinned. He said, "I'm asking for it. And it's for keeps."

Lee looked at him a minute, and then shrugged. His face went blank as he picked up the deck. His fingers, as he shuffled, reminded me of a violinist's fingers on the strings of a violin. I tried to follow his movements, but it looked like a straight shuffle to me, although the cards moved so fast they almost blurred.

He pushed the deck to Hoagy. "Cut," he said.

Hoagy cut them. Lee picked up the bottom half and put them on top, and I watched for the pass that would put them back in order, but I couldn't see it. The motion of Lee's hands as he moved the deck back toward him must have covered it.

He dealt five cards to each of them.

Lee took a roll of bills out of his pocket and put a single with Hoagy's in the middle of the table.

Hoagy picked up his hand. I asked him, "Mind if I look, Hoagy?" and he shook his head, so I slid my chair around until I was behind him. He held his hand so I could see it; he had aces and eights—two pair, and the jack of clubs.

He said, "Okay, I'll open," and put five dollars in the pot. Lee took a ten from his roll. I think he was going to raise, but he changed his mind. He looked at Hoagy a minute and then put the ten into the pot and took Hoagy's five for change.

Hoagy leaned toward me and said in a stage whisper, "We got him scared already, Ed." Then, to Lee, he said, "Three cards."

He threw away the jack and the pair of eights, holding only the two aces.

Lee looked at him again, and then picked up the deck. While he dealt Hoagy's three cards I listened for the click that would indicate dealing seconds, but I couldn't hear it.

I looked back over my shoulder. Uncle Am still hadn't moved; his eyes were still closed. I figured he really must have dozed off or he'd be over watching this.

I looked back as Lee was picking up his own hand. He threw down one card from it and picked the top one off the deck.

Hoagy fanned out his hand so I could see it. With his two aces he now had a seven and a pair of treys. No better than it had been when he opened; a little worse, in fact.

Hoagy asked me, "Should we bet it, Ed?"

I didn't answer, of course; he hadn't expected me to. He put his cards face down in front of him and picked up the wallet. He took all the bills out of it; there were a lot of twenties and tens and a few singles. He counted it out into a stack on the table on top of his hand. There was a hundred and eighty-four dollars.

He hesitated, or pretended to hesitate, just a second, and then he put it all into the middle of the table. He said, "I'll bet it. One eighty-four."

Lee Carey looked at his own hand, and then at Hoagy. His face was a nice job of deadpanning, except for his eyes. They looked puzzled, cagy.

He said, "Hoagy, what the hell's the idea? You're throwing away your dough. I don't want it. God damn it, I told you this was a cold hand."

Hoagy said, "You're not calling me, then?"

"I didn't say that. Look, I dealt you aces and eights and me a four-card straight. Maybe you think by tossing away the eights to draw to your bullets, you gummed my draw. You didn't."

Hoagy said, "I can deal seconds myself. I can't run up a hand, but I can deal seconds. No, I know you filled."

"Then a bet like that is crazy."

"You're calling?"

Lee looked at all the money on the table; he looked at his own hand, and then at Hoagy. He didn't seem to get the answer he wanted from any of them. You could almost hear the wheels go around.

He'd known the first twelve cards after that shuffle; he wouldn't have stacked them any deeper than that. So he knew what Hoagy's first card had been on the draw; he didn't know the other two. The odds were long against it, but Hoagy *could* have a full house. Those two unknown cards could have been aces, for that matter, to give Hoagy four of a kind.

But the odds were almost impossibly against either of those things. What really worried him was *Hoagy*—his offering, even suggesting and insisting, that they play this. There must be a gimmick somewhere; never bet a man at his own game. But, damn it, that was silly too; Hoagy was betting *him* at his own game; *he'd* dealt the cards.

Lee picked up his roll of bills and folded them out flat. He started counting. He got to a hundred dollars, and one ten dollar bill past it, and then he hesitated again and looked at Hoagy.

Again you could almost hear the wheels go round. Hoagy wasn't a sap; there *had* to be an angle somewhere. Nobody but a magician can possibly realize how many angles and gimmicks there are—or know better that he doesn't know all of them.

Lee looked at his wrist watch and swore; it must have been almost time for his act to go on again in the side show.

He started counting again, and got to a hundred and fifty. And stopped.

He said, "To hell with it. I can't figure your angle, but I'm not going to donate all that money, in case there is one."

"You're not calling?"

"No. To hell with you." Lee stood up.

Hoagy nodded calmly. He said, "Openers," and threw down his two aces. He picked up the money and put it in his wallet. His own and the six dollars Lee Carey had put in—the ante and the call on the openers.

Then he picked up the three cards Lee hadn't seen and put them on top of the deck. Lee asked, "Care if I look?"

Hoagy said, "You didn't pay, Lee," and picked up the deck with the three cards on top of it, and gave it a quick shuffle. Then he grinned at Lee. "But I don't mind telling you. I had two pair. Aces and treys."

Lee looked at me, but I didn't nod or shake my head. He hadn't paid to see the cards, I realized, and Hoagy hadn't wanted him to know for sure, or he'd have shown it instead of telling him.

Lee started out, frowning. At the door, he turned again. He said, "Okay, so if you're telling the truth, you bluffed me out. But all you won was the ante and the opener. What's six bucks?"

"Six bucks," Hoagy said.

"But you stood to lose almost two hundred."

"But I didn't, did I?"

Lee said, "N-no, but— Hell, I've got to get back. Skeets will be having fits."

He went out.

Uncle Am was sitting up on the edge of the cot. He said, "Want to play a hand with me on those terms, Hoagy?"

Hoagy laughed. *"You?* Think I'm crazy, Am? You wouldn't

call; you'd raise me back and that would make me think I *had* gummed your draw and that you didn't have anything, and I'd have to call."

He stood up and stretched. "Guess I'll see if Marge is back at our joint. She was going to shill on Walter's wheel for a while. By now, he's probably got a six-deep tip without sticks."

He went out, stooping to get through the doorway. He called back, "You staying here, Am? I can bring Marge back for some cards."

"Got things to do, Hoagy," Uncle Am told him. "We're leaving in a minute."

"What things we got to do?" I asked him.

"Well—one more drink, for one thing. You want one?"

"I guess so."

We had a drink apiece. I asked, "What would Hoagy have done if Lee'd called him on that hand?"

"What do you mean, what would he have done? He'd have lost some money. But Lee didn't call, did he?"

"No," I admitted. "What do we do now, though?"

"Kid, you got a one-track mind." Uncle Am frowned. "Look, Ed, if I had all the answers I'd know what to do. But then—if I had all the answers, I wouldn't have to do anything at all."

"You mean, you got some of the answers?"

"I think so, Ed."

"Will you tell me?"

"No."

I said, "Thanks."

He grinned. "You want to do something, huh? Okay, come on, let's take a ride."

"On what?"

"The ferris wheel."

I didn't know whether or not he was kidding, but when he started out, I strung along. We went out to the midway and turned right.

He wasn't kidding. We went over to the ferris wheel, talked a minute with one of the ride boys, and got on. They were loading and unloading and it took us a few minutes to get up to the top.

I looked over and down at the dark surface of the water in the diving tank where, Tuesday afternoon, the mark had looked down from one of these cars and seen Susie floating. There wasn't anything floating there now.

I wondered if that was why Uncle Am had thought of the ferris wheel—to look down at the water? But he didn't seem even to glance that way, as far as I could tell. Our car started down again and this time the ride boys had finished changing passengers, and the wheel went round and round for a while, and we went round and round with it.

After a while Uncle Am passed a signal to the ride boys when we were on the down side, and the next time around they stopped the wheel and let us off.

I still didn't see this as a substitute for Indianapolis. I asked him, "What next? Do we ride the merry-gee or buy some floss candy?"

"I been thinking about that. How about the train?"

I said, "I'm thrilled to death. Listen, Uncle Am, it's all right to be eccentric if you want to, but aren't you working too hard at it?"

He laughed, but didn't answer me. Instead, he started off in the opposite direction from the terminus of the scenic railway. I thought my crack had changed his mind for him, and tagged along, wondering what crazy thing we'd do instead.

We headed for the main gate, and through it. A taxi was letting out some customers, and Uncle Am got in and said, "The railway station," and it wasn't till then that I realized he hadn't been talking about the carnival's railroad, but a real one.

I stopped with my foot on the running board. "Hey," I said, "where are we going?"

"You heard me tell the man," Uncle Am said.

"But where from there?"

"Cincinnati."

"I can't, Uncle Am. I talked to Rita on the phone. She's going to be back here tomorrow evening, just for a few hours. And I promised to meet her at the train around seven. I can't break—"

"That's okay; we'll be back long before then. Shut up and get in."

I got in. While we were heading for the station, I told him about Rita's father dying, and most of what she'd told me. I mentioned the insurance and that she had some business in mind, but I didn't say much about her implying she wanted me to go into it with her. No use talking about that, I thought, until I knew what she'd meant.

Then I asked him what we were going to Cincinnati for.

"Kid, we got to start somewhere. And that's where Lon Staffold started from. That's the farthest back we've got anything on this mess—the time he left Cincinnati five days before he turned up dead on the Evansville lot."

I said, "Weiss went to Cincinnati. Can we do anything more than he did there?"

"There's only one way to find out."

At the station, we learned we were lucky; there was a train out in a few minutes that would get us to Lima, Ohio, in time to transfer to the fast train of the B. & O. that high-balled between Detroit and Cincinnati. Our only stops would be Dayton and Hamilton, and we'd be in Cincinnati by two-fifteen in the morning.

At least, Uncle Am said we were lucky to get a connection like that. Personally, I didn't see that we were any better off getting in at two-fifteen than a few hours later; we couldn't do anything at that hour in the morning. Except maybe get a few hours sleep before we started doing whatever we were going to do.

We didn't talk much on the train. Uncle Am apparently wanted to think, and answered only in monosyllables whenever I said anything.

So I gave up talking, and tried to think, too. But I wasn't a success at it; midgets and monkeys and kids went in circles in my head and didn't get anywhere. The more I tried to make my ideas into a pattern the more confused they got. After a while I gave up thinking and tried to sleep instead, but I couldn't do that either.

At the big railroad station in Cincinnati, Uncle Am headed for the telephones. He didn't make a call, but just looked up an address in one of the phone books.

We took a taxi and he gave an address on Vine Street.

I said, "Vine Street— That must be where the midget lived. Weiss said a rooming house on Vine Street, didn't he?"

"That's right. Mrs. Czerwinski's."

"Two-thirty in the morning," I said. "A hell of a time to call on somebody."

Uncle Am said, "Yeah," absent-mindedly.

He was looking out of the window; the cab had just turned a corner. He said, "Ed, this is Vine-Street-Over-the-Rhine. That's what they used to call this section back in the old days before the first world war, and before Prohibition. It was all German beer gardens, and little German bands and orchestras playing German music. Full mit *Gemuetlichkeit*. The 'Rhine' was the old canal—they've got a parkway over it now, and it's gone. The whole thing's gone, and it was like a cross between the Beer Barrel Polka and a Strauss waltz. They say some of the places had signs that read 'English *sprechen* here,' but I never actually saw—"

The cab swung in to the curb in front of a brownstone front that was gray with age. There was a sign in the window, "No Vacancies."

Uncle Am paid off the cab and we went up to the door, and Uncle Am held his finger on the doorbell button awhile. There wasn't any light on in any window at the front.

Behind us, the cab slid off into the night and nothing else happened for a minute. Then a window went up, on the second floor right over our heads. A woman stuck her head out and looked down at us.

She had red hair, bright red hair; the light from the street lamp on the corner caught it, and made her head look like a stop light. Her face, bent down toward us, was in the shadow and I couldn't see it.

She called out, "Whadda ya want?" Something in the tone of her voice confirmed my idea that two-thirty in the morning isn't the right time to make a call.

But Uncle Am took a few steps back from the door, so his face would be in the light, and looked up. He said, "Hi, Flo. You decent?"

Her voice dropped a couple of notches. "Damn if you don't look familiar, but—" Then it went up three notches, shriller than it had been at first. "My God, *Am Hunter!* Be right down, Am." Her head disappeared.

I looked at Uncle Am. I said, "Is that Mrs. Czerwinski? Why the hell didn't you tell me you knew her?"

"You didn't ask me."

"Nuts," I said. "You didn't tell Weiss, either."

He grinned. "He didn't ask me, either. Flo and I were both mentalists with the same carney once, years ago. She ran the mitt camp, and phrenology. I was in the side show; I made with the madball."

"What's making with a madball?"

"Crystal-gazing, Ed. Hell, I thought you talked carney by now."

"Give me time. Say—you didn't ever know the midget, did you? That's another thing I never asked you."

"No, Ed. Weiss did ask me that. No, I didn't know Lon Staffold." His face was serious now. He said, "Kid, never take for granted that people are going to volunteer information, if they've got any. Like—well, those marks that Hoagy saw on Susie's arm. He didn't tell us that until we asked him if he'd noticed anything unusual about her."

A light went on inside the downstairs hall, making a yellow rectangle of the glass pane in the door and the pulled-down curtain behind it. Footsteps shuffled toward us and the door opened.

"Am, come on in and let me get a look at you! My God, where have you been all these years?"

I think she was going to throw her arms around him, but Uncle Am pushed me in ahead of him as a buffer.

"You haven't changed a bit, Flo," he said, "except maybe to put on five pounds or so. But on you it looks good."

"Liar." But she said it with a smile broad enough to block a street. She'd put on more than that, I judged. And most of it was around the hips and bust. She must have weighed a hundred and sixty or seventy pounds, and she wasn't over five feet three tall. But, surprisingly, her face was still pretty. She'd put make-up on, rather hastily and too much of it, but through that she had really pretty features, laughing eyes, and a skin as smooth as a baby's backside. Her teeth were pretty, too, and

THE DEAD RINGER 141

looked like they were still her own. If she'd ever weighed less than one-thirty—and she must have, once—she must have been really beautiful. I don't know if it would have been because of or in spite of that brilliant shade of red of her hair. Or maybe it hadn't been that red, then.

Uncle Am got behind me again as she closed the door.

He said, "Flo, this is Ed, my nephew. Same name, Hunter. He's Wally's boy; you remember my brother Wally." And before she could ask, he said, "Wally died a little over a year ago. Ed's with me now. We're running a ball game with the Hobart shows."

"Hobart? Say, isn't that the carney where Lon—" Her voice trailed off.

Uncle Am nodded. "I want to talk to you about it, Flo."

"Sure, Am. Say, what are we standing here for? Come on up to my room. Go on ahead; I take my time on these stairs."

"Ladies first, Flo. Go ahead; we got all night."

"And trust *you* behind me on a flight of stairs? Git on up here before I kick you up."

Uncle Am laughed and we went up the stairs first. She took us into the front room at the end of the second floor hallway. It was a pleasant room, nicely furnished—although a bit garish in choice of colors—and it was as neat as a pin. Except for the fact that the bed was rumpled and the covers thrown back, it looked as though it had just been house cleaned.

She waved us to chairs and sank down into a rocker that creaked under her weight.

"Staying awhile, Am? Look, I'm full up here right now, but I can make a couple of these monkeys double up and get you a place to sleep for tonight, and then tomorrow—well, there's a guy on the next floor two weeks back in his rent. Besides that he's a creep. I'll move his stuff out and—"

Uncle Am put up a hand to stop her. "Nix, Flo. We aren't staying. Hobart's in Fort Wayne; we got to get back there. We just ran down for a talk with you. About Lon."

"Sure, Am." She'd got her breath back now, and got up out of the rocker. She tightened the blue quilted bathrobe—or housecoat or whatever it was—around her and started for the back corner of the room where a screen with bright parrots on it shut off most of the view of a kitchenette. "You'll have a drink; I don't have to ask you that. God damn it!"

What sounded like an icebox door slammed shut. "God damn it; I forgot—it's all gone."

She came around the screen and headed for the door. "Well, just a minute. I'll get some. One of these damn roomers'll have a bottle—"

"Forget it, Flo. Sit down."

"Sit down, hell. We'll have a drink, or I won't talk. What's the use of being a landlady if you can't wake up people to borrow a drink?"

She closed the door, and a few seconds later we heard her pounding on another door down the hall.

Uncle Am grinned at me. "Some gal, Flo."

I said, "She scares me, but I like her. How long did you know her?"

"Two seasons. Then she married a ringmaster with the Big Top. Ted Czerwinski. I heard he died a few years later. And somebody told me Flo had quit the game and was running a rooming house. But I didn't know where till Weiss told us." He shook his head slowly. "She was sure a looker in those days."

"How well did you know her?"

"Kid, you ask the damnedest questions sometimes."

"You told me to, never to take for granted people will volunteer information if they've got any."

He laughed, and didn't have to answer because the door opened and Mrs. Czerwinski came back, carrying a fifth-size bottle of clear liquid.

"Gin," she said. "Don't remember whether you like it or not, but if you don't, the hell with you. You'll drink it anyway. You open it, Am. You'll find glasses back there."

She handed over the bottle and sat down again, and this time she looked at me. She said, "Am, you got a good-looking nephew. A likelier kid than you were at his age. I'll bet the carney girls are nuts about him."

From back of the screen, Uncle Am said, "He drives them off with a baseball bat."

She looked at me again. "Can he talk?"

"Sure," I said, before Uncle Am could answer her. "What do you want me to say?"

She sighed. "Just like you used to be, Am. Except he's taller." She reached over. "Let me see your hand, Ed."

I held it out and she took it, looked at the back of it, and then turned it over. She held it down a little so the direct light from the table lamp fell on the palm. She said, "You like music, Ed, don't you? It gets you, gets inside you, does things to you. But—I don't think you'll be a musician. It isn't there."

Uncle Am came out from behind the screen, with a tray with three glasses and the bottle. He said, "Cut it out, Flo."

"Put mine down here on the table, Am," she told him, and looked back at my hand. "You're going to have a long life, Ed, but there's a lot of trouble in it. How old are you—twenty, twenty-one?"

"Not quite twenty."

"Then there's trouble coming soon. I think you're riding for a fall. It's something to do with a death, but—"

Uncle Am spoke sharply. "Cut it out, Flo. Damn it, you know better than that."

I was looking at the woman; her face was serious, dead serious. She let go my hand, though.

Uncle Am said, "He doesn't believe that stuff, Flo. And if somebody doesn't believe it, it's bad. Because the good things you tell him will slide off since he doesn't believe them—but the bad ones will worry him, even if he doesn't believe them. You know that as well as I do."

She said, "Yeah, Am. Sorry. I was just ribbing you, Ed." She leaned forward and reached for her glass of gin. Her hand shook just a little and she spilled some of it on the carpet.

Uncle Am looked at me sharply and then took his own glass to the sofa and sat down. Gradually his face relaxed into a smile.

He said, "The years have been good to you, Flo. Damn it, you're still pretty."

"They've been better to you, Am. You're still *with it*. But hell, let's quit throwing bouquets at each other and have a drink instead." She lifted her glass and her hand was steady. "To—to—"

"To Lon," Uncle Am said. "I didn't know him, but let's drink to him anyway. We're going to talk about him."

Flo Czerwinski said, "Okay, Am; to Lon. He was a nasty little bastard, but—I liked him a little anyway."

They drank and I took a sip at mine. It tasted raw and pretty fierce.

CHAPTER XIII

THE CONVERSATION for a while after that drifted into reminiscences and I didn't pay any attention. They had a few more drinks, but I didn't like gin much, so I kept working on my first.

Then I heard the name "Lon" again and I came back from thinking about Rita and started listening again.

"Yeah," Flo was saying, "he was hard to get along with—most midgets are, the ones I've known, anyway. But once you got inside his guard, he wasn't so bad. But he'd never talk about himself. The little I do know about him, I just picked up and put together from here and there; you know what I mean."

"How long had he lived here?" Uncle Am asked.

"Four—it'd be five years this coming November. He was—let's see—he was almost thirty then. Something had soured him on show biz. He hated it and swore he'd never go back on the road. He hated being a freak; Lord, how he hated it. If you wanted to get along with him, you had to forget he was a midget and never mention it or mention anything that had to do with size."

"What had he been doing before he came here?" Uncle Am asked her. "Weiss said he'd been away from the carney business six or eight years; he was here, you say, less than five. What about in between?"

"He was in Toledo. Didn't say so, but I think he ran a newsstand or paper corner there. Anyway, he knew the racket; it wasn't new to him when he started here."

"Did he do good at it? Have much in the grouch bag?"

"Hell, no. He made a bare living and was always broke—or most of the time. Always squawking about lack of money. Half the time he'd be on the cuff for a week or two, and then gradually catch up. I even lent him money a time or two—a fin or so."

Uncle Am said, "He couldn't have been broke when he left here; Weiss said he paid two weeks in advance, so you'd hold his room."

She nodded. "That's right. Because he sold his paper corner for a couple hundred bucks."

"Weiss told me that," Uncle Am said. "I forgot. That'd mean he expected to come back to Cincinnati—but not to selling papers. Did he say anything to show what he did expect to do?"

"No, Am. He was a close-mouthed little son of a gun. But —well, little things he said and did added up to that he expected to come back with his pockets lined. Maybe not enough to retire on, but enough to take a good long rest and not work for a while."

"That was two weeks and five days ago, Flo. He was killed two weeks ago tonight—right about this time, I guess— Ummm—when he left here Hobart was just starting for Evansville. You think he went there?"

"I don't know, Am. I think the cops covered all the railway and bus stations trying to find out where he'd bought a ticket to. You'd think they'd remember a midget. But if they did remember him, they didn't remember where he'd bought a ticket to. You think he went to Evansville, to Hobart?"

Uncle Am shrugged. "Hard to figure how he could have been there—either in Evansville or with the carney. Dammit, a midget can't hide; he's too small to hide. He sticks out like a sore thumb. He *must* have been somewhere else until he turned up dead. Look, Flo, do you know how many suits he had?"

"Yes. Three. Weiss said they found him naked. That right, Am?"

"Yeah."

"Well, he wore a suit all right when he left here. He left his two other suits here, though. He traveled light; just took a brief case with a few things in it. Toilet articles and maybe a couple extra shirts and sox and stuff. I think he left most of his linen here, but took some."

I said, "You'd think if he figured two weeks, he'd have taken more stuff than a brief case would hold."

Mrs. Czerwinski looked at me and back at Uncle Am. She said, "He *can* talk, by God."

Uncle Am said, "And say things, too. The kid's right, Flo. Wasn't a brief case traveling pretty light for a two weeks' trip?"

"Midgets' clothes aren't big, Am. You can stuff a lot of 'em in a brief case. If he figured on getting by with the suit he was wearing and the shoes he had on— Besides, he didn't really figure on two full weeks. Said he might be back in a few days, but it just might be longer so he paid two weeks. I'd'a held his room anyway, but since he had the money I took it."

"Did he ever mention the Hobart shows?"

"No. Not that I remember, anyway."

"Or anybody with Hobart shows? Weiss talked to everybody with it, but nobody there admitted knowing Lon. First, before he had a name, he showed everybody the picture— Say, did he show you?"

"Sure. It was Lon all right."

"And then after he'd been here, he—or the South Bend cops —went all down the line again, with the name that time instead of the pic."

"Hell, Am, you know better'n that. Pour me another drink, will you? Outa several hundred carneys, however many Hobart shows have got, at least a dozen of 'em would've come across Lon somewhere or other. But why *would* they stick their necks out—just to tell the coppers he'd been with the same show they'd been with, once."

"Sure, I figured that. That's why I'm asking you, Flo, if he ever mentioned anyone with Hobart."

"Nope, Am. He never talked about the past, I tell you. And he didn't get any mail, as far as I know, so he must not have kept up contacts. He didn't really have any friends."

"Good Lord," Uncle Am said. "How did he spend his time, outside of selling papers?"

"He read a lot, and he liked movies. He saw a movie nearly every night. And every week he brought home a big armful of books from the public library. Yeah, if he wasn't working, then he was either at a movie or in his room reading, or maybe writing poetry."

"Huh?" said Uncle Am. *"Poetry?"*

"Sure, poetry. He was smarter'n most midgets, Am. Had an education, I think—or anyway he knew a lot; maybe just from reading so much. He was smart, Am. If he hadn't been a freak, he might have made something of himself. But, outside of show biz, who'd hire a midget?"

"About the poetry, Flo. He ever show you any of it? Was it any good?"

"He never showed me, but I saw some of it. He never showed anybody, that I know of. But a few times, he'd forget to clear off the table he was working on and I'd see some of it when I straightened his room."

"Was it any good?"

"How the hell would I know, Am? I'm no judge of poetry. It was funny stuff—I don't mean the kind of funny that makes you laugh. Some of it I couldn't understand, and some of it was—well, not so much sad as—uh—"

"Bitter?" I suggested.

"That's it, Ed. That's the word I wanted. Bitter. And a lot of it about death and stuff. It doesn't rhyme. You want to read it, Am?"

"Is it here? Didn't the police take his stuff?"

"No, it's all in a trunk up in the attic, with the lock busted. When that Indiana copper was here, he and some other cops went through all of Lon's stuff, with a fine-tooth comb, and said they didn't find anything to help them at all. And none of it's valuable to anybody else; they told me to hang onto it for a while in case somebody turned up to claim it. But nobody will."

"Flo, can we look through that trunk?"

"Why, sure, Am. There's a light in the attic. Damn if I'll climb two flights of stairs with you, but I'll give you the key to the attic and you can't miss it; the door's right opposite the head of the stairs that take you up to the third floor. And the trunk's the little one with the busted lock, right near the head of the steps."

"Swell, Flo. Listen, it may take us a long time to go through it, so you go back to bed. I'll slide the attic key under your door on our way out."

"But Am—I'll see you again?"

"I'll drop back sometime tomorrow. I'll be in town till noon, anyway. Say, how you fixed on *Billboards?* Back copies, I mean."

"Got a few of 'em. Two-three months back, anyway. Why?"

"Did Lon read *Billboard?*"

"No. I told you, Am, he was sour on show biz. And he didn't have any friends to keep track of."

"Well—I guess I'd like to look at them anyway, Flo. We can do that up in the attic, too. Then, shall I leave them there?"

"Or take 'em along if you want to. I'm through with them, all but this week's. I haven't finished with that."

She pushed herself up out of the armchair and went over to a cupboard and opened it. There was a stack of about a dozen *Billboards* there, and she brought them back and put them on the table.

She said, "There they are, Am, and here's the key. But don't go yet. I'm good for a lot of talk yet and there's still some gin left. Here, I'll pour 'em while I'm up."

I tried to guard my glass, but didn't get to it before she'd filled it again. She said, "Don't be a pansy, Ed. That's only your second. It'll put hair on your chest. Say, Am, remember that blowdown in Bridgeport? . . ."

And they were off again. But not for so long this time; in about fifteen minutes Uncle Am made a break. I took the stack of *Billboards* and he took the key, and we got away.

The trunk was where she'd said it was. When we opened the top all we could see at first was clothes. Two tiny suits were on top; one was fairly new and neatly pressed, the other—his work suit—shabby and almost worn out.

Uncle Am found newspapers and spread them on the floor beside the trunk. He said, "Put the stuff here as we take it out, Ed, in order; then we can put it back the same way."

"Okay," I told him. "But what are we looking for?"

"I don't know, kid. But maybe we'll recognize it if it's there. It won't be anything obvious; Weiss has been through it before us. Hell, we probably won't find a thing. But going through it will help us round out the picture, anyway. You know what I mean."

"Yeah," I said. I was beginning to get his idea, all right. The questions he'd asked Mrs. Czerwinski hadn't got us a thing that had tied Lon Staffold to the Hobart carney or had given us anything new about the murder. But we'd begun to see the midget as a human being instead of an unknown quantity.

I mean, he wasn't just a picture any more. A picture of a dead wizened little face against a background of trampled grass. He was a man, with the thoughts of a man, trapped in a pint-sized body that kept him from ever *being* a man, and he was bitter as hell about it. Taking out his bitterness by avoiding people and losing himself in books and movies.

I thought, I'd like to have known him. If he was still alive, I'd like to try to get through that guard of his that Flo had told us about and try to make friends with him. He might have been interesting. If you could get under the bitterness, he might have had something on the ball.

But it was too late to think about that. All that was left of him now was the contents of this little trunk and—buried in a Potter's Field near Evansville—a dead little body.

Uncle Am had picked up one of the two suits and was going through the pockets of it. I took the other and did the same. The one I had was the worn-out one. There wasn't anything in the pockets except a broken toothpick in the breast pocket of the coat. I felt around the linings, too. And before I put it down I looked at the label.

I said, "She was right about Toledo. This one has a Toledo tailor's label in it."

Uncle Am nodded. "This one's Cincinnati; bought since he came here."

We put them down on the paper, neatly. I don't know why; he'd never wear them again. A year from now, probably, Mrs. Czerwinski would stuff them into the furnace.

Under the suits were tiny shirts and children's socks—those at least he could buy ready-made. And a tiny topcoat, overcoat and raincoat. Below them, underwear—child's underwear, size six.

We got near the bottom of the trunk. In one side of the bottom was an ancient portable typewriter—one of the oldtime folding Coronas with only three rows of keys. It took up half of the bottom of the trunk. In the other half was a pile of papers and a ream of eight and a half by eleven bond paper, unopened.

I took out the typewriter, looked it over, and put it down outside the trunk. There wasn't any carrying case for it, but it seemed to be in working condition. Uncle Am was looking at the unopened ream of paper, examining the sealing; apparently he decided it hadn't been opened and resealed, for he put it down without opening it.

"There aren't any books," I said, "except this dictionary. Wouldn't he have any books, if he read a lot?"

"Not necessarily, Ed. Some people who read a lot don't like to own books. Especially people who've traveled and figure some day they may travel again. Books are an anchor that tie you down, once you start accumulating them. I guess he felt that way, and got all his reading from the library."

I started to put the dictionary aside, and then remembered and riffled through all the pages, looking for any slips of paper or any markings or notes. It was a small dictionary, but it took quite a while to go through it thoroughly, and I was glad now that there weren't a lot of books to go through; it would have taken all the rest of the night.

Uncle Am had picked up the pile of papers, all eight and a half by eleven bond, a neat stack of it. I could see there was typing on it as he leafed through, most of it was in irregular length lines, like poetry.

He said, "No letters, kid. He didn't have any correspondence at all, it looks like. Well—"

I went back to the dictionary and he started reading the poetry. I didn't find anything in the dictionary and finally put it down and started examining the inside of the trunk, which was now completely empty. There wasn't any false bottom or secret compartments.

I sat back and watched Uncle Am. He was reading, and there was a funny expression on his face; I couldn't quite tell what it was. He said, "Ed, will you stack the rest of the stuff back in? We can put this on top, last."

"Sure," I said. "Is that all poetry? Nothing else?"

"Nothing else. But—some of it's good, Ed."

I started filling up the trunk. "How good?" I asked.

"I don't know. I'm not good enough to judge; I'm no poet. But off-hand, I'd say this isn't great poetry—whatever that is— but that some of it is damn good poetry. It's better than I expected."

He handed me over a piece of it. I read:

> The sere leaves of despair flutter down
> And heap about my feet and the roots of trees;
> A cool voice stirs them and they whisper
> With soft lutevoices like the never-weres
> In dreams under a pale dawn.

I read it twice. I said, "It doesn't mean anything. It's just words."

"Sure it's just words. What'd you expect—an organ background?"

"Maybe it's over my head. I don't see anything in it. What are 'lutevoices' and what are 'never-weres'?"

Uncle Am grunted. He said, "Don't be so damned literal, Ed. How the hell would I know what 'lutevoices' are? But someday you'll run into a flock of 'never-weres'; I'll guarantee you that."

He handed me another one. Like the first, it didn't have any title on it. The first line, I saw, was *"Cover my coffin slowly."*

It was very quiet there in the attic, and the far corners were dim and shadowed. For some reason, a little shiver went down my spine, thinking that he—the dead midget—had written this. It was silly; everybody dies sometime; everybody has his coffin covered, doesn't he?

I took time out to light a cigarette before I read it. Then I sat down on the spread-out newspapers. I read:

> Cover my coffin slowly
> That I may hear the thud of every striking clod
> With ears now dead to every other sound.
> And quiet shall I lie, nor dream.
>
> Soon, then, shall come the rains
> And make of earth one vast mud pie
> Wherein I shall be one of many raisins. So.

That was all there was to it. I read it again and then handed it back. Uncle Am held out another, but I shook my head.

"I don't want to read any more of it," I told him. "Too morbid. I don't like it."

He glanced at me and then went back to his reading. I finished my cigarette, watching Uncle Am, and thinking—but not about him. About the poetry.

I hadn't liked that last poem, but I had a hunch I hadn't been supposed to like it. There was something about it that made something inside me squirm, and maybe that was what the poem was supposed to do.

Anyway, I thought of Lon Staffold sitting alone in his room, writing that, *feeling* that, and it gave me the willies, a little. And it *had* rained, in Evansville, since they'd buried him.

And, damn it, the earth really was—if you thought of it that way—one vast mud pie, with the buried dead a million raisins in it.

Finally Uncle Am put the stack of poetry back in the trunk, and closed it.

He said, "Well—that's that."

"Learn anything?" I asked.

"About the murders, no. But I got to know why he wrote poetry."

"Am I supposed to ask why?"

"I don't give a damn if you do or not. I couldn't answer you if you did. It's something you can feel, but can't explain. Like— Well, could you explain why you play trombone?"

"I guess not. I see what you mean. Say, Uncle Am, I've been thinking about what Mrs. Czerwinski said, that I'll never be a musician. I think she's right."

He looked disgusted. "My God, kid. *You*, falling for a mitt reading."

"Hell, I don't mean because she said it. Only I've been thinking the same thing. I don't intend to give up the tram, but I'm going to figure it for a hobby and not a profession. What it takes to be really good at it, I haven't got. But I'm curious; what was her idea in giving me a reading at all?"

"Ed, it's why I dropped the mentalist racket. Even though it's easier and pays more than running something like a ball game. But if you keep it up, you get to believing in yourself. Even when you know you're guessing, there's a feeling you get that there's something mysterious inside of you that tells you which way to guess. You make a few lucky hits, and that feeling grows. And pretty soon you're believing in yourself."

I said, "She made a good guess on the music angle. Unless —well, the only way she could have known anything about me was through Weiss. He talked to her."

Uncle Am shook his head. "Weiss didn't know I knew Flo; there's no way we'd have come into the conversation. But hell, kid, that wasn't an especially good guess, as guesses go. Most guys your age go for music, and a damn small percentage of them become musicians. The odds were with her both ways.

"But in your case, because you play an instrument, it seemed to you like a miraculous hit. If you liked music—either hot or classical—it would still have gone over all right, even if you didn't even play a mouth organ. She couldn't miss."

He picked up the stack of *Billboards* and put them on his lap.

He said, "Kid, that's what makes the mentalist racket easy for anybody with the gift of gab. There are so many things you can say to *anybody* and hit close, even before they give you the slightest clue. You can make predictions that are bound to come true, because the interpretation of them can be twisted to fit whatever really does happen. Oh, hell, we got to go through these *Billboards*. Get me going on mentalism again, sometime."

He divided the stack of magazines in his lap and gave me half of them. "Here, Ed. Get going."

"Want ads?"

"Yeah, take them first; they're the best bet. Especially the helped wanteds, at libertys, and personals. Anything that concerns a midget. Or—well, we don't know exactly what we're looking for, but we ought to know it if we see it."

"Okay," I said.

I took the top one and went through the ads. There wasn't anything there that I could find. In the second, among the at liberty ads, I found a midget. But he gave a name and a Birmingham, Alabama, address, so it didn't look likely. Just the same, I checked it and turned down the corner of the page.

In the third magazine, I found it. The ad we were looking for, I mean. I didn't even have to look for it, because it was circled in heavy black pencil.

It was a personal, and it read:

> LON S.—BIG DOUGH, WRITE SHORTY,
> Box D-4, Billboard, Cincinnati 1, O. au17

I was still staring at it when Uncle Am said, "After the wants, Ed, look through the Letter List—he could have had a letter waiting for him at—"

"I got it," I said. "Look." I handed him the magazine and he read it and then looked at me.

"That's it all right, Ed. Did you circle it, or—?"

"No, it was already circled. What does the 'au17' mean?"

"That's the last issue it was to run in. Let's see, this is the August third issue, and I've got the last issue in July and it wasn't in there. So the ad was placed in time to make August third and was scheduled to run three issues—that'd be the third, the tenth, and the seventeenth. You've got those issues; take a look."

I did, and the ad was in both of them, but not circled as it was in the first issue it appeared in.

I showed Uncle Am. He said, "Let's find out about that circle, Ed. Flo said the midget didn't read *Billboard*. I wonder if he managed to read her copies without her knowing about it."

"Could be," I said.

"Couldn't be, on second thought," Uncle Am said. "Because if he read them secretly, the last thing he'd do would be to circle the ad in heavy pencil like that, to show he'd read it. That wouldn't make sense. Well, come on."

He gathered the *Billboards,* with the important one on top, and started for the stairs. I folded back the newspapers we'd spread on the floor and put them where they'd come from, and then followed him. From the head of the stairs I took a last look back at the trunk. It looked, I thought, almost like a child's coffin. Or a midget's.

And, in a way, it was. A coffin not for a body but for the thoughts that had once been in that body. Thoughts on a sheaf of paper that would someday be thrown away or burned, and then both the thoughts and the body would be dead forever. The thoughts would be smoke from a furnace fire, and the body that had held them was already one of many disintegrating raisins in a vast mud pie. . . .

Uncle Am was waiting for me at the foot of the attic steps. I turned out the light, leaving the attic dark behind us, and he locked the door that led to it.

I wondered if anybody would ever again read those dark poems up there in the dark attic.

Going down the stairs to the second floor, I asked, "You aren't going to wake her up again, are you? We were up there a long time. It's about four o'clock in the morning."

"Sure I'm going to wake her. This is important, maybe."

He knocked on the door of Mrs. Czerwinski's room. The bed creaked and a light went on. Then there was a shuffle of footsteps and the door opened.

Uncle Am said, "I'm sorry as hell, Flo. But I've got to know about this tonight. About this ad." He handed her the magazine, opened to the ad, and pointed it out to her.

"Oh, that. Damn it, I'd forgotten all about that. Come on in, Am."

"No, we're leaving. Won't bother you any more tonight. But about the ad—?"

"There's nothing much about it. I saw it that Saturday when I was reading the issue and it said 'Lon S' so I thought it was for Lon Staffold, naturally. I marked it, and when he came home that evening I showed it to him. But he said it couldn't be for him, that he didn't know anybody named Shorty, and didn't know what it would mean anyway. Said it must be for someone else."

"That's all that was ever said about it?"

She nodded. "Sure. It was in the next issue or two and then it quit running. Since it wasn't for Lon, I forgot all about it, till you showed it to me just now." Her eyes got a little less sleepy. "Say, it *could* have been for him, couldn't it. And if it was, he didn't want me to know. But it's such a short ad, he could have remembered the whole thing, and the box number, just from reading it once, and just pretended it wasn't for him but maybe answered it anyway. Think so, Am?"

"I don't know, Flo. I'll try to find out. Anyway, thanks to hell and back. Here's your attic key, and the *Billboards*."

"I'll see you again, Am, before you leave town?"

"I hope so. I'll at least phone you; that's a promise. 'By, Flo."

We walked south on Vine Street, toward downtown. A cab or two went by, but Uncle Am didn't try to hail them. There was a first faint gray of dawn in the sky, and a cool wind was blowing north from the river.

I shivered a little, but it wasn't from the pre-dawn coolness. I was still thinking about the two poems I'd read, and they were growing on me, now that I was away from them. I remembered them, I found, word for word.

Uncle Am asked, "Cold, Ed?"

"Nope. Hungry, though."

"Okay, we'll eat. Then we'll check in at a hotel and get a few hours' sleep. Next thing is 25 Opera Place, but we can't go there until nine or ten tomorrow. Today, I mean."

I nodded. I didn't have to ask what 25 Opera Place was; it's the one address every carney knows—*Billboard*. I asked, "You think they'll tell us who put in the ad?"

"I used to know a guy who worked there. If he still does, he'll get me the dope—what there is of it."

"And if he isn't?"

"If I can't find out myself, we'll have to let Weiss in on it. He can get the police here to make the request official. But—hell—I'm afraid it isn't going to get us anywhere. I mean, if they still have a record of the holder of that particular box on those dates, it'll be a fake name and a general delivery address."

"Then why bother?" I asked.

"Got any better ideas?"

"Guess not," I admitted, "except to eat and sleep. I'm starving to death."

Near Sixth and Vine we found a restaurant open and put a meal under our belts. Then we checked in at a hotel on Fountain Square and got a double room. Uncle Am left a call for nine.

In our room, he said, "No use your getting up at nine, Ed. I can handle things at *Billboard* better alone. I'll wake you up when I get back from there. That'll give you an hour or two more sleep."

"Swell," I said. "But don't let me sleep *too* long. I can't miss getting back to Fort Wayne by seven tonight, to meet Rita."

"Don't worry, Ed; you'll be there."

I was already in bed by then. Uncle Am switched out the light and lay down beside me. He groaned. "After all season on that cot, I'll never get to sleep on a bed as soft as this. I feel like I'm drowning."

But when I asked him a question less than a minute later, he was already asleep.

CHAPTER XIV

I HEARD THE PHONE ring at nine, but I realized that I didn't have to get up yet, and dropped off to sleep again. But the instant it stopped ringing, Uncle Am started shaking my shoulder. I opened my eyes and said, "What the hell, I thought you said I could—" Then I saw that he was fully dressed.

He grinned at me. "It's noon, kid. You better pile out if you're going to be sure of being back in Fort Wayne in time."

I sat up on the edge of the bed, and saw that he had a package. He tossed it down on the chair where I'd hung my clothes the night before, only my suit wasn't there any more.

He said, "You don't have to hurry; the train's at two. But there's the transfer and it won't get in much before seven, so I figured you'd want to clean up here before you start. Room Service is pressing your suit; it'll be back by the time you take a shower."

He was opening the package and I saw that it held a new shirt, socks, a pair of shorts, and a really snazzy necktie.

I said, "You're a swell guy, Uncle Am."

"Sure I am. But I've been up three hours and I could use some breakfast. Get going."

It wasn't until I'd had a shower and was putting on the suit that the bellboy brought back freshly pressed, that I remembered to ask what luck he'd had at *Billboard*.

"What I figured, Ed. No better, no worse. The name was John Wilkins, which I take to be a slight variation of John Smith, and the address was General Delivery, Louisville, Kentucky. The ad was placed by mail and paid in advance, with cash enclosed in the letter. Their records show there was an answer to the ad and it was forwarded to the General Delivery address."

"Louisville," I said. "That was about the time we played Louisville, wasn't it?"

"On the head. We opened in Louisville on Monday, August fifth, two days after the date of issue of the first mag the ad ran in. Yeah, it ties it to the Hobart carney, Ed."

"What if the answer had come after we'd left Louisville? The ad was for three weeks and we were there only one."

"Whoever placed it would have left a forwarding address from Louisville General Delivery to Evansville General Delivery, that's all. And the next week to General Delivery, South Bend. But he got his answer right away—since Flo showed the ad to Lon on the third of August."

While we were eating breakfast in the hotel dining room, I asked Uncle Am if he'd phoned Flo Czerwinski yet, as he'd promised he would.

He thanked me for reminding him and called her from a lobby booth as soon as we were through eating. After that we got ourselves shaved in the hotel barber shop, because we

THE DEAD RINGER 159

hadn't brought razors with us, and then took our time about getting around to the railroad station by two.

On the train, Uncle Am was quiet for a while. So was I, listening to the click of the wheels and thinking that every click was bringing me closer to seven o'clock.

Uncle Am took an envelope out of his pocket and began writing on the back of it with a pencil. He'd write a word or two, stop and think awhile, and then write another word or two. I looked over to see what he was doing.

He asked, "Kid, what night was it Lon was murdered?"

"Thursday," I said. "Evansville. Two weeks ago yesterday. That'd make it August fifteenth. Or—wait, I guess it would be the sixteenth, because he was killed after midnight. Yeah, Friday the sixteenth."

He had the entry, in the middle of the envelope, "L. S. killed," and he added a "15" after it. He said, "If it was Thursday night, we'll call it Thursday, after midnight or not. And Susie?"

"She disappeared the night of our first day in Fort Wayne—last Monday, the twenty-sixth. It was Tuesday afternoon they found her in the tank, but it would have been Monday night she was killed."

He put a "26" after his next entry. "And Jigaboo—day before yesterday, Wednesday, the twenty-eighth." He made another entry. "And the night you saw Susie—or a dead ringer for her—looking in the trailer window?"

He said, "What else have we got, kid? Lon left Cincinnati—how many days before he was found murdered?"

"Five. He'd have left on the tenth—a Saturday. That would have been our second last day in Louisville." I watched him make an entry for that, up ahead of the "L. S. killed" entry, in chronological order. "L. S. left Cin.—10th."

I said, "We can put one more date on there, the earliest one we got—August 3rd. That's the issue of *Billboard* Mrs. Czerwinski showed Lon the personal in."

He put it down. "Lon sees ad.—3rd," and looked at it. He said, "And if he answered it right away—and I'd guess he did—the letter would have reached the General Delivery window in Louisville on Monday the fifth, which is the date the carney got to Louisville. Kid, it's all adding up—but God knows to what."

"The carney would have been in Frankfort, Kentucky, then, when the ad was placed," I said. "That's the farthest back date we can tie in—late in July. Or it could have been late the week before—Lexington, Kentucky."

He made another note. Then he sat looking at the list, and I stared at it, too, but it didn't give me anything I hadn't known before except a clearer picture of someone with the carney, *our* carney, sending the ad to *Billboard*, hearing from Lon, then contacting him to make arrangements that ended with Lon leaving Cincinnati on the tenth and turning up—five days later—dead, in Evansville, four days after the carney had reached there. Where he'd been during those five days was still a blank.

The train pulled into Lima, and we got off for our transfer to the Pennsylvania, which took us the last lap to Fort Wayne. We had a wait between trains, so we ordered coffee, across from the station.

The envelope came out again.

Uncle Am put it on the table where we could both see it. He said, "Ed, there's a pattern there. There's got to be. But we can't see it because there's a piece missing. There's *something* that you could drop into there and then all of a sudden the rest of the pieces would fit together."

I nodded slowly, and took another sip of coffee. Out of the corner of my eye I could see the station clock. It was five-fourteen, one hour and forty-six minutes before seven o'clock.

Uncle Am said, *"Think,* kid. What do we know about the missing piece?"

I took my eyes off the clock. I said, "For one thing, it ought to provide a motive. You don't like the idea that these are a madman's crimes and neither does Weiss, so I guess they aren't. But if not, we don't know of any reason *why* they were committed. Nobody, as far as we know, gained anything at all by *any* of the killings. Unless—and we haven't found anything to back it up—someone had a grudge against Lon from way back when."

"Ed, I don't like a grudge for a motive. People kill in the heat of anger, but this wasn't that, because it was planned. Somebody stood to gain something; you're right that the missing piece would provide a motive. What else?"

I said, "It ought to explain the screwy business of all the victims being the same size. They were, damn it. That's what—"

I stared at the list again. It still didn't mean anything.

Uncle Am said, "Kid, you're the one of us that's got a good memory. Close your eyes and think. Think like hell— Wait, don't; make your mind a blank. Then take those two angles you just mentioned: gain, money—and size, the size of a midget, a young chimp, a child. Think, remember."

I closed my eyes and tried. I couldn't get a thing. After a while I shook my head.

Far off, a train whistled.

Uncle Am said, "Once more, Ed. Here comes our train, but try it. What's the missing piece?"

I didn't close my eyes this time; I was looking out of the restaurant window at the station across the street. I said, "I thought of something. But I don't see how—"

"Forget how; what?"

I said, "The day after Lon's murder, while I was in town in Evansville, I read the newspaper to see what it said about the night before. I remember reading that a boy was kidnaped somewhere; there was a ransom demand for fifty grand. It happened the night before I read it—that would have been the night Lon was killed. The kid was seven, it said—that fits for size—same size as Jigaboo, Lon, Susie. And—fifty thousand bucks in money."

"Where? Where did it happen?"

I thought back, and remembered. It put a little chill down my spine. I said, "Louisville."

The train was getting close to the station and I stood up. I said, "Come on, or we'll miss it."

I took a few steps toward the door but I didn't hear Uncle Am move, so I turned back. He was still sitting there, with his eyes wide open, looking as if he'd seen a ghost.

I called, *"Uncle Am,* the train. Come on."

He turned slowly in the booth. He said, "Go ahead, kid. I'll join you later. Tomorrow. I—"

It didn't get it; what I'd told him must have meant something had, hard. His face had something of the same expression I'd seen on it the first time I'd ever seen him, when I'd had to break the news that my father—his brother—was dead.

It was the same look on his face now.

I didn't get it; what I'd told him must have meant something to him more than it had to me.

But the train was pulling in, slowing down, and in a minute or less it would start without me, and it was the only one that would get me to Fort Wayne in time, and I'd definitely promised Rita I'd meet her.

He saw the indecision on my face and helped me out. He said, "Get the hell out of here or you'll miss that train. I said I'll see you tomorrow."

"But—"

He picked up the salt shaker as though to throw it at me. "Get the hell out of here."

The train highballed.

I got the hell out of there and made the train.

Rita wore a black dress. It did things for her. It made her skin whiter and her hair more golden. It made her look like an angel—but not the kind of angel you want to worship from far off. There was enough of devil in her eyes and her face, as she looked at me across the table, to keep me from getting any ideas like that.

I'd mentioned her father, and she said, "Let's not talk about that, Ed." And then she went ahead to talk about it anyway.

She said, "Ed, I don't want you to get a wrong idea. I want to be honest with you. I didn't love my father. He was—well, he's dead now, so I hate to say it, but he wasn't much good. He was cruel to my mother. Oh, I don't mean he beat her or anything like that, but in little ways, little things. I don't even know—or care—if he was unfaithful to her, but I do know he cared more about drinking than he did about her, or me.

"I think she stayed with him only because of me, so there'd be a home for me to grow up in. She had a little income of her own, and that's what she kept his insurance up with and that's why she fixed it so he couldn't cash it in, and took paid-up insurance on him when she knew she was going to die. She died of cancer, Ed, and she must have known it was coming for a long time before. She—"

I put my hand over hers, on the table. I said, "You don't need to tell me all that, Rita. It doesn't matter now."

"But it does, Eddie. I want you to understand why it—it hit me so hard that we've been away from each other so long, just when we found each other. It hurt me to have him dying like that, because I *hadn't* liked him. But then—sometimes when it's too late, you get to know people. He wasn't a bad guy, Eddie. I found that out, visiting him every day at the hospital. He was just weak—about drinking. And he was my father. He—"

"Don't talk about it, Rita."

"I thought I didn't want to, Eddie, but I find I do. He knew he was going to die, even right away, after the accident, while all the doctors thought he was going to get better. And he was glad when I came. He—he cried. And after that, I— I just had to stay there until it was all over, one way or the other."

"I understand, Rita . . . What about Chicago? Why are you going there?"

"Business. I'm going to put *us* in business, Eddie." She smiled, mysteriously.

"Huh?" I said.

"We've got money. The insurance was five thousand, Eddie. I've got over four thousand left—I gave him a good funeral, and I spent some I needed on clothes and— How do you like this dress, Eddie?"

"It's beautiful," I told her. "But—five thousand bucks! That's a lot of hay."

"It's capital, Eddie. The four thousand of it, anyway. If I just lived on it, it wouldn't last more than a year. And if I put it away to try to save it and kept on working, I'd draw against it—I know—and it wouldn't last long either. But I know how I can invest it so it'll bring us plenty. An illusion show."

"A what?"

"*You* know what an illusion show is, Eddie. It's got five features—a sword cabinet, a headless lady, a guillotine act, spider girl, and one other—I didn't get what it was but it's a newer one than those. And a top, and banners. It'll be *big* money for us, Eddie."

So many things were going through my mind, I didn't know which of them to say first. But she didn't give me a chance to say anything.

"I want Am to go in with us, if he will. And we'll need one more girl; four of us can handle it. You and Am—one on the inside and one outside; and myself and another girl for the acts— How do you think I'll look as a headless lady, huh?"

"Marvelous," I said. "But—look, the season's almost over. It's late to start a new show."

"After Milwaukee and Springfield, the carney's heading south; there's almost two months left. We'll make enough to get off the nut, and next season—"

"Off the nut?" I interrupted. "Your four thousand won't cover it?"

"The top and everything? Of course not. The guy wants eight grand, but I think I can get it for six. And I'm going to put up only three—we'll need some for a starter, and for a stake for the winter. I'll have a year to pay off the rest, and that gives us most of next season, for that."

I opened my mouth to say that Uncle Am had some money, too, and might have enough to swing the deal for cash, but I didn't say it. I wasn't going to stick his neck out for him by even admitting he had anything in the grouch bag. That was his business, if he wanted to suggest it.

I said, "It sounds swell, but—"

"But what, Eddie? Don't you want to?"

"Sure I want to, Rita. But— Well, I wish it was my money instead of yours. I don't like—"

"Don't be like that, Eddie. It's *our* money. If I'm going to belong to you, what I've got goes along with. Or—if you don't want me in with the bargain—I'll pay you a hundred a week flat, for managing and spieling. How's that?"

I laughed. I said, "I'll take fifteen cents a week, if you go with it. But don't jump into this, Rita. You might be buying a clunker. Let my uncle look it over for you before you put up any money. Or get Maury's advice—he's been in carney biz since the year one. He can tell you what you're getting."

"Maury *does* know about it, Eddie. A couple of nights before the night that—that I met you, Hoagy and Marge and Maury and I went downtown for a few drinks after the show, and Maury was talking about this deal. It's a show with a carney that folded, and Maury said the rest of that carney stank, but this show is good. Said he wished Hoagy or someone would buy it and run it with the Hobart shows; it was what they needed and a real money maker. He mentioned the name of the guy who owned the illusions—he's sick in the hospital in Chi and that's why he wants to sell instead of taking the show out with another carney."

I said, "But, Rita—"

"So when I got the insurance money, Eddie—or rather when I knew I was going to get it, I phoned Maury and asked him about it again, and he said it was a swell deal if I could get it for under ten grand. He said I ought to clear a couple of thousand just the rest of this season."

I said, "Then it sounds all right, Rita. But can't you wait and get my uncle's advice, too? Especially if you want us to go in with you. We're doing all right on the ball game deal. Maybe he wouldn't want to gamble."

She smiled. "Your uncle Am? Not want to gamble? Don't be silly. But, all right, I'll talk it over with him first. And I want to see Maury again, and pick up a few things I left with the posing show. So let's go out to the lot, huh?"

"Uncle Am isn't there," I told her. "He's out of town on business. I—I don't even know how long he's going to be gone. I guess he'll be back about tomorrow."

"Oh—then if I leave tonight I won't get to see him. But I want to catch the midnight train to Chicago. I—I think I'd better catch it, Eddie."

I looked at her, and I thought, I can talk her out of it. But I said, "Yes, you'd better catch it, Rita. Okay, let's go."

In the taxi, as soon as we were out of the downtown section, I kissed her. We seemed to melt together; it wasn't like any kiss I'd ever had before. It—it was like a bonfire. It was the real thing; I knew then I hadn't been kidding myself. It was worth waiting for. I wished, suddenly, that I'd done a better job of waiting; I was sorry now about Estelle. But it didn't really matter; it hadn't meant anything, and it hadn't counted. Just the same, I knew I'd never do it again; from here on in, it would be Rita and me against the world.

Even Uncle Am—but I hoped like hell we could stay with him somehow. And it had been swell of Rita to know I felt that way and to figure him in on a deal that would keep us all together.

I know that that kiss did things to her; she was breathing fast when I took my lips away from hers. Her eyes were closed and with my face only inches from hers I could see in the dim light in the taxi how beautiful she was, how perfect, and I thought, this can't be happening to *me*. But it was. And it was wonderful, and awful, to know—and I did know for sure, after that—that if I only asked her to stay, she wouldn't take that midnight train.

But I didn't ask. I don't know why, really, unless there was a vague idea somewhere in the back reaches of my mind that, as penance for my slip with Estelle, I should let Rita catch that train, that I should wait. That didn't make sense, exactly, but a lot of things don't.

She whispered, "It's going to be wonderful, Eddie." Her face was alternately in light and shadow as the taxi went by the lights and the darker places between them.

I said, "It's been worth waiting for." And I felt guilty because I hadn't waited.

Then we heard the sounds of the carney lot, and the taxi was pulling in to the curb before the main entrance. Just inside the gate, we stopped, looking down the midway. I don't know why we stopped, or which of us did it first. But we stood there, Rita holding tightly to my arm.

I don't know what she was thinking about. I thought of the recent night when I'd seen the midway and heard its sounds through a haze of white mist that muffled the sounds and made rings around the lights. I thought of it because it was a little that way now—only it was my mind, the mistiness of my mind, that did the muffling and haloing. It was, again, as though I were seeing the lot, hearing it, for the first time. Again, everything was different—only in some funny way I couldn't exactly explain or put my finger on.

Physically, at least, there wasn't any muffling of sight or sound. It was a clear night, with just a touch of coolness in the breeze, and the noises were strident through it.

But it seemed strange and alien to me, as though I hadn't been with it all season—and part of the season before. As though, too, I wasn't going to be with it much longer. It was almost as though I was seeing the carney as a stranger, for the first and last time—and yet with understanding, seeing deeply into it, through the canvas, into the lives and thoughts of the people who *were* the carney.

Beside me, Rita said, "I *like* it, Ed. I didn't know how much till I got away from it. Those two weeks in Indianapolis, I missed the carney. I missed you worse, but I missed the carney, too. I think I might have come back, even if you weren't here, even if I hadn't got the money and would have had to go back to the posing show. There's something about it, Ed, that *gets* you."

I nodded. I knew what she meant all right. I said, "It proves that one thing they taught me in high school—in plane geometry—is wrong. *The whole is equal to the sum of its parts.* It isn't, when the whole is a carney lot. It adds up to a lot more than that—I don't know how or why, but it does. It does with a lot of other things, too, I guess."

"What do you mean, Eddie? What other things?"

"You and me, for instance. Won't we add up to more together than we did separately?"

She squeezed my arm a little. "Yes, Eddie."

I said, "Anything worth while adds up to more than the sum of its parts, Rita. Music. Ever hear a great violinist, Rita, and think what he's doing?—scraping the hair of a horse's tail across the dried guts of a sheep. It's—"

Rita's laughter stopped me. She said, "You *are* funny, Eddie. I never knew anybody like you."

I laughed with her, feeling a little foolish for having talked that way, but inside my thoughts were going on. A carney, I thought, is a lot like a violin. It's made up of things as unromantic as horses' hair and sheep's guts, and Weiss is right; it's pitched to appeal to the nasty instincts of the public, the lust and morbid curiosity and avariciousness—but it adds up to magic, too. There's *something* there that's more than neon and gambling wheels and human flesh and misshapen freakishness and—hell, I can't explain it, but it's there.

It was as though I were really seeing and feeling it for the first and last times.

After a moment Rita stirred. She said, "Eddie, you don't want to go to the posing show with me. I'll have to talk to the girls awhile, and—shall I meet you at Hoagy's trailer?"

"No!" I said. I hadn't meant to say it that strongly. I backwatered as quick as I could. "I don't think anybody's there," I went on. "I think Hoagy's out of town, making arrangements for our next jump. And I heard Marge is helping out at one of the wheels."

"Oh. Well, where then?"

"At Lee's," I told her. "About an hour?"

"I guess so. Yes, it'll take me at least that long. Don't get lost, Eddie."

I grinned at her. "I'd rather come along," I suggested.

"Inside the dressing tent? Even with me to watch you, I wouldn't trust you." She patted my cheek lightly and walked away. I stood there watching her until she was lost to sight in the crowd.

And I kept on standing there because, in a way, I was afraid to move. There was one place on the lot that I knew I shouldn't go; and yet I knew that as soon as I started walking, my feet would take me there.

But I couldn't stand there forever, and I did start walking, and my feet did take me to Hoagy's trailer.

I don't know exactly what I'd expected. I knocked on the door; it was closed. Hoagy called out for me to come in.

Weiss was there. He was sitting astraddle of a chair, leaning on the back of it. His face looked as though he hadn't slept for a long time. Hoagy was jammed again into the breakfast nook with a bottle in front of him. From his face, I couldn't tell whether he'd been drinking or not. But the bottle was only half full.

Marge was back at the end of the trailer, sitting on the bed. She looked huddled up, as though she were cold—or scared.

Hoagy said, "Hi, kid," when I came in. "Have a drink?"

I said, "No thanks, Hoagy."

Weiss nodded to me without speaking. There was a silence and I wished I hadn't come. But I couldn't walk out again right away, now that I had come here.

After a while, Weiss said, "Where's your uncle, Ed?"

I'd have felt foolish saying I didn't know, so I said, "In Cincinnati. On business."

He stared at me and I knew he was wondering what the business was, but I looked back at him blankly, and he didn't ask. I kept my eye on Weiss, because I didn't want to watch Hoagy or Marge.

Why didn't I have sense enough to stay away from here, I thought. Hell, I *had* had sense enough to stay away, but I hadn't used it. It was like a funeral parlor in that trailer.

When Hoagy poured himself another drink, the sound of the whisky coming out of the bottle and going into the glass— a sound you don't even hear ordinarily—was like an exaggerated sound effect in a play on a radio that's tuned too loudly.

He drank it—and you could hear that, too. Then he turned around and looked back at Marge. He said, "Isn't it about time you gave Pete a hand again, honey?"

Marge got up quickly from the edge of the bed. She said, "Sure, guess it is. Be back pretty quick." She went out in a hurry, as though she was glad to get away.

Hoagy said, "Sit down, Ed." I went over and sat down on the edge of the bed, where Marge had been. That way, I figured, when she came back I'd have an excuse for getting up and I'd make my getaway. She'd be gone only a few minutes if Pete already had a play at his wheel and didn't need a shill. Otherwise—well, I'd have to stay ten or fifteen minutes more and then leave.

Anyway, where I was I didn't have to watch Hoagy; I was behind his back.

Suddenly, Armin Weiss raised his head and looked at me. He said, "Kid, what about the hypo marks on Susie's arm?"

"What do you mean, what about 'em?" I asked.

"Did you know there were any?"

"Sure," I said. "Hoagy mentioned it last night."

Weiss said, "They were there all right."

He looked disappointed, and another piece of the pattern fell in place in my mind. I saw now why Hoagy had told us about those puncture marks on the monkey's arm; he'd known that the police would dig her up, even as I had, and that their examination would be more thorough than mine.

He said, "We dug up the chimp this morning and the coroner looked her over. She was full of morphine."

"You mean she didn't drown?"

"Sure, she drowned—or, she *was* drowned is a better way of putting it. She had too much morphine in her to make the trip by herself. Somebody doped her so she wouldn't struggle and then carried her to the tank and held her under."

"Oh," I said. I'm afraid I didn't make it sound very surprised. I think I'd known all along that Susie's death hadn't been any accident. I think I'd been sure of that even before I'd had a faint glimmering of the reason for it.

It was quiet again. So quiet that I heard the tiptoeing footsteps outside the trailer. I don't think anybody else heard them. Anyway, neither Weiss nor Hoagy seemed to hear anything. I guess I've got pretty good ears, and I could barely hear them.

They came to the door, paused, and then seemed to go around the trailer.

I looked up toward the window behind Weiss's back. There wasn't anything there, and then Uncle Am's face appeared outside the window, looking in. He caught my eye and shook his head slightly, so I didn't move or say anything.

He looked at Hoagy, who was staring down at the bottle in

front of him. Then he looked back at me. I knew he wanted
to get Hoagy's attention without letting Weiss know.

I said, "Hoagy, remember that night I thought I saw Susie
looking in the window?"

He said, "Yeah, Ed?" And then, as I'd hoped, the mention
of a window made him glance up at the one in front of him.
He caught Uncle Am's eye, and Uncle Am jerked his head
backward in a signal.

Hoagy glanced toward Weiss and saw Weiss wasn't watching, so he nodded slightly.

I was stuck with the remark I started, so I tapered it off: "I
was wondering if— No, that's crazy. Skip it."

Hoagy stood up, and poured himself another drink—a full
glass—and raised it. He said, "Marge hasn't come back—
means Pete needs a stick. I'll wander over and give a hand for
a few minutes. Be right back."

Weiss nodded and didn't move.

Hoagy stood perfectly still for a moment. Then he lifted the
glass and drank it as though the whisky were water. He put the
glass down, and went out.

Weiss looked up again. He said, "Ed, what did you and Am
do in Cincy?"

"We saw Mrs. Czerwinski. We went through Staffold's
trunk. And Uncle Am went to the *Billboard* office."

"You found that ad, then? The one in *Billboard* addressed
to Lon S.?"

I nodded. I was surprised that Weiss knew about that; he
hadn't mentioned it. But then he could have found out about
it since the last time we'd talked to him.

He stood up and kicked aside the chair he'd been sitting on,
and started to pace back and forth the length of the trailer.
He stopped in front of me.

He said, "Ed, I know who did these murders. I know damn
well who did 'em, but I don't know *why*. I can't make a move
till I know *why*. I haven't got a case."

"Hoagy?" I asked.

"Sure, Hoagy. But for God's sake—a midget, a monkey,
and a Negro kid! What's the pattern? I can't find it."

I didn't say anything.

CHAPTER XV

THE DOOR OPENED behind Weiss, and he wheeled around. It was Uncle Am. He came in and shut the door behind him.

He said, "Hi, Cap. You talk pretty loud; I could hear you halfway to the ferris wheel." He moved to the chair Weiss had kicked aside and sat down, straddling it, his arms folded along the back of it.

Weiss asked quietly. "Got all the answers, Am?"

"Enough of them. How much has Ed told you?"

"Nothing," Weiss said. "Does he know too?"

Uncle Am glanced at me. "He's figured out most of it by now, haven't you, Ed?"

"I guess so," I said.

Weiss looked from one to the other of us. He said, "Hoagy did it. *Why?*"

Uncle Am tilted his chair toward the table, reached over, and got the whisky bottle. There were still a few inches left in it. He tilted it up, and then there was less of it left.

Then he said, "Go ahead, Ed. Give him a start. I'll fill in anything I can, that you can't."

I said, "Cap, the night the midget was murdered, there was a kidnaping in Louisville. The whole thing revolves around that. The son of a rich manufacturer named Porley was snatched from his bed about nine that evening, when his parents were at a party and only two servants were in the house. The kid was seven—just about the size of Lon Staffold, the monkey, and Jigaboo. That's the missing piece; with that, the rest can be fitted in."

"Hoagy did the kidnaping?"

I nodded. Uncle Am said, "I checked Louisville papers this afternoon. The kid was returned on the twenty-sixth, for forty thousand dollars ransom; that was a compromise figure. The kid was alive and in not too bad shape, but he showed evidence of being kept under drugs the eleven days he was gone. He's recovering; he's still under a doctor's care, but he'll be all right."

Weiss said, "The twenty-sixth—last Monday. That was when Susie was drowned. My God, Am, my mind's tired; I could go off and dope out the details, but if you've got 'em, save me the trouble. Give it to me in order."

Uncle Am looked at me, so I took over.

I said, "Hoagy must have been working on the idea for at least a month before the kidnaping, all the time we were playing towns in Kentucky. He figured on one big gamble for a big chunk of dough, and then a break with the carney.

"The hard part of a kidnaping is keeping the kid under cover, while you're negotiating. If there's a kidnaping, you can't suddenly have an extra kid around without somebody putting the two things together. Hoagy figured out a way around that."

I wasn't too sure about the next part, so I watched Uncle Am's face while I went on:

"But Hoagy kept the kidnaped boy right in his trailer, in plain sight, only nobody saw him. Because he was under drugs, and in a monkey suit. There wasn't any real monkey—then. The Porley boy was the monkey for the whole eleven days he was gone, while Hoagy was fixing it up to return him and collect.

"He was in a dim corner, behind wide bars so nobody could see him plainly, and nobody even guessed there was an extra kid around the carney. If the kidnaping had been traced to the carney, you still wouldn't have found him."

Weiss grunted. He looked up at the door of the trailer. Then he looked back at me. "What about the midget?"

I said, "That was part of Hoagy's careful advance planning. He didn't want to turn up with a monkey suddenly right after the kidnaping. He wanted that sick monkey planted in everybody's mind *before* he got the kid.

"For the five days before the night of the kidnaping—and the first murder—Hoagy's sick monkey was Lon Staffold in the monkey suit. In his case, not drugged, just playing sick.

He was Hoagy's accomplice. Maybe he helped in the actual kidnap—"

"No," Uncle Am said. "He was found naked, remember? That means he was wearing the monkey suit up to just before he was killed. Probably he'd just taken it off when it happened."

Weiss asked, "But why a midget? Why didn't Hoagy get a real chimp right away, for a stand-in up to the time of the kidnaping?"

I didn't see why, either, so I looked at Uncle Am. He said, "I think he figured there'd be too much difference between a real monkey, and the Porley boy in a monkey suit. Somebody might notice. And then there'd be the problem of what to do with a real monkey while the kid was playing the part. Lon would have gone back to Cincinnati, then returned again to stand in for the monkey a few days *after* the kid was returned, to avoid any coincidence of dates again. Then the monkey would have disappeared or something."

Weiss nodded.

I said, "Hoagy must have known Lon a long time ago, somewhere. He and the midget must have pulled something crooked together once before. That would be why he thought of Lon for a stand-in, and advertised to reach him through *Billboard*. Hoagy must have had the nickname 'Shorty' then; case of opposites, like a fat guy will sometimes get called 'Slim' or a guy who never talks, 'Gabby.' "

"And you think he found out the midget was going to cross him up?" Weiss asked. He looked at the door again; I knew he was beginning to wonder when Hoagy was coming back. I saw him reach under his arm and loosen a gun in its holster.

I said, "I'd guess that when the kidnaping actually happened, when he came back that night with the boy, the midget demanded half of the take—instead of whatever Hoagy'd offered him, a few thousand bucks, probably. Or maybe he hadn't known, till then, just what his impersonation job was for, and wouldn't stand for a kidnaping. Maybe Hoagy'd lied to him what the real reason for the business was, and he threatened to turn Hoagy in unless Hoagy took the kid back home."

Uncle Am said, "That's my guess. Your second one."

I said, "That takes us up to the twenty-sixth, the day Hoagy traded the Porley boy back for the forty thousand dollars. He'd found out, meanwhile, where he could buy a real chimpanzee, and bought it on his way back from Louisville. Only he didn't want to risk keeping it. He had drugged it, and the minute he got back he drowned it in the diving tank. Then he told us it was missing, and we spent the rest of the night hunting it.

"Up to that time, everything was okay—except for his having had to kill Lon. But on the twenty-sixth, he must have thought he was safe. The kid was returned, he had the money, the monkey was accounted for, and you hadn't got to first base on Lon's murder. Then something went wrong again, and he had to kill once more. This time—Jigaboo."

Weiss said, "The monkey suit!"

"Sure," I said. "Jigaboo found the monkey suit. When I saw it—while Jigaboo was looking in the window of Carey's trailer, wearing it—it had dirt on it, so it had been buried; probably Hoagy buried it somewhere in the same woods he buried the chimp in. Likely Jigaboo was playing around in the woods and saw him bury it, that afternoon. Or maybe he just came across a place where something had just been buried, and dug for buried treasure.

"Anyway, he found the suit and took it back to the van he slept in and hid it there. And that night, after the show, he went to his bunk, undressed, and put on the monkey suit; it was just the right size for him. He started out, in kid fun, to play a joke on someone."

I shivered a little, thinking about it. "On me, as it turned out. He was a dead ringer for Susie, all right, when he looked in the trailer window and I saw him. Then—somehow—Hoagy got hold of him, and after that he wasn't a dead ringer—he was just dead."

Weiss said, "A dead ringer for a monkey that didn't exist, but that had one stand-in after another—the midget, the Porley boy, the monkey he drowned, the kid— No wonder it didn't make sense." His voice was ugly. He looked at the door again, and stood up. There were, I noticed, a few beads of sweat on his forehead.

He said, "What the hell's keeping him?" Suddenly he turned

and glared at Uncle Am. "God damn it, Am, did you tip him off?"

Uncle Am didn't look at Weiss, nor answer him directly. He said, "He won't try to get away. Guy with a build like his; you could trace him to Patagonia. He'll—take care of it himself, I imagine. He wouldn't want to fry."

"He *ought* to fry. God damn it, Am—"

Uncle Am said mildly, "Sure, he ought to. But how about Marge? Maybe they wouldn't give her death, but they'd give her worse. Life. And knowing about it when Hoagy sizzled. . . . Even if he was a son of a bitch, she loved him, Cap."

Weiss frowned. "Past tense, already. You're that sure?"

Uncle Am didn't answer. Weiss started for the door. As he opened it, Uncle Am said, "Cap," and Weiss turned.

"Look, Ed and I aren't in on this. You doped it out, the whole thing. Don't mention us."

Weiss looked at him a moment and then said, "Thanks." There was still sullen anger in his voice, but not so much. He'd get over it. He went on out.

We sat there and didn't say anything, Uncle Am and I. We sat there and waited. There was a deck of cards lying on the table, and after a while I picked it up and shuffled it. I played a game of solitaire, and started a second one.

Then Weiss came back. There were two men with him, Fort Wayne detectives.

He said, "You'll have to get out. We're going to search the trailer. He didn't have the money with him. We got to find it."

Uncle Am looked at him, without asking. Weiss glared at him, and then said, "Yeah. Two miles down the road. Head-on into a concrete abutment at about eighty miles an hour. Both killed instantly."

Uncle Am nodded and we started to leave. But the Fort Wayne detectives wanted to search us first to be sure we weren't walking off with the kidnap money, and we didn't argue about it. I don't think Weiss would have thought of searching us.

We went back to our sleeping tent, and about ten minutes later Weiss came in to tell us they'd found the money. "Anyway," he said, "the bulk of it, thirty-four thousand. We'll find the rest."

Uncle Am nodded. "Have a drink, Cap?"

"No, thanks. . . . Say, Am, maybe it was best that way. On account of the woman. Well—I got to go and wind some red tape. Be seeing you."

He went out.

A few minutes later I suddenly remembered Rita was waiting for me at Lee Carey's trailer. I told Uncle Am, and hurried over there.

I was late, almost an hour late, but she was there, sitting on the steps outside the trailer, crying. I knew then that I wouldn't have to tell her the news, and I was glad of that.

It was almost time to start to the railroad station, and we were lucky in finding a cab that got us there in plenty of time. We sat in the station, and didn't talk much. Once Rita mentioned the illusion show, and I said, "It does sound good, Rita, but why don't you wait? Go look at it, maybe take an option on it if you can get one, but don't go the whole hog until we've all had time to think it over."

"All right, Eddie, I'll not do anything more till I see you again. Monday afternoon, in Milwaukee."

"Shall I meet your train?"

"I don't know which one I'll take, Eddie. I'll phone you from a hotel when I check in."

The train pulled into the station and I put her on it. We didn't kiss good-by; I wanted our next kiss to be something more than one could have been just then, with our minds full of what had just happened.

But when the train pulled out again, there seemed to be a hole in my life, and I found myself counting up how many hours it would be from Friday midnight to Monday afternoon.

I went back to the lot, and the carney was just closing. Uncle Am was still—or again—in our sleeping tent. He hadn't undressed; he was sitting on the cot, with his hat shoved back on his head.

He said, "Hi, Ed," when I came in, and then he yawned. "I'm trying to convince myself that I'm sleepy, but I can't."

I felt the same way myself. There wasn't anything I wanted to do, but I didn't want to turn in, either.

He said, "Want a drink, Ed?"

"No, thanks," I told him.

He shook his head. "Ed, did you like playing detective? It's a nasty business, sometimes."

I said, "Murder is nastier. I'm sorry as hell about Marge, but I'd do it again—my part in it, I mean. Damn it, Uncle Am, I think maybe I *would* like to be a detective."

"It's a hell of a life, Ed. It's not what you read about in those magazine stories. It's long hours for not much money, and nine-tenths of what you work on is peanut stuff, anyway. It's a hell of a life."

"That's what you told me about being a carney, before I joined up. It isn't; I like it. But I just don't think I'm cut out to be a carney. All my life, I mean."

"How are you going to fit Rita into the idea of being a detective, Ed?"

"I don't know," I admitted.

I thought about it awhile, and the two things didn't seem to fit at all.

I said, "All right, I'll forget it. Being a detective, I mean."

Uncle Am stood up suddenly. He said, "I'm going out awhile, Ed. I'll be seeing you."

I sat there, thinking, after he'd left. I thought, he's going out to get drunk. I wished I could do the same, but I'm not cut out for that, either.

I wondered again if I really had what it took to be a detective. Maybe there was some way I could have both that and Rita. But maybe, anyway, I didn't have what it took? Could I do routine shadow work, for instance? I'd never shadowed anybody in my life.

On a sudden impulse I got up and went out. For a gag, why not? Uncle Am had been gone only a minute or two. I'd find out if I could tail him for a while, without losing him or without letting him spot me. Anyway, it would kill some time.

When I reached the street, I could see him a block down, walking toward town. I crossed over to the other side of the street and kept about a block behind him, keeping him in sight and making myself as inconspicuous as I could, so he wouldn't notice me if he turned around.

He walked all the way in to town, although a late inbound bus passed us, and several empty cabs went by.

When we got to town there were still a few people on the streets, so I closed up a little. I was getting proud of myself, for I knew he hadn't seen me.

Then I quit feeling proud and felt foolish, for he stopped and turned into a building—but it wasn't a tavern. It was a church, one of the big ones that stay open all night. I felt foolish because I'd figured he was going out to get drunk, but instead he'd wanted to go somewhere and pray for Marge and maybe for Hoagy, too.

I stood there a minute, wanting to go in and join him, but knowing I couldn't because I'd followed him there and would be ashamed, now, to admit it.

A cruising taxi went by and I grabbed it back to the carney lot. I felt like kicking myself, in a way, but in another way I was glad; what had just happened proved that detective work can find out good things about people as well as bad things, if there are good things to find out.

We opened up the ball game booth again the next day, Saturday, and then and on Sunday the lot was jammed and we worked like the devil, so the time went quick. Sunday night we tore down late and it was after three when we got the vans loaded. Uncle Am and I were too tired to go into town to try for Pullmans, so we found a pile of canvas in one of the vans and slept most of the way to Milwaukee.

It was almost noon when we got there and we worked like hell pitching our tops so I'd have time to get cleaned up before Rita called. I checked right away that the office car had a telephone run into it.

I didn't quite make it; the call from Rita came while I was taking a sponge bath in our sleeping tent. He came back and told me, "She just got in and she's taking a room at the Wisconsin Hotel on Third Street. She'll meet you in the cocktail bar there in an hour or so."

I set a record getting dressed.

Rita was waiting there when I went into the bar, looking more beautiful than ever. She was in one of the booths, and I sat down across from her.

I said, "I don't believe it. There's a catch somewhere."

"You're too far away, Eddie. Come on over."

I shook my head firmly. "No, positively not. We're still in public and if I get any closer than this— Nope, I've waited this long so I can wait a few minutes more. Must we have a drink?"

The waiter was coming over, so it appeared that we must, and we ordered martinis.

When they came, I lifted mine. "To us," I said.

She smiled. "Love me, Eddie?"

"I don't know yet," I said. "I'm waiting to find out. How long should we sit here and act civilized?"

"I'm shameless, Eddie. I registered for two, and took a double room."

I said, "I shall now make the greatest understatement of my life: That's nice."

"How is Am, Eddie?"

"Fine," I said. "Rita, I don't believe this. There's a big catch somewhere. You're a beautiful liar; but you aren't what you seem. You're—"

Something in her face stopped me. Just a quick flicker of something that might have been fear.

She leaned forward a little, dead serious. "What do you mean, Ed?"

I hadn't meant anything at all. I'd been going to say that she was really a beautiful international spy, pretending to love me so she could wheedle from me the secret plans of the fortifications of Peoria, Illinois. God help me, that was what I'd started to say.

I stared at her, and didn't answer. Her face cleared and she smiled at me. She said, "You're kidding, Eddie."

I was; I had been. But that little flicker of something *had* been fear. And a thought that I'd pushed to the back of my mind ever since Friday evening crawled out of hiding and looked me in the face, and I couldn't make it crawl back.

I said, "Rita, you knew about the kidnaping, didn't you?"

Her eyes went wide, but it was because she made them so.

I said, "I don't mean you were *in* on it, Rita. But you spent so much time in the trailer with Marge, you must have seen something. During those five days when the midget was playing chimp; he, or Marge, must have given something away to you. And you were afraid; that's why you carried the gun that night. And when you stumbled over the dead midget you must have known, more or less, who it was, and that Hoagy had killed him."

She wetted her lips with the tip of her tongue. She said, "Eddie, I did suspect something. I didn't *know*. Yes, I knew from something that happened that Susie wasn't a real monkey. It—he—must not have known I was in the trailer once when I was there with Marge, and he talked to her. Marge was scared stiff of Hoagy. She made me promise not to tell."

I said, "But then when the midget was killed, you knew where he had been—in the monkey suit. And you must have known Hoagy killed him."

"I didn't *know*, Eddie. And I'd promised Marge—"

My hand was lying on the table; she put hers over it. The shock of the contact jarred me. The touch of her hand was like fire. She said, "Let's not talk about it here, Eddie. Let's not talk about it at all. But if we have to, let's go up to our room where we'll be alone."

It was sensible, but it was too sensible. Upstairs, I wouldn't want to talk about death.

I said, "Let's have one more drink, Rita. It's—well, I want a minute to adjust my mind to something new; that's all."

I didn't want to look away from her face, but I turned and caught the waiter's eye and signaled for two more martinis.

I looked back at Rita and I thought, it doesn't matter. I can believe her. I can believe she hadn't read about the kidnaping and put the two things together. And if she didn't *know* anything for sure, she wasn't under obligation to tell her suspicions.

I sat looking at her and I believed it, while I looked at her. Then, deliberately, I closed my eyes a moment.

When I opened them, I said, "Rita, that night in Evansville, you couldn't have known about the kidnaping. But you could have read the papers next morning, before I met you in the hotel lobby at noon. And you had an errand at the bank, then, while I waited for you, and later you had another appointment with a banker—

"Let me guess. You were afraid Hoagy might kill you because you knew and guessed too much. He'd already done murder. So you left something with the bank—let's say a sealed envelope to be opened only in case of your death. And then, after that, you wouldn't have to be afraid of Hoagy."

Her tongue licked her lips again. She said, "Eddie, I'm almost afraid of *you*. You talk like—like a detective. If I didn't love you so much, Eddie, I'd—"

Our martinis came and I paid for them, but I didn't touch mine yet.

Rita took a sip of hers, and then put her hand back on mine. "Eddie, let's forget about all that. It's over. I got the envelope back Saturday and burned it. And I did it because I really was afraid of Hoagy."

I thought, maybe. It could be. I wanted to believe that much and no more, and forget it. She was as beautiful as hell and I could say, "Okay, Rita," and forget it and we could go up to our room.

But instead of saying it, I asked a question.

I watched her face, and asked, "Rita, what insurance company paid that five-thousand-dollar policy on your father's life?"

She jerked her hand away from mine.

I'd had to know, and now I knew. Until I'd asked, there was an outside chance, a hope, that it *had* been a coincidence that Weiss had found only thirty-four thousand dollars of the forty thousand Hoagy'd got from the kidnaping—and that my beautiful Rita had so suddenly acquired five thousand dollars.

Now, I knew, that the only coincidence had been the death of Rita's father, giving her an easy way to account for suddenly having so much money.

She was glaring at me across the table. She said, "Damn you, Eddie."

That didn't mean anything. I could say, "Okay, Rita, let's forget it; I just wanted to know."

And, in our room, it would be easy to forget. Oh, we could have fun, Rita and I, spending that blackmail money. Except that that money had come from the kidnaping of a little boy and had led, indirectly, to the death of another little boy—a very black little boy who could dance like mad.

I said it. I said, "Okay, Rita, let's forget it; I just wanted to know."

But I didn't mean it that way. I meant that I couldn't prove where she *did* get the money, and didn't intend to try. I meant, let's forget everything. I meant, good-by.

I never did touch that second martini.

I went away from there, and walked. I knew the lake was east, and I went that way until I came to it, and I sat down on a grassy slope in the park, looking out over the water. A cool wind came in off the lake and after a while it began to get dark and I started back.

From a drugstore I phoned the carney lot and asked for Uncle Am. The girl in the office car said, "He went into town, Ed. Said something about taking you and Rita to dinner."

I knew he might have been to the hotel and left, but I went there anyway. He was sitting in the lobby.

He said, "I was trying to figure out where to look for you, Ed. They told me at the desk Rita had checked out. You—uh—split? You figured out what happened?"

"You *knew?*" I asked. "And didn't tell me?"

He shook his head slowly. "I didn't know, Ed. I was afraid, but I wasn't sure. You knew her better than I did, and I knew that if she blackmailed Hoagy for that dough, you'd dope it for yourself."

"Let's skip it," I said. "Shall we go back to the lot and open up tonight? It's only eight o'clock."

"We're through with the carney, Ed."

"Huh?"

He nodded. "That's what I came downtown to tell you. That wasn't any rumor about Maury selling. And the new owner is Skeets Geary." Uncle Am grinned a little. "He wanted different terms for our running a concession; it seems he doesn't like us. I told him to hell with it, and I sold our props and stuff to Pop Janney and had our trunks sent to the station. We're free as air, Ed."

I said, "Skeets can't change terms in the middle of a season. Your contract holds good; he can't change it."

"I told him that, kid. With gestures. If you'll look closely you'll see the beginnings of a mouse on my left eye. But you ought to see Skeets." He grinned reminiscently. "We wouldn't have worked under him anyway, Ed, under any terms. And don't worry; the grouch bag is in good shape. We won't starve for a few months."

"What shall we do?" I asked.

"I was thinking about holing in for a while in Chicago. How about it?"

"Okay," I said.

He put his hand on my shoulder. He said, "You'll get over it, kid. You'll be all right."

I said, "I *am* all right. I thought it out. I'm over it. I'm okay."

"Good. Look, Ed, let's stay in Milwaukee tonight, then, and go to Chi tomorrow. And we don't want to hit Chi with *too* much money; they take it away from you there. So let's paint Milwaukee a light pink this evening, huh?" He snapped his fingers. "And I just thought, Ed. Estelle's going to jump the carney, too. She hates Skeets's guts as much as we do, and he's taking over the posing show to run himself. So let's go out and get her, and make it a real evening."

I grinned. I said, "That leaves you without a date, though. Why don't we all three take a plane to Cincinnati and get Flo Czerwinski for you?"

I was kidding, of course, but I should have known better. That's just exactly what we did.

The Okefenokee swamp, with its bear and deer, alligators and cottonmouths, was a lifelong lure to Ben Ragan. He thought he knew all the hidden dangers of the swamp until he stepped ashore on a small island.

Gun in hand he passed through the sinewy thicket. Hearing a footstep near him, Ben whirled, but he was too late ...

"SWAMP WATER ... is not only a very good tale but ... a brilliant one." —New York TIMES

DON'T MISS—

Swamp Water

by Vereen Bell

wherever BANTAM BOOKS are sold

This Bantam Book contains the complete text of the original edition. Not one word has been changed or omitted. The low-priced Bantam edition is made possible by the large sale and effective promotion of the original edition, published by E. P. Dutton & Company, Inc.